TAKE
THESE
Broken
Wings

TAKE THESE Broken Wings

natalie corbett sampson

clubhouse press

For my AP
(you'll have to actually read this to get it).

prologue

Sometimes I try to imagine how they *all* ended up in the car, headed to the hospital. To see me. The scenario changes, depending on my mood, depending on what I'm thinking about, what I'm doing and what makes me wonder, again, why they were all in the car.

Scenario One: They were all in the car, headed to the mall. Or a movie — though if they were going to see a movie I think they'd have texted to ask if I wanted to go, and there was no text. Dad said, "I feel like getting a burger, who wants one?" and they hustled about finding shoes (Penny never knew where her shoes were) and keys and wallets to leave the house. Dad would have been driving, as usual, and the hospital people probably called his phone, but Mom would've answered, because she hated it when he talked on the phone while he was driving. I don't know what she said — the nurses never told me — but once they heard I was there, they would've forgotten about the burger or the mall or the movie and headed to the hospital. In my imagination, my little movie for myself, Mom is telling Dad to hurry up, and Dad is acting all calm, saying, "Margo, we'll get there as soon as we can."

Scenario Two: They were all at home when the nurse called, and when Mom answered the phone, she got all frantic and panicked. She stood in the living room after hanging up the phone and couldn't think what to do next. She might have yelled "Matt! Matthew! It's Layne! Matthew, it's Layne!" and he would have come running, not having any idea what she was talking about. And Penny, too. Maybe she was reading in her room, or studying — her chemistry book was open on her desk when I got home — and she heard Mom yelling and ran into the living room too. Maybe Dad made Mom sit down, and he made calming sounds — "shhh shhh shhh" — like he used to say to us when we fell off a bike or had a nightmare. He would've squeezed tightly on her arms and stared into her eyes. And once she was calm, Mom told him where I was and that she had to go. He would have insisted on driving her, because she was panicked and frantic. He asked Penny to go with them to keep Mom calm. Or maybe Penny insisted on going too.

Scenario Three: Mom's not frantic or panicked. She's pissed. They were having a nice, relaxing afternoon. It was a beautiful, sunny day, so they were in the garden working together on their new bed, where they wanted to put in herbs and vegetables — the one that's covered in grass and weeds now. Mom was annoyed that the phone interrupted her, and then more annoyed that her phone got dirty from the mud on her hands when she answered it. When she hung up, she swore and told Dad, "Well, Matthew, I guess we'll have to do this later. Layne's gone and gotten herself hurt. Again." Sometimes that "again" isn't there at all, and sometimes it's there in a really angry voice. *Ah-gain*. Penny was just hitching a ride. She came out of her room and asked to borrow the car, but Mom said, "I wish, but we have to go to your sister. If you're ready now, I can drop you off on the way. C'mon."

However it happened, they were all in the car when the pickup crossed the centre lane and hit them. I was waiting in the hospital. The same emergency department, actually, that they were brought to in ambulances, though of course I didn't know at the time. It wasn't until way later I found out that while I was waiting, everything changed.

chapter 1

I only got on that stupid skateboard because Asher told me I was too chicken to try it. I mean, how elementary-school-dumb is that? But I fell for it — like I always do — and got on the stupid thing and went down the stupid hill, and now I'm waking up in the ambulance with Asher and some paramedic with terrible breath gawking at me. Asher is sitting there by my head, staring down at me with his eyes all wide and scared. He isn't saying anything, just staring. Why is he staring like that? I reach up to touch my face, to see if all the parts are in the right place, and the paramedic starts asking me questions:

"Can you tell me what day it is? What's the date? Where does it hurt? Does this hurt? How 'bout this? And this?" I mumble the answers, but all I can think of is how twisted and yellow his front top teeth are, and OMG, his breath! With each question a poof of air puffs out at me. Rank! I know, it's not very gracious of me to think nastily about the person who is trying to help me, but I'm not a very nice person.

That's Penny. She's the nice one. The pretty one too. And the smart one. I'm the funny one — if you think sarcasm is funny. And the fearless one. When we were little and we went to Canada's Wonderland, I went on all the roller coasters. Being daring was cute when I was small. Dad would say, "Did you see her, Margo? Laynie isn't scared of anything. The bigger and faster the ride, the more she loved it." It was true. And he was proud of me for it. He didn't call me "reckless" until I was older. I *am* the reckless one. Penny has the common sense.

It was as if, when those first cells divided into two identical people, all the personality traits got divvied up too. We're each a half. Even our names. Dad wanted to call his daughter "Penny Lane" — yes, after the Beatles song. I asked Mom once why she agreed to it, and she only shrugged and said, "You know your father if he gets his mind on something. Besides, it was his turn." His turn. He said Mom had her chance with Zac. Dad always says he wanted to name him "Ringo." I don't know if he's joking or not. Mom named him Isaac after the violinist Isaac Stern. (Whenever this came up, Dad would say to Zac, "At least she didn't name you Yo-Yo," and laugh and laugh.) But we always call him Zac. So the story is that when Dad found out there were two of us, he split the name in half too: Penny and Lane. Mom added the "y" to make Layne look more like a real name than a street sign. At least most of our friends didn't know about the Beatles or the song, and so they didn't make the connection between our names. Until their parents told them, that is.

We arrive at the hospital, and the paramedic wheels me into the ER, past the busy waiting area and into a space with a curtain that does little to block out the noise. Asher follows and stands in the corner while the paramedic tells a nurse all sorts of numbers and long medical words. The doctor flashes a light in my eyes and runs his hands over my body, squeezing at points and asking, "Does this hurt?" Everything hurts, but my arm most of all. And my head. Trying to watch the people moving around the bed makes me dizzy, so I focus on Asher by the door. Maybe they should check on him; he's white as a ghost.

Then the doctor leans close. It takes effort to get my eyes to focus on his face. "Layne, you've bumped your head, and I'm pretty sure you broke your arm, but everything else looks good. You're going to be fine. Wait here and we'll get you all patched up." Wait here? Where else would I go? The doctor stands and pats my shoulder. As he lifts the curtain to leave, he says to Asher, "Call your folks."

"I did," Asher says. I don't remember that.

"You did?" I ask when the doctor is gone. He nods. "What did you say?"

He shrugs and steps closer. "That you fell and hit your head, that we were headed here."

"Did you call mine?"

Asher was so abnormally white to begin with, it's hard to say if he blushed or his colour was just coming back. "Um, no. I should've. I don't have their number, and they took your phone."

Longer sentences are confusing. I summarize what he said to make it clear: He didn't call. They took my phone. "They who?"

"The paramedics. Sorry, I should've —" I'm not sure what he thinks he should've done, because he stops there. I try to nod my head reassuringly, but it hurts. A lot. "What's their number?"

I think for a minute. Why can't I remember? It's a favourite on my phone, not one I dial often. "I, um, don't remember."

He goes white again and steps back toward the crack in the curtain. "I'll go tell the nurses." He's gone before I can ask what exactly he's going to tell them. The lights hurt, so I close my eyes until he whispers, "You awake? I'm back." I try to smile, but it hurts my head. "The nurse said she was looking up your folks' number and calling them."

"What did they say?"

"I dunno. I didn't wait. Want me to go ask?"

"No. I just hope they aren't mad."

"What? Why would they be mad?"

Because I'm the reckless one.

FLASHBACK: *I was sitting on the counter pressing a wet paper towel to each bloodied knee when Dad walked into the kitchen. "What happened to you?" he asked, but the casual words didn't hide the tight pitch in his voice that showed he was worried.*

I shrugged. "Rollerblading."

His worry-widened eyes pinched into a frown. "Weren't you wearing your knee pads?" I shook my head, my arguments for not needing them obliterated by the blood oozing from each knee. He sighed. "Laynie, why do you have to be so reckless?"

Asher and I wait. And wait. I sit on the bed, holding my sore arm against my chest. Asher sits beside me sometimes and then paces by the foot of the bed when he can't sit any longer. He keeps looking at me every so often, his face white and his eyes wide. We chat a bit about nothing. We've been there a whole forty minutes before a nurse shuffles into my curtained space. She studies the chart and adds some notes. "Shouldn't be too long," she says. For the cast? For my parents to arrive? I want to ask for what, but she's already gone, leaving the curtain waving in the gust her exit made.

Asher tries to smile at me, his lips curl up on the edges, but his face is still white and his eyes are still wide. "That's good," he says, and I nod again. The silence in the curtained square is awkward. But it's not like silence with Asher is ever comfortable lately. I mean, it seems I've always got this tight knot in my middle when it's just him and me together. If we're in a group and there are others around, I'm not so edgy, but more and more lately when we're alone, I don't know what to say. I never used to be that nervous. It would seem really creepy if I just watch him and don't say anything, so I'm staring at my feet trying to think of something unlame enough to say. "It's a Mom Race," Asher says, and it takes me a minute to realize he means between our mothers to arrive. "Wanna place bets?"

"Mine," I say. So sure. But where is she? The nurses called them at least a half hour ago.

Asher's mom gets there first. She rushes in and hugs him long enough that his pale face finally gets a bit pink. "Oh, Asher, are you alright?" she asks, pushing him away from her, holding his shoulders at arms' length and looking him over.

"Yeah, Mom, I'm fine. Layne was the one who fell."

She looks at me then and says a small "Oh!" as if she hadn't seen me sitting there at first.

Asher says, "They think she broke her arm. She needs X-rays." X-rays? Did I forget that too? I smile and shrug to show it isn't that big of a deal. Moving my shoulder makes a pain stab in my arm, but I make sure I don't wince.

"Oh, dear, Layne, are you alright?" she asks. It's a pretty dumb question, considering we're sitting in emerg and Asher just told her I broke my arm. I nod, because my throat is tight all of the sudden. I wish it were my mom who was here instead. "Where are your parents?" she asks, and I feel guilty, like she read my mind.

"The nurse called them, they're on their way," Asher said. "I'm going to wait with her."

Asher's mom looks at him a moment, then at her phone, and says, "Okay. We'll wait," before giving me a too-sweet smile.

More awkward minutes. Nobody talks. Asher keeps glancing at me. When our eyes meet, he smiles and sometimes shrugs as if to apologize. Asher's mom keeps checking her phone and her watch and pacing. The space is really too small for a hospital bed and three people who aren't talking. When the nurse returns, Asher's mom looks relieved. "Are Mr. and Mrs. Wheeler here?" she asks. I'm not sure where she thinks the nurse would be hiding my parents.

"Not yet," the nurse says and smiles at me.

Asher's mom gives me a sympathetic smile too, as if *she* were hiding my parents and felt a little guilty for it. "They must have gotten caught up in the traffic. I was able to slip out and around before they closed the road."

Closed the road? What for? The nurse stepped closer. "The doctor wants you to get your X-ray done now, though. Think you can go down without them?"

There's a part of me, an embarrassingly huge part, that wants to cry and stubbornly insist that I wait until my mother can come with me. But she isn't here. And Asher is, and he doesn't need to see me act like a crybaby. So I smile as calmly as I can and say, "Yeah, sure, no problem."

Asher's mom sighs loud enough that everyone turns to look at her. She says, "In that case, Layne, I have to get back to work. You're in good hands with the doctor, and your parents will probably be here when you get back from the X-ray department."

I squelch the tantruming child that is making my heart start to race. "Of course! You're right. They'll be here any minute. There's no sense you waiting here."

"Well, good luck and feel better. Asher, come on then."

Asher looks at me and stays seated. "I'm going to stay here with Layne," he says, and my middle does a little flip-flop that may not be related to the pain in my arm or bump on my head.

"Asher, Layne is fine. She said so herself. You know I have too much on my schedule today to worry about how to come back and pick you up. I've lost too much time already. And you have exams to study for."

Asher crossed his arms. "It's fine, I'll get a ride home with Layne. I can study later."

Her voice is cool. "The last thing they are going to want to do is drive out of their way to take you home. I really would prefer if you come with me now while I'm here and not make an issue of it in front of your friend."

For a moment Asher stays seated, and his lips press together so that they are white against the reddening in his cheeks. He can't get into trouble on my account. "Yeah, Asher, I'm fine. Go while you've got the chance," I say instead of *Please, please,* please *stay here so I'm not alone.*

He looks at me for a moment then stands up and takes a step toward the bed. His fingers brush the back of my hand where it rests on the mattress, and suddenly I'm frozen, afraid to move and break the buzzing connection. "Okay. Text me later?" I don't trust my voice to stay even, so I nod. Head hurts.

Asher follows his mom out of the curtained space, and I can hear their arguing voices fade as they walk away.

"Ready?" the nurse says, and I nod again. She pulls back the curtain to reveal a wheelchair and pushes it toward the bed. "You get valet service," she says with a smile. I try to smile back, push myself up from the bed with my good arm and sit down in the chair. A single tear slips out and runs down my cheek to my neck. I wipe it away quickly, but the nurse says, "Is your arm hurting worse?"

"Yeah," I say, thankful for the excuse.

My parents are not waiting for me when I get back from X-ray. They don't show up in the hour I wait after that. Nobody comes. Maybe they are mad. Maybe this is a grand display of tough love. They'll come when it's convenient. I can hear footsteps and muttered conversations on the other side of the curtain. There's a slit where the curtains hang apart by a few inches, and I make a game of trying to guess who might be zipping by the space by the sound of the voices and footfalls on the linoleum. That one's a woman for sure. Two men. A man? No, a woman in a winter jacket, which is strange because it's hot outside.

Footsteps coming with no voice, so it's only one person. Heavy, like a man, but they stop before anyone passes through my narrow view. I hear papers shuffle, and finally a doctor pushes the two curtains aside to come in. "Good news? Bad news?" he asks, but before I can answer he goes on, "The bad news is it's broken, right about here." He points to his own white-sleeved arm, about halfway between his wrist and elbow. "The good news is it's a clean break that will heal quickly and easily. Bad news? You'll need a cast, so no swimming or summer sports for the next while. Good news, no cleaning toilets either." He smiles, seemingly proud of his wit.

"Where's my mom?" I ask, and my voice cracks. I feel tears building in my eyes and blink fast to push them back. I'm not sure if I'm more upset that she's not there or that my cool, independent facade is crumbling.

His smile does not falter. "Did you call them?"

"Asher, my friend, he went to the nurses' station. He said someone called them ..."

"Ah yes. They probably meant to and got distracted. I'm afraid it happens — it can be busy around here. I'll get someone to call them to be sure."

Well, that makes more sense than my silly Tough Love Conspiracy Theory. I use the hand on my good arm to pat my pockets for my phone. My pockets are empty.

"Where's my phone?"

At that his smile slips a bit and his eyes narrow. "You didn't get it back?" He steps around the small space, looking along the counter, moving tubes and bandaging in shrink-wrapped packaging. "The ambulance guys would have had it. They should have left it here. Maybe they left it at the nurses' station. I'll find out for you." I try to smile, but I don't think it works. "A volunteer is going to come and take you down to the orthopaedic department so they can get a proper cast on that arm. By the time you're done with that, your folks and your phone will be here waiting for you."

"Okay, thank you," I manage to say as he's backing out between the curtains.

He has only been gone a few minutes before a man comes through the curtain with a clipboard and a wheelchair. "Layne Wheeler?" he asks, looking from it to me.

"Yes."

"Hi, Layne. I'm Keith. I'm going to take you to the ortho clinic."

I sit in the chair, and the volunteer pushes me to and then from the orthopaedic department. I'm now sporting a fresh orange fibreglass cast that is wrapped around my hand and arm up to my elbow. The curtained area is still empty when we return, and my phone is nowhere to be seen. My arm and head ache, and I'm feeling sick to my stomach, so I lie down on the bed and close my eyes against the fluorescent light. Urgent shouted orders reverberate from another corner of the emergency department over the hushed muttering I've heard so far. I turn on my side, gently cradling my newly casted arm, and pull the pillow over my head to block out the sounds. I close my eyes and start to cry.

I must have fallen asleep. When I open my eyes the doctor is standing beside the bed. His smile is gone, his face tense and tired, but his voice is gentle when he asks, "How are you feeling?"

I shrug. "My head hurts," I admit. I don't tell him my eyes hurt from crying. The curtains hang open a bit behind him, and I catch a glimpse of movement: Penny's ponytail. Finally, they're here. "My parents?"

He studies me a minute and shakes his head. I must be seeing things. He says, "Concussion," as if the one word holds all the answers to the unknowns of the world. I guess it explains a lot about my situation: headache, queasy stomach, falling asleep, easy tears, seeing things. "I'm going to keep you overnight for observation. We'll get you a room upstairs." I look at my fingers poking out of the cast to see if they are turning blue or green or swelling up huge or in danger of falling off. I can observe them myself at home, I think, and come back if they do anything strange. I must've said it out loud because the doctor sighs and says, "Just the same, we'd like you to stay the night."

He reaches into the hall behind the curtain and rolls a wheelchair into the cramped space. "Hop on," he says. His voice is light in a fake, strained way, like I'm six and he's trying to make everything fun — even the horrible bits. Especially the horrible bits.

And I'm getting sick of other people pushing me in a chair. "I can walk," I say. After all, it's my arm in the cast, not my leg. I swing my legs to one side of the bed and push myself up onto my feet. The room spins, and I lean back against the bed again.

The doctor doesn't laugh or say I-told-you-so, which is nice of him. He smiles at me, still like I'm six and difficult, and says, "Hospital policy," as he puts his long fingers around my bare elbow and steadies me toward the chair. I shut up and sit.

He pushes me through the ER to an elevator and hits the fifth-floor button on the inside. The ride up is short and silent. From the corner of my eye I see

Penny sitting beside me, but the wall of the elevator is a mirror, and it's just me with messy strands of hair falling loose from my ponytail. I raise my good hand and try to smooth it out. My face is so white that my freckles look darker than usual. When the elevator doors open, the first thing I hear is screaming. Not horror movie sounds, but toddler screaming — somewhere too close, someone is not getting their way. Or maybe far — toddlers can be loud.

I'm fifteen, almost old enough to drive and just a few years away from being a legal adult who can drink and vote and all that, but in the hospital fifteen is still a kid, I guess. He steers me down the hall into a dim room. The curtains are open, but the sky outside is dark, so I see the doctor behind my chair in the reflection. How long was I in the ER anyway? Before I can ask the doctor, a nurse rushes in and says, "Thank you, Doctor," in dismissal, and he obliges without saying anything further to me.

The nurse turns to me and says, "Here you go." She holds out a pair of ugly hospital pj's. When I don't reach for them immediately, she says, "You must be tired." She stands there holding them out until I take them, then she says, "You can change in here," and opens the bathroom door. Her words are abrupt. She doesn't seem to be the soft, gentle kind of nurse. Her perma-frown has creased the lines between her eyebrows into deep crevices.

"Resistance is futile," I mumble to myself, but she hears me. Her eyebrows meet over the fissure, but I can't tell if she's confused or annoyed. It's probably better to shut up and go along with her. I step into the bathroom and shut the door — there's no lock on it. I pull my T-shirt up, and my casted arm gets caught in the sleeve. I pull and tug, and the pain in my arm shoots from under the cast up to my shoulder. But there's no way I'm asking for her help. I stop for a minute, take a deep breath and slowly slide my good arm and head out of the shirt, then untwist the material and slip it off over my cast. Victory comes at the cost of a throbbing pain from my shoulder to the tips of my not-yet-green fingers. I look at my orange-plastered arm and wiggle my fingers. My watch.

I come out of the washroom with my T-shirt and shorts folded and set them on the chair by the bed. "I still don't have my watch or phone," I say to Nurse Hatchet.

She looks at me for minute then pats the bed with her hand. "I'll call down and see who has them. The paramedics usually collect that stuff and give it to the staff in emerg."

"When are my mom and dad getting here? The doctor called them before he brought me up. They should've been here by now." My voice catches on the last three words. Nurse Hatchet looks at me and sighs again, a big enough sigh that her whole upper body rises and settles. I must be fulfilling the self-centred, ungrateful teenager image. Maybe they weren't able to drop everything and come running right away. There's a quiver of guilt in my chest. Penny's the thoughtful one. I'm more often selfish.

"Your family will be along as soon as they can," she says without looking at me. And then, "How about you lie back and relax." She strides out the door without saying anything else. If I never see her again, I'd be good with that. I lie back against the pillows and close my eyes.

When I open my eyes, Zac is sitting beside the bed, his head lying on his folded arms by my leg. I must've been more tired — or maybe my concussion is worse — than I thought, because I don't remember anything after closing my eyes. There is light coming through the window, so it's close to morning. I must've fallen asleep. Or, a scarier thought, maybe my smushed brain didn't make any memories.

Zac's asleep. What's he doing here? Besides us, the room is empty and quiet. Maybe Mom and Dad were here and stepped out for a minute. Why would they call Zac? Maybe my hit to the head *is* bad. It had to be something for them to call Zac; they haven't talked to him in months.

His hair is longer than the last time I saw him, flopping over his arms and touching the bed. He needs a haircut, badly. But it's good to see him; it's been way too long. "Hey," I whisper, but he doesn't move. I say it again, just a bit louder, and he wakes up, looks up.

His eyes.

Something's wrong.

His blue eyes are green, like they turn when he's been crying. And the whites are red. And his face is puffy.

I'm going to puke.

And he's here. And my parents aren't. I don't know what's happened, but nothing about Zac sitting here crying can be good news.

Something's wrong.

He says, "Hey," then makes this hard clumping sound in his throat, like he's trying to swallow the world. Like the whole sphere full of plants and animals and people going about their regular days working or jogging or playing with their kids or studying or falling in love or falling out of love or cleaning their cars or playing sports or walking the dog is stuck in his throat, and he has to swallow it down before he can open his mouth again to tell me what I already sort of know, because his blue eyes are green.

And he is there and they are not.

He puts his forehead down on the side of the bed and mumbles it away. I try to listen closely, but opening my ears to hear him just makes me hear the kids screaming in other rooms and the beeps and buzzes that seem to be the breath of the hospital. His words come out jagged and sharp so that I don't really need to hear them with my ears. They pierce me through my chest and cut straight into my heart. A drunk. A pickup. They were all in the car. Mom. Dad. Even Penny. All of them. In the car.

My brain is searing. Screaming. Someone's screaming. It's me.

People rush in.

Colours, flashes, swirl in my head.

Maybe it's the concussion.

chapter 2

I wake up groggy later in the morning after the skateboard and the drunk in the pickup and Zac crying and mumbling and someone giving me a needle. I slept — dark and dreamless and heavy. It takes me a minute to figure out where I am (hospital) and why (stupid skateboarding dare resulting in concussion and orange cast), and why Zac is here beside the bed instead of Mom (oh, yeah). The light is streaming through the flimsy curtains, making my stinging eyes water. I squeeze them shut, but that makes them hurt worse — stiff and puffy and prickly. Zac is stretched out on a cot that must have appeared sometime in the night. He's breathing fitfully in his sleep, twitching and moaning a little. So it wasn't some dream. Or maybe it was? Maybe it's still possible that since I wiped out on the skateboard and hit my head, the doctors are holding me in some medically induced coma, and the drugs they are using create super real and terrible dreams about pickup trucks. Maybe. I lift my left hand to pinch my right arm, but my fingers bump into a cold solid substance. The cast. Right. I reach up and pinch my ear. Ouch. Okay I'm awake. *Crap.*

The door pushes open, the bottom swishing on the tile floor. A woman in Winnie the Pooh scrubs walks in, her head bent over the clipboard in her hand. Stringy strands of her brown hair that pulled loose from her ponytail hang down so that I can't see her face. Just before she reaches the bed, she stops and looks up from her notes.

"Oh, you're awake. Good morning." Really? Is it? There's nothing I can say in response to that, because Zac in the cot; the pinch hurt; the pickup and the drunk were not a dream. "I'm Andrea."

"Hi," I say, because saying nothing just feels too rude. Sheets shuffle and a groan slips from the cot. I turn away from the frantic-haired nurse to see Zac rubbing his eyes. He freezes then sits up like a catapult. If his head wasn't attached, it would have zipped across the room and hit me. Guess he forgot for a moment there too. More proof it isn't a coma-drug-induced dream. He sits staring at me. Through me.

"Layne," the nurse says and waits until I turn back to look at her. "The doctor said he can discharge you to go home, if you want."

If I want? Are there options? Instead of home, could I go back in time? I would tell Asher to piss off instead of getting on the skateboard; no crash plus no call from the ER plus no mad dash to the hospital equals no drunk in a pickup. Yes, I'll take the time travel option, please.

"We're good," Zac says, and I turn back to glare at him. We are far from good. One puffy eyelid drops down over his red-rimmed eye, and someone inside my head screams at him. SO not good.

The nurse doesn't seem to believe him either. She looks between us and chews her lower lip then pushes the straggly hair out of her face. It just falls back in the same place again. "Okay. I'll finish up the discharge paperwork and call the social worker."

"Social worker?" Zac says in a high-pitched voice. I hear his feet hit the floor. "We're good, why do we need to speak to a social worker?" He perches on the edge of my bed. He starts to cross his arms but then stops, and they move awkwardly for a moment, trying to find a resting place before settling in fists on the mattress on either side of him. "We're good." *Why* does he keep saying that?

"Your sister is a minor," the nurse says, looking down to where her finger points to a place on her notes, as if to be sure.

"I'm not," Zac says. Now he crosses his arms. I see Dad then as a shimmery layer over Zac like when we did cartooning in art class and used tracing paper to draw pictures just a little bit different from each other to create movement when the pages flipped. Zac is a tracing of Dad. His feigned casual manner in the relaxed-bed-perch posture is sabotaged by his defiantly crossed arms and jutting jaw.

"I understand, but your sister is underage … you're not legally —"

"I'm her brother and her guardian. I have papers. Plus I called our aunt, she's on her way from out of town. She … she doesn't know the city, so we're meeting her at home." Zac's voice is low and even, like a warning growl a big cat may give out before an attack. "We're good," he repeats. He isn't only trying to assure the nurse of our sufficient level of goodness, he's trying to convince me too. And probably himself.

"I see," the nurse says, balancing the clipboard on one hand and writing something with her other. "I'll go confirm with the doctor and with the worker on call. Just give me a few minutes." She turns around and walks out without looking back up from her papers. I sort of hope for a minute that she'll walk into the doorframe, but apparently she has had too much practice reading and walking for that.

"Let's go," Zac says the minute she's gone. He tugs on my uncasted arm to pull me off the bed. He steps to the chair and tosses me my shorts and T-shirt then purposefully turns his back. "Hurry."

I pulled my shorts on under my johnny shirt then carefully swap the hospital gown for my T-shirt so I don't get tangled up again. I step into my flip-flops. "But she said —" I'm shivering and rub my free palm from my shoulder to my elbow to try to warm up. My pinky finger hits the top of the cast with each rub. The pressure hurts my broken arm, but I keep doing it because it seemed to be the only part of me not floating in a pool of numbness.

"I know, I know. But we're not waiting. They can find us if they want." He turns around and gives me a genuine Zac-crooked smile and offers a Ziploc baggie that holds my phone, watch and forty-seven cents. "And besides, now I have to call Aunt Carole," he says, and I try to smile back.

"I don't get it, what's the hurry?" I say, putting the coins back in my pocket and slipping my watch on the wrong wrist. My phone is dead. Dead. The word ricochets around in my head.

"Social worker, Laynie. You're a minor. I don't know what they'll say or do, but I don't want to wait and find out." Good point.

We walk to the door, but he stops and I bump into him. He peeks out left then right then left again. He waves his hand to say c'mon, as if we're some spies in a movie. Or art thieves sneaking out of the gallery. I follow him down the hall at a near run on my tiptoes to the end, where he pushes a door open into the stairwell. He doesn't look back to see if I'm following. He just knows I probably am, because I always have. I keep the distance between us as short as possible without tripping one of us up. Down the stairs, winding around three floors until he pushes the door with a large "L" on a blue square. We step out into the lobby, and he ploughs ahead through a few lost-looking people. The automatic exit doors slide open, and hot air blasts me in the face. My eyes sting. The parking lot is just past the driveway that passes in front of the doors for quick drop-offs. He stops to look both ways, and I reflexively do the same, scanning right to left, looking for a car.

No car, just a blonde girl exactly my height standing there waiting. For us.

"Laynie, finally," Penny says.

I stop. Shake my head. Blink hard — twice — and Zac's already across the driveway and heading to the cars.

"Zac! Wait!" He stops and waves his hand for me to hurry up. I take a step toward him. Then another. I force my eyes forward to follow him through the cars until Mom's blue Yaris beeps and flashes its lights. I climb in the front and only then chance a glance around. Penny is settling into the back seat. Maybe running away from the hospital isn't such a great idea. My concussion is obviously worse than anyone realized.

Zac doesn't talk until we are buckled into the car. "I hate that place!" he spits. He rests his forehead on the steering wheel, and his shoulders lift up as he takes in a deep breath.

"Me too," Penny whispers in the back seat. I put my hands over my ears and squeeze my eyes shut, but her voice continues inside my head: "I'm so glad you're finally out of there."

"Laynie?" Cold fingers brush my arm, and I jump back against the door. My eyes open against my will, but it isn't Penny touching me; it's just Zac. "Laynie, what's wrong? Does your head hurt? Do you want to go back in? Maybe we should go back in." His eyes shoot around in a frantic search for something. I don't know what.

But: social worker. "No, I'm fine. Let's go. Go." I stare straight ahead out of the windshield as Zac backs out of the spot and drives out of the parking lot. He glances at me every few minutes, but I stare straight ahead, trying to work out what's going on. Penny is dead. Zac said so. She was in the car with Mom and Dad. There was a drunk in a pickup truck … she was in the car. I peek into the back seat, and Penny smiles at me. "Zac?"

"Yeah?"

"They're all gone." I meant it to be a question, but it sounds like a statement. A surrender.

The word kind of slips out of him when he sighs. "Yeah."

None of us talk the rest of the way home. Zac drives, and I keep staring out of the windshield, feeling the world rush toward me. Cars and trucks and bikes and signs and houses and people walking dogs seem to hurtle toward the car, when really we are rushing past them. I don't look back, but I know Penny is sitting there with us, silent and thinking.

We pull into the empty driveway, and Zac turns off the car. We sit for a moment, not talking. I stare at my fingers sticking out of the orange cast, squeezing each fingertip and watching it turn from white back to pink when I let go. "Ready?" Zac says finally.

No. "Yeah."

Zac uses his key and unlocks the door. Silence. I strain my ears to hear something, anything, that could indicate a mixup. Nothing. Penny's hoodie hangs from the doorknob of the closet; one of mine is nearby on the floor. She is the tidy one. Mom hates it when our jackets are left where they fall on the floor. *Hated* it. "Hey, you okay? I've got to call Aunt Carole," Zac says and seems to be watching for my reaction. I nod, too queasy in the stomach to say anything.

"It's too quiet," Penny says. I turn and stare at her until she shrugs and says, "Well, it is!" It is too quiet — that's no less true even if the person saying it isn't real. She can't be real. She was in the car. "You should rest," Penny says.

I walk down the hall, past Mom and Dad's room. I'm glad the door is closed. Too soon, I'm standing outside my bedroom door. *Our* bedroom door. I put my hand on the knob, trying to work up the, the what? Courage? Gumption? Effort? to turn it and walk in. I don't know what I'm expecting to find. Penny is dead (and standing right behind me), but if I open the door I will find *her* in the room. Her stuff; all the little things that painted a picture of who Penny is. *Was.* Her books. Her clothes. Her stereo that would call up the last song she played. The twenty-five most played songs playlist. Her big stuffed hippo — that she bought when she was way too old to buy stuffies — sitting on the top of the bookshelf. Maybe her stuff would smother me with signs of her.

Behind me, Penny finally says, "Oh go on, loser," which peeves me off enough to twist the knob and shove the door open.

The room is silent, of course. And still. Her things sit tidily in the places where she left them. She is the tidy one, after all. *Was.* Her chemistry book lies open on her desk, a pencil resting in the crack between the pages. Chem exam on Tuesday. Her charger is plugged in, the cord lying on her desk, but her phone is missing. Of course she would've taken it with her. The yellow novel with the red and white spine isn't on her desk, or her side table, or her bed; she always carried her current read with her. Always and everywhere.

"You should lie down," Penny says, flopping down on her bed so that her ponytail bounces behind her.

I ignore her and sit at my desk. The surface is hidden by a clutter of school books, papers, candy wrappers, hair ties, headbands and a seemingly endless list of stuff I'd tossed there to put away later. I shift things around until I find the charger cord and can plug in my dead phone. The battery appears on the black screen, and I stare at it so as not to look over at Penny's things or Penny sitting on her bed. "Penny, you're … I mean, why are you … I mean, what's going on?"

"You know," Penny says. I don't. I really don't. But I can guess.

Reasons Why Penny Is Sitting on Her Bed Even Though She's Dead

1. She's a ghost.
2. She's a concussion symptom.
3. She's a hallucination.

Whichever is the truth, the bottom line is obvious: I've lost it. Crazy. Cracked.

The white apple pops on my phone and then the home screen. A red circle with white number "52" covers the corner of the green text app icon. The red circle over the phone square says "14." Fifty-two texts, fourteen missed calls. I open the texting app and flick through the list of conversations. Texts from Sara, Melissa, Abby, Asher, Adam, Julie; all the people I'd expect to get a text from if I disappeared from the cyber world for a day. Which I guess I did. But there are also texts from people who haven't talked to me in years. They are full of exclamation marks and OMG's and X's and O's and teary emoticons and coloured hearts — broken and whole — and praying hands. And none of them say anything at all. I slide my finger from right to left on each conversation and hit "delete" on each one. Then I go into my voice mail and delete each message without listening to them.

Penny is here our room, even if she is just some cruel side effect of my concussion, sitting cross-legged on her bed. For a moment I can pretend she's real if I erase the evidence on my phone. I lay back and she whispers, "Sleep tight, Laynie."

chapter 3

FLASHBACK: **When we were little we had a band. We weren't quite** *the Beatles, but that didn't stop Dad. He had already shown us "I Want to Hold Your Hand" a bazillion times on YouTube, so we knew the words. The first time we played it for him, Zac played the guitar and Penny and I were singing. Sometimes Dad would play piano, but that time he just sat on the couch "directing" us, which really meant "watching" us, mesmerized. He perched forward with his elbows on his knees and his hands tied together as if each was holding the other back from reaching out to us. His eyes were like Zac's, bright and blue but glowing green when they were wet. They glowed then. His smile beamed behind his folded hands. Every so often he'd mouth the words as if willing them into our brains.*

My favourite songs are always the ones that conceal a sucker punch. The upbeat tempos with the fun runs and harmonies that held a story so so so … *haunting*. Haunting isn't the right word. Neither is poignant, because sometimes the emotion is happy or hopeful, not always sad. But one song — three verses, three minutes — can hold all the emotions that one of Penny's novels takes three hundred pages to reveal. There's just something about adding music to words that makes an impact. Penny can sing, she has a beautiful voice, but she likes funny songs. *Liked.* I'm the sentimental one. I'm the one who cried burying the bird we found in the backyard when we were seven — Penny dug the hole.

I keep thinking about our band when I'm supposed to be helping plan the funeral. Dad's sister, Carole, flew in and swept us up in the planning. Sort of. At least she dragged us along. She had already made the appointment to meet with the funeral director when she arrived this morning. She said Monday afternoon was the most efficient time to meet with someone "in that business," whatever that means.

She insists Zac and I go to the funeral home with her and drives her rented car, deeming my mother's Yaris to be too cramped. When we arrive at the door of the funeral home, a tall, lanky man in a too-big suit opens the door for us. He smells of something strange that I can't place, a musty combination of old fragrance and dust. "Hello, Ms. Wheeler? And you must be Isaac and Layne?"

Zac reaches out his hand and says, "Zac," with a wince. The man's skeletal hand turns toward me, and I shake it, though I'd really rather not. It's cool, smooth, dry. Lifeless.

"I am so sorry for your loss," he says. I would think someone in his profession would've come up with a more imaginative platitude by now.

"Thank you, it really has been terrible," Carole says with a sniff.

By the time those rote pleasantries have been said, we're standing in a main hall of the funeral home. "If you'll follow me," Skeletor says and walks away toward an open door at the end of the hall. He ushers us in, and Zac and I sit on a couch while Aunt Carole claims the chair across from the desk.

Aunt Carole takes a folded piece of paper from her purse and says, "I've already done some planning that I think you will find adequate …" and here starts our discussions about the funeral plan.

The Plans for the Funeral

1. Cremation. (No choice in the matter, really after the damage done by the drunk and the pickup.)
2. Service in the funeral home chapel. (Since we do not have a church family.)
3. Readings by Dad's friend, Dave (Ecclesiastes 3:1-2) and Mom's friend, Robyn (Isaiah 41:10).
4. Abby and Emily (grown children of the chapel's recommended organist) to sing "The Old Rugged Cross" and "Amazing Grace" —

"What about 'In My Life'?" someone says. I look around. Zac is sitting on the couch next to me, nodding with wide eyes. It was me. I said it. I'm not sure who's most surprised to hear me speak up — Aunt Carole, Zac or me.

"Yeah, that's a good choice," Zac says and leans forward, looking from me to Aunt Carole.

"Which hymn is that?" she asks, flipping through the hymnal in her hand. Her voice is sharp with impatience, as if I'm wasting time with the interruption.

Zac looks at me, but my mouth won't open. I don't know what I'd say anyway. "'In My Life' by the Beatles …" he says and starts to sing the first line in his easy, low tenor. Aunt Carole puts her hand up, her perfect red nails pointing at the ceiling.

"Isaac, please, this is a funeral, not one of your father's jam sessions. We will have hymns." She mutters something more, but I can't make out the words.

FLASHBACK: *All of us were sitting around the dining room table with dirty dinner dishes scattered and stacked on the table. "Oh, Matt! You know what Carole thinks … I'm the evil heretic who lead you astray."*

Dad winked at me then trained his eyes on her. "You're right, Margo. I'll follow you anywhere, even to Hell." He laughs at the easy exchange, the tried and tested and familiar family joke.

Carole didn't find it funny. She managed to make comments about our heathen ways any time she was around for Christmas or Easter or even if she happened to be visiting on a Sunday. "It's a shame these children don't go to church" or "Mother would be so disgusted, Matthew" or "How will they understand the true meaning of Christmas?" She never even called my brother Zac, like everyone else. She always called him Isaac because she preferred to believe he was named after Isaac in the Bible, not the Isaac with the violin.

She's probably muttering that wanting a rock and roll song played at a religious memorial ceremony is just more proof of our spiritually doomed status and wholly expected of her sister-in-law's ungodly children.

And so back to The Plans:

5. Carole to give the eulogy. (She's already working on something.)
6. Reception in the hall of the funeral home. (A discount if both are held there.)
7. Family-only interment service. (It'll be a small gathering, since our family is quite small now.)

Zac places his hand over my casted one where it rests on the couch between us and gives my sticking-out fingers a squeeze. I stop helping with The Plans and go back to singing Beatles songs in my head. There are enough songs in the Beatles anthology that I can move from one to the next throughout Aunt Carole's meeting with Skeletor. I'm so engrossed in my one-woman concert that I'm startled when the other three stand up. They are looking at me.

"I knew she wasn't paying attention," Aunt Carole says under her breath to nobody but plenty loud enough for everyone to hear.

"I'm sorry." I'm not sorry. "What?" I ask and Aunt Carole rolls her eyes.

Zac squeezes my fingers and says, "Mr. Robertson is going to show us the chapel and our choices for burial urns." Burial urns. For Mom and Dad and Penny. My breath catches, and the air seems too thin. I try to suck more in, but my throat is tight. "Laynie? Are you okay?"

I do my best to smile and nod. "I think I'll just wait in the car," I say to Zac, trying to ignore Aunt Carole behind him.

"The car is locked," she says.

"It's okay. I need some air anyway. I'll just sit outside."

"I'll come with you," Zac says and turns to Aunt Carole. "I'll go with her."

"For Heaven's sake, children, this is your parents and sister we are talking about. Can't you demonstrate some interest in the plans I am making? Must I make all the decisions on my own?"

Zac looks back and forth between us, seemingly lost for words. Knowing him, he feels caught between us, between keeping Aunt Carole happy and being there for me so I'm not alone. I bet I won't be. "Really, Zac, you go with them and I'll wait for you outside," I say, hoping he'll just go along with it. He studies me a minute so I say, "Really," again.

Before any more argument can be made, I back out of the room and go down the hall, concentrating on walking, not running to the front door. I open it slowly, careful not to swing it open in haste or anger or frustration. Across the driveway is a green space with a large oak casting shadows on the grass. Penny is sitting with her back against the trunk, braiding three long pieces of grass together. See? Not alone. I go and sit down in the cool shade, the rough bark scratching my back as I slide down beside her.

"Hey," she says.

"Hey," I reply as if talking to a hallucination is something I do all the time.

"Want to talk about it?" she asks, and I shake my head.

"Let's sing," I say instead, and she starts in easily with the first words of "Eleanor Rigby."

chapter 4

The doorbell wakes me. I squeeze my eyes more tightly closed and lie still on my side on top of the covers on my bed. I'm turned toward Penny's half of the room with the fingers of my free hand still curled around the neck of her guitar. The doorbell rings again and my eyes open, and for a moment I am sure it was all a joke. They were ringing the doorbell instead of just walking in so we'd open it and they'd laugh and say "SURPRISE!" and we'd laugh and hug them because even though it was a really sick, mean joke, we'd just be happy they were okay. Maybe it's not a joke, but a way to get Zac to come home. They knew he'd come home, and when he did they'd come back and yell "SURPRISE!" He'd be so relieved it's not real that he'd stop being mad and come home. But he's been home for three days. They'd have come back by now.

The window lets in sunlight, bright enough to throw shadows on the ceiling. There're no indications to help me know what time of day it is. "How long did I sleep?" I ask Penny, who is sitting with her back to me at her desk. She shrugs without turning around. Maybe I slept for days or even weeks. There's a knock on the door. I hear the door open, then close again, and Zac's voice says, "Layne? They found us." Is he trying to be funny? His voice is too shaky to sound like a joke.

I push myself up and turn to face him. He smiles at me, but his eyes are wide and jumpy, and his nervousness plants a nauseous whirl in my middle. "Who?" Penny and I ask at the same time.

"A social worker. She's here."

"Where's Aunt Carole?" I run my fingers through my hair and retie the ponytail. Try to smooth the wrinkles in my T-shirt. When's the last time I changed it?

"Grocery store," he says. I check my phone on my bedside table — 11:37 a.m., still only Tuesday. "Come on, she's waiting. I want to get this over with before Aunt Carole gets back."

"Why?" My head is still foggy from sleeping.

Zac makes a face that says "shut up and hurry up" and says in a hurried whisper, "She wants to take you home with her."

The social worker? That doesn't make sense. "No, moron, Aunt Carole," Penny says. She's beside me on the bed.

The words register first, then the implication: moving away. To live with Aunt Carole. "What? But ..."

Zac rushes to say, "We don't want that, right? I want you to stay with me, here, but I don't want the social worker to talk to Aunt Carole until I have everything figured out."

He watches me for a minute, and I guess he's waiting for me to say something. "I don't want to go," comes out whiney and petulant. I feel my face burn.

"I know. So come on, let's go get rid of her." My mind is racing, but I can't think of anything else to say, so I follow Zac down the hall.

A woman stands in the living room. She's dressed in a dark suit and is still wearing her shoes. Rude. She's skinny. Not healthy skinny but blow-away-in-a-brisk-breeze skinny. She reaches out her hand to me, and I can see each bone leading to her knobbly knuckles. A weird thought pops into my head: maybe she's really dead, a skeleton to go along with my ghost sister who is already sitting on the couch. The absurdity of the idea makes me laugh, a manic, out-of-control giggle, and she frowns and takes her hand back without shaking mine. "Hello, Layne, I'm Rebecca Sturge."

I open my mouth to say hi but my breath catches in my throat, and I make a squeaky grunt sound instead. She sits in Dad's armchair and waves her hand toward the couch. I sit beside Penny.

"I'm a social worker with Children's Services. It seems you and your brother did not understand that we needed to conduct a short interview before you left the hospital on Sunday," she says, glaring at Zac. I look at him too, and when she looks back at her clipboard, he winks at me.

"I'm her guardian," Zac says, but she doesn't look up.

"Layne. Do you understand the role of a legal guardian now that your parents are no longer able to care for you?" *Dead. Say dead.* The word feels foreign in my head, and I'm still trying to pair it up with my parents. And Penny. My eyes fill with water. I nod. "Your brother claims that your parents named him as your legal guardian. How do you feel about Isaac being your legal guardian until you are an adult?" My throat is tight and blocked by something thick and sharp. I swallow, but it doesn't clear. I nod again. "I'm terribly sorry to have to discuss this with you right now, but arrangements need to be made. I need to hear it in your own words. Is this what you want?"

I manage to push out enough air to say, "Yes." A tear falls from each eye with the effort, and I swat at my cheeks to wipe them off. "I want to stay with Zac."

She nods and writes something on the paper fixed to the clipboard. "Alright, then. It is my responsibility to make sure this is an appropriate arrangement. Isaac, I'll have to see your parents' paperwork. Do you have that here?"

Panic. I close my fists tight. My hands are warm and sticky. I glance at Zac, and he looks so casual. It's an act, I can tell that it is, but I don't think she can. "It's in our parents' safety deposit box. We have an appointment later in the week to get the papers and go through them with their lawyer."

The lady stares at him for a minute, as if she is trying to see into his brain to determine if he's telling the truth. "Are you sure, then, that you are named as her guardian?"

Zac's hands curl into fists in his lap, but that's the only indication that the question makes him angry. "We talked about it before." His voice is low and even. "They said it was just a precaution. They wanted to make sure I was okay with it."

The room is silent for a minute while she scribbles something else. Without looking up, she says, "Okay. I will schedule a follow-up meeting to make sure you are both well and managing. You can show me the documentation then." She tucks the clipboard into her bag and stands up, reaching her boney hand out toward Zac, who also stands up to shake it. "I'll be in touch. Here is my card. If you need anything at all, please let me know."

Zac takes the card and makes a show of pulling his wallet out of his back pocket and tucking it safely away. "Thank you, Ms. Sturge, I will," he says, but I know from his voice he is lying.

She studies him a minute. Maybe she heard the lie too. "Isaac, Layne, I'm not the bad guy here. It is not my intention to make things worse for you. But I have a responsibility to make sure that Layne, as a minor, is in a safe and supportive environment." Minor. Child. Me. Beside me, Penny giggles and whispers, "You're such a child!"

FLASHBACK: *Me hidden behind the shower curtain with an old Halloween mask that smelled like cheap rubber and Dad's cordless drill trying to stifle a laugh while Penny, unsuspecting, brushed her teeth at the sink. When she turned on the water, I silently pulled the curtain back, knowing — because I knew her — that she dipped her head down to spit in the sink when she ran the water. It was my chance to make my macabre presence appear in the mirror behind her. She looked up and screamed. And screamed and screamed and screamed. Even after I took off the mask she kept screaming. Loud enough that Mom, Dad and Zac came running and found us in the bathroom: me doubled over in the shower, laughing hysterically, and Penny covering her face, shivering and leaning against the counter.*

Mom tried to chastise me, but I could hear a tinkle of her laugh in her effortfully stern voice. "Come on, Penny-girl, let's get away from her," she said, guiding Penny out of the washroom with her arm over Penny's shoulders.

"You're such a child," Penny hissed at me on her way out.

Remembering the prank and a hundred more like it, I feel another manic giggle rising up and swallow hard to suppress it. I'm the joker. Penny is the gullible one. *Was.*

"She is safe and supported," Zac says. And this time he's totally convincing. My eyes prick again, and I blink fast to hold the tears back.

Zac walks the social worker to the door, but I stay rooted on the couch beside Penny. "That was *weird*," she says finally. Talk about understatement.

"Everything's weird," I answer, realizing talking to a hallucination of my dead sister feels like the most normal thing to have happened in days.

chapter 5

I expect the funeral to be pathetic and desolate. It feels like it was Zac and me left alone in the world — well, and Aunt Carole, too — so who would come? But people did.

Turns out the drunk in the pickup truck was in the news. Aunt Carole bought copies of the paper from Sunday morning — the day after. Three copies, in case we needed an extra. The story was on the second page with a full-colour picture of Dad's SUV busted and twisted. It reminded me of Play-Doh, how once we were done creating our work of art — a cat, a person, a car, a house, a dragon — we'd punch it and twist it and stretch it and squish it until the recognizable cat-person-car-house-dragon shape became nothing but a blob. On the road in front of the SUV-blob was Penny's book. I don't think anyone else would know what it was, but I did, because I'd picked it up that Saturday morning before I went out with Sara and studied the yellow cover that clashed with the red and white spine. "Is it good?" I asked her, which was a dumb question, because my sister never met a book she didn't like. She nodded and told me I should read it and I said I would, but we both knew I was lying, because she was the reader, not me.

Aunt Carole showed me the papers on Monday after we met with the funeral director. Then she went for a shower to wash off the travel grime. I took the three newspapers out to the backyard and set them on fire. They burned quickly, the pages turning black and curling into the middle before breaking off in brittle flakes. Penny crouched down in the grass beside me, watching the glowing red line move from the outside edges of the paper inward as the black and white text disappeared. "You should have brought marshmallows," she said.

So I suspect the funeral is so full because the story was in the news. Zac and Aunt Carole and I are waiting in a small office near the chapel. I can see the full chapel through the inch the door was left ajar and hear a murmuring that is just above a shuffle.

"Look at the books," I whisper to Penny.

"They're beautiful," Penny says. She stands by the bookshelves, running her fingers along the spines. The walls of the office are lined with books, organized so that the height shrinks from left to right along the shelf. Most of them are black or dark brown with lighter lettering. Some are leather-bound, soft and matte, and others are shiny, reflecting back the bright overhead light and obscuring the text of the title.

"What was that, Layne?" Aunt Carole asks.

I have got to be more careful. "Just praying," I say, and Penny bursts out laughing. Aunt Carole frowns at me, suspicious and annoyed. Even Zac shakes his head when I look his way.

Almost in the middle of the third shelf down is a red spine with white letters. I want to step closer to see if it's a copy of Penny's book. The book she was reading. My fingers itch to pull the book from the shelf to read the cover, but my feet seem to be nailed to the floor. And then the funeral director says, "It's time," and my feet follow Zac's out of the little office into the chapel of the funeral home.

I look over my shoulder at Penny. "I think I'll sit this one out," she says.

The place is packed. The chapel itself is full of chairs that are full of people. People are even standing along the back. A side wall has been opened into another room with chairs and people. Some of the faces look familiar, but I don't know who they are — maybe people from Dad's work or the school where Mom taught? Could be the guy at the grocery store for all I know. And some kids from school. I wonder briefly if they got out of their exams too. Zac's friends Chase and Corey are sitting in the second row, looking strange all cleaned up in suits. Abby is between them, along with Sara and Asher, who are side by side, their faces chalk-white and eyes red. Both try to smile when their eyes meet mine, but they fail, leaving their lips twitching like some weird spasm. It makes me think of zombies. Asher raises his hand and wiggles his fingers in a small wave.

Behind them in the third row are Chloe, Jaime, Willow and ... I forget the redhead's name. The four of them always sit together at the corner table in the cafeteria.

FLASHBACK: *I walked into the cafeteria, looked around for Sara and Penny. Sara wasn't there, but Penny was sitting alone at a table in the corner. I walked past one table and heard giggles and a voice say, "Such a loser." When I looked at them, Chloe stopped laughing, suddenly like she was choking and her hand covered her mouth. The others kept laughing until she tipped her head in my direction and they looked at me, like puppets on the same strings. I didn't even realize I had stopped walking and stood there staring at them. Olivia — that's the redhead's name! — smiled at me and waved. I used all my willpower to turn back facing Penny and walk away instead of toward their table. "It's not worth it," Penny kept saying, but it would feel good to do something. Anything.*

The four girls crane their necks to see me as I walk into the chapel, their flushed red faces, streaked with mascara tears, peeking around Sara and Asher in front of them. I check to make sure Aunt Carole isn't watching and flip them the bird. There are a few gasps and mutterings above the sniffles, so I can't hear exactly what Zac hisses in my ear. But Asher laughs and gives me a thumbs up. I turn and sit in my special front-row seat. How lucky we are to have reserved seating for the show.

I don't want to hear the service, so I look around the chapel for something to focus on. I count the red pieces of glass in the mosaics in the front windows — one hundred forty-seven. One hundred and fourteen blue. Only ninety-seven purple. I am counting yellow when Aunt Carole rises beside me and walks up to the front. At the podium she shuffles through some papers, smooths them flat with shaking hands and starts to talk. "My brother would be so grateful to you all for coming today." Her voice catches, and I start to sing "Hey Jude" in my mind to block her out. I wish Penny were here to sing with me, even in her state as a hallucination, but I guess I get it. I do. It would be creepy to attend your own funeral.

At the front of the chapel are three white urns. They look sort of like cookie jars but without any cute cookie decals or retro letters. Instead, on the front of each is a metallic gold cross, tangled up with white lilies. Behind each urn is a picture in a black frame. Aunt Carole picked those too. Penny doesn't look like Penny in hers. It's a school picture from last year — one she hated and Mom only ordered to tease her. It wasn't a *bad* picture. I mean, my sister was pretty, so there weren't many bad pictures of her ever taken. But she hadn't liked the way her hair looked, and she thought her glasses were crooked, and she didn't like her smile. She looked at the picture and used the word "nerd" and I had said "but you *are* a nerd," and she had punched me on the arm and almost laughed. Aunt Carole found *that* picture in a pile on Mom's desk and said, "This one is lovely." I tried not to make a face and showed her a picture on my phone that I took at the beach a couple of weeks ago. A couple of weeks ago? Impossible. Her hair was loose and blowing up behind her in the wind. Her laugh was natural. She had just told the worst joke about a pelican and a racehorse — it made literally no sense. But Aunt

Carole pointed her knobby finger at Penny's bare shoulders (she was wearing her bathing suit!) and said it was unacceptable for a funeral.

I thought Penny was unacceptable for a funeral. And a funeral was unacceptable for Penny.

"I think this one is perfect," Carole said holding up the Nerd Penny Picture.

And Zac agreed. "Yeah that's great." But he was looking at me. What he was really saying was "Not worth it, Laynie," and I heard him loud and clear. I put my phone away, but later I printed out the Beach Penny Picture and tacked it to the wall beside my bed. It's a better place for it anyway.

Sitting in the front row, I wonder how they know which urn is which and if the pictures are actually beside the right ones. What would happen if I went up there and switched them around? It would be like that carnival game where you try to follow the marble under the cup. I could ask the mourners (and the gawkers) to guess which urn is which. I'd have to come up with a prize. For my ingenuity I'd probably win an all-expenses-paid trip to the looney bin. At least there no one would think twice of me talking to Penny. Luckily, my butt is nailed to my chair. My brain seems separate from the rest of my body, floating detached from the muscles and bones that would be needed to wreak havoc.

A shuffling beside me interrupts my crazy plan, and Zac stands as Aunt Carole returns to her seat. It's almost over, thank John Lennon. Zac convinced Carole to let him play the piano for the recessional hymn while the funeral directors carried the cookie-jar-urns out of the chapel. He sits at the bench, still for a moment, then his shoulders rise and fall.

FLASHBACK: *Sitting on the piano bench, I was distracted by the trees waving in the breeze outside the window. And the sound of the TV voices in the other room. And the smell of dinner — what was Mom cooking? And the clicking of the cat's nails on the hardwood floor and ... I played the wrong note. Again. And slammed my fingers on the keys in frustration. I heard the scratching of claws scramble to catch hold and carry the startled cat away from the clash of notes. Dad settled behind me, and I braced for the "respect the piano" lecture. "Take a deep breath, Laynie," he said instead. I did, lifting the hand he laid on my shoulder. "There. Better. Always take a deep breath before you start. It brings you to the moment. You have to be present to play music. Right here, right now. Go on, take a deep breath and then try again." And the trees and voices and garlic and cat faded and my fingers fell on the notes.*

Zac's long fingers hover over the keys for a moment and then press down the first notes. The C, A, CDEG trill out. "In My Life." So that's why he thought the argument for him to play was worth fighting when the Nerd vs. Beach picture one wasn't. Zac's voice rises up over the shuffling sounds in the congregation, singing about places and faces and memories. I smile. And I think maybe that was the first time I really smiled since waking up in the hospital with Zac crying beside me. Aunt Carole shifts in her seat to my right. I glance her way. Her face is flushed red and blotchy, her eyes narrow as if focusing laser darts on a target on the back of Zac's suit jacket.

Without my direction — actually, against my will — my body stands up, and my feet move one in front of the other toward the piano. I sit beside Zac on the bench and add my voice to his. The suits come and pick up the urns, tuck them under their arms as if they are footballs and head down the aisle. I turn my attention to Zac's music. I can't read the words. Everything is blurry but it doesn't matter, I know them by heart.

I totally plan to go into the hall where people are mingling for the reception but don't. I only meant to go into the washroom for a minute to catch my breath, but now I'm in here with the silence and calm, I just can't leave.

Flashback: *Last summer, Penny and I at the lake. Like a million other days. We dove in and swam to the floating dock then climbed out and lay in the sun as our skin dried and became hot to the touch. We chatted about nothing until Zac called out from the shore that it was time to go back. I dipped my toe in and shivered. The lake seemed so much colder than before. Penny waved and gestured and called out to Zac until he seemed to understand. He pulled the canoe to the edge, gingerly stepped to the middle and pushed off the sand with the oar. He paddled out and held it steady as Penny climbed in in front of him and I settled in behind. Expertly, he steered us away from the dock, then, in a motion too quick for us to react, stood to one side and tipped the boat over, dumping unsuspecting us into the icy water.*

The bathroom is safe, the crowd outside of it tortuous and overwhelming.

And maybe Penny will show up here.

I sit on the couch in the restroom — weird, but there *is* a couch in here. A deep red, velvety couch with curled arms on either side and dark wood trim along the top. Beside the couch is a table with a box of tissues conveniently placed. My fingers ache to be busy, fiddle on the piano or pluck at my guitar, but all that's in here is the box of tissues. I pull out one tissue, then another and another after the other, watching how the next tissue clings to the one being pulled and is lifted out of the box only to be left standing alone and vulnerable, exposed and within reach. I fold one tissue into a paper airplane, the soft material too limp. I throw it anyway. It floats unfolding to the floor and lies there shaped like a tent.

"Nice try," Penny says.

"You do better." Can hallucinations move things? Fold paper airplanes?

"What song is that?" she asks. I listen. The speakers play muffled notes at an in-between volume, where I can hear some of the music but not enough to make out the song.

"I can't tell," I say, still straining to hear some words or a complete sequence of notes that will tell me what song it is, but it's just out of reach within the static of the noise coming through the walls.

The door swings open, and Aunt Carole comes in. She stands in front of me with her arms folded. She's actually tapping her toe, clicking her dress shoe on the tiled floor. I thought that only happened in comedy movies and cartoons. Penny laughs and starts tapping her toe on the floor in front of the couch where we sit. When I don't say anything, Aunt Carole finally says, "You're making a spectacle of yourself, Layne." And then, "All those people came here to see you, to pay their respects to you. You owe them the decency of your presence." I don't argue. I don't think my voice would turn on if I had the first clue what to say. I don't even look up. I stay melted into the velvet cushions, folding the tissues I had pulled from the box back in half, placing one over the other in a neat, even pile. I try to block out the tap-tapping of her toe to hear what song is playing in the background. It could be "Yesterday" ... or maybe not. Finally, she huffs and mumbles something under her breath and stomps out of the room with a click click click.

"You can go out if you want," Penny says.

"No, thanks." There's no way.

Fifteen folded tissues after Aunt Carole left, Sara comes in and sits down on the other side of me so I'm between her and Penny. She puts her hand on my knee for a moment then takes it back. She pulls out her phone, and her thumbs wiggle over the screen. Without looking up, she says, "Asher was looking for you. I'm just telling him where we are."

We don't say anything after that. Sara stays with me, slouching on the velvety couch. Penny sits on the other side, humming different Beatles songs. I'm safe sandwiched between them until Zac comes in and tells me it's time to go home.

chapter 6

At the funeral, my list of What To Do Next was long but only covered a couple of hours, but my list of What To Do Next when I got home was shorter and had to last forever.

What To Do Next at the Funeral

1. Block out the service.
2. Keep it together.
3. Avoid the crowd.
4. Put the tissues back in the box.
5. Get out of the washroom undetected.
6. Survive the car ride home with a fuming Aunt Carole.

What To Do Next for the Foreseeable Forever

1. Stay under the blanket.
2. Go back under the blanket when forced out.
3. Convince Aunt Carole not to let people in when they show up uninvited.
4. Avoid everyone (except Zac sometimes).

So I hide in my room. Our ensuite lets me avoid everyone for hours — literally no need to leave my room. Zac brings food every so often and guilts me into eating. Penny is here with me, lying stretched out on her bed or curled up on her side facing me, or sitting in her desk chair, pushing her foot off the bed, then the desk, then the bed, the desk, the bed to spin herself around and around and around. Sometimes we talk. Sometimes we're silent. It takes all my courage and every ounce of my energy to find the breath and strength to ask, "Why were you in the car?" I manage it three times. She doesn't answer. The first time she shrugs. The second time she gives me a small smile and shakes her head, just a tiny bit. The third time I ask with my eyes closed, and when I open them the room is empty.

There are a lot of people to avoid. Outside my room, voices shift and come and go. Some are familiar — I hear friends of Mom and Dad in groups or one at a time. Corey and Chase seem to be there a lot; I hear them laugh over the voices. In five days Asher shows up four times. Sara three. Once they show up together. Each time I hide in my room under the blanket and pretend to be asleep until Zac or Aunt Carole give up tapping and go back to the door to tell them to come back another time.

I'm hiding like that when, instead of knocking on my door and then creeping away, Zac pushes the door open and "wakes me up." I'm pretty sure he knew I was faking.

He kneels on the bed and tugs at my shoulder. "Layne. Layne, get up. Sara's here," he says to trick me into opening my eyes.

I squeeze my eyes shut then squint and blink, trying to make it look like the light is unbearable because I'm still mostly asleep.

"Hi, Layne," Sara says from the doorway where she's waiting, twisting her rings around her fingers.

"Hi," I say out loud and add, *Now that you've seen me you can go away*, in my head. I hope it was just in my head.

"Be nice," Penny says. She's sitting cross-legged on her bed.

I close my eyes again. Feet move from the bed to the door, and Zac says something too quiet for me to hear. The door shuts. Thank John Lennon in Heaven. I sigh and open my eyes, roll onto my back and see Sara standing *in* the room looking at me. Geez. "Sorry, I'm just really tired." It's all I can think to say. I roll back to face Penny's bed, my back to Sara and the door.

"No, no, *I'm* sorry," she says, and the mattress dips down behind my knees as she sits on the bed.

Sorry for what? It's so stupid for people to say sorry. *She* wasn't the drunk in the truck, so what is she sorry for? Interrupting my pretend nap? Ignoring me when I texted to say *I'd rather be alone right now*? Being the one sitting on my bed when Penny is only an unreliable hallucination that shows up and disappears on her own schedule? And what am I supposed to say in response? "It's okay"? That's what people usually say when someone says "I'm sorry." But it so isn't okay. And I don't trust my voice to stay even and nice and flat instead of angry or breaking or catching or strangling me completely. So I don't say anything at all.

"Zac's back?"

Wow, your observational skills and deductive reasoning are top notch! is my first response. Luckily I have just enough willpower to say, "Yup," instead.

"Stop. You're being a bitch," Penny whispers. I stick out my tongue at her. "Easy for you to say."

The bed shifts, and Sara asks, "Pardon?" Crap. I must've said that aloud. I sit up and face Sara. Her eyes meet mine with this weird look of awkward hope.

"Huh?" I ask, trying to keep my face blank like she's the one hearing things.

"I thought you said something."

"Hm. Nope."

She stares at her hands and I chew on my thumbnail, peel it back until it splits from the skin with a sharp stab of pain and a bubble of bright red blood. I suck on it, and the metallic taste makes my stomach lurch.

"Want to go out somewhere? Get some ice cream? Or the mall? Or maybe …"

I'm shaking my head before she stops talking. "I'm too tired," I say. "I just want to sleep."

She nods, looks down. She's blinking fast, but it doesn't stop a tear that falls out of her eye onto her hands.

"This sucks." Truest thing anyone has said to me in almost two weeks.

"Yeah," I whisper, and she gives me a sad smile. For a second the silence around us is comfortable and familiar, like it has been since we met in primary.

FLASHBACK: *Sara and I were sitting on swings in the school playground, each holding a chain of the empty swing between us. Margo stomped toward us, gave the rubber seat a tug and whined, "I want to swing!"*

Sara yanked the chain she held, snapping the swing seat up between her fisted clench and mine. "No, it's for Penny. We're waiting for her."

It's like we're still sitting there waiting for Penny. And I think Sara may be thinking that too, because her smile slips away and she closes her eyes. And just like that, the quiet is edgy and strained again, and I can't think of anything to say.

"Hey you should check out New Landers, the post from yesterday is epic." Sara wipes at her face and looks at me. New Landers, the advice blog we love to laugh at. Used to. Viewers would write in about their problems, and the host acts out the situation someone asks about, then creates a few solutions for the viewers to vote on. Most of the solutions are comically ridiculous, and the way they act it out is hilarious. Will anything ever be funny again? I guess it's a misery-loves-company sort of thing. We could relate to the awkward uncertainty that drove people to ask a complete stranger about school and relationships and sex and family. But the host usually has a good suggestion to end the show and seems to have a good head on her shoulders. She gives good advice. Sara seems to take my silent apathy as encouragement to continue. "It started out the usual way; some guy wrote in saying he needs help with some asshole at school giving him a hard time."

"Yeah? What did Ann do this time?" My voice is flat, almost rude. I swallow the sigh that threatens to come after my words.

"She's trying," Penny says. I am too.

"Well, in one skit she suggested he contact Taylor Swift and ask her to sing a breakup song to the guy to end their bully-victim relationship."

Who cares? "Was it really Taylor Swift?"

"Yeah! And she was hilarious!"

"I'll check it out." I kind of laugh, because Sara's laughing just thinking of it, but it's not enough to ease the silently nervous pauses between us. She goes back to staring at her hands. I wait. We've never had to think about what to say before, but when you're trying *not* to talk about one thing — or one person — it makes it hard to think of anything else.

"Anyway, I'll let you sleep," she says finally and stands up. "Text me if there's anything I can do."

I nod and say, "Sure," but really there's nothing anyone can do. Really. She watches me for a minute until I say, "Really, I will."

"Okay," she says and stands up. Without looking back, she clears the distance from the bed to the door in three long strides, opens it and slips out of the room. We're alone again, and I'm relieved.

I stop answering calls and stop answering texts and threaten Zac he'd better not to let anyone else in. Or else. I have no idea what the "or else" would be. I spend the time between meals — when Aunt Carole insists I come out and join them at the table, even though I'm never hungry — curled up on my bed. Zac sneaks in a few times every day, saying he has to hide from Aunt Carole, but he could do that in his own room if that's the truth. He sits on my bed or in my desk chair, reading or playing Penny's guitar. Time warps and twists so that sometimes it stops and sometimes it's lost, and I never know what time of what day it really is.

Sara and Asher keep texting but stop looking for replies. They stop asking questions like *how r u?* or *what r u doing?* and just send me reports of what's going on in their still-normal existence in the world outside my blanket cocoon.

Asher: *Best ice cream in town* (with a picture of a melting cone attached)

Asher: *He2 He2 He2 — thot Id send some laughing gas.* (with an LOL and laughing emoticon)

Sara: *Watch this* (with a video of a puppy rolling down some stairs)

Sara: *Check it out* (with a picture of an East Coast Hoodie and a sale ticket marking it 50% off)

Sara: *Watch this* (with a gif of an emu chasing a woman at a zoo)

Asher: *Wish you were here* (with a picture of his feet in the sand at the beach)

Sara: *Watch this* (with a clip of a penguin sliding down a hill)

So now What To Do Next is every ten minutes. I don't even think about a long-term What To Do Next plan until Aunt Carole forces me to at breakfast. I'm pushing each little Cheerio life buoy down under the milk with the tip of my spoon to watch it bounce back up. "I'm going to go grocery shopping," Aunt Carole says. "Write down things you'd like to have in the house."

She puts a note pad and a green-inked pen beside my bowl. The note pad is long and thin, with "Life Is Better in Flipflops" across the bottom. I run my fingers along the top page. I can feel the divots and grooves left from writing on pages before it. Penny and I used to write a list each Saturday morning. The ToDah! list of things we wanted to get done that weekend. We never wrote our own lists, just added both lists together in one long collection of brainstorming. That's how Saturday morning is supposed to start. We wrote the last list together two weeks ago. Two weeks? Only two weeks? I can see Penny's square letters embossed in the soft pad. I trace them with the pen so our last list appears. "Skateboard crash" and "collision with pickup" are not on that list.

The Last ToDah! List Ever

1. Finish last three chapters. *(Penny usually started with a reading goal.)*
2. Study for Chemistry exam. *(She didn't really need to, I did.)*
3. Go for a run. *(I preferred to be impulsive with running, she liked to plan and log hers.)*
4. Bake cookies. *(The way to Dad's heart: Penny's oatmeal chocolate chip cookies.)*
5. Practice guitar. *(I had a song I was working on. Lost it now.)*
6. Study for math exam. *(Penny wrote that for me, I didn't want it there.)*
7. Flunk math. *(I scrawled that on the bottom under Penny's neat script)*

I pull off the top page. I don't know how to start a ToDah! list on my own. Instead I write "milk, bread, cheese, eggs." I have no idea what groceries we need.

Aunt Carole is standing at the sink, washing dishes that could go in the dishwasher. She clears her throat in an I'm-about-to-say-something-important way, so I look up at her. She says, "I need to return home." I look at Zac, who stops still, a piece of toast halfway to his mouth. Some melted peanut butter drips off the bread and lands on his plate.

"About time," Penny whispers beside me, and I'm glad no one else can hear her. Aunt Carole is tough to take sometimes, but she dropped everything to come out here and help us. She means well.

"Um, okay," I say, not sure what else is warranted. I know I owe her a thank-you, but it seems like saying "thanks for coming" right at this moment would sound like a "don't let the door hit you on the way out" invitation to get lost. My brain flashes through quick video clips of how it could be fixed on the New Landers; a marching band crashing through the kitchen wall to escort her out, or maybe an old *Star Trek* scene of Scotty beaming her out of the house, or an off-screen bellow of a Harry Potter spell that zips her away in a cloud of smoke. Any of those would work.

Zac is better with words. "We really appreciate you coming to go through all this with us." That's the right way to put it. Penny snorts beside me, and I want to kick her under the table, but it's impossible to kick a figment of your own demented imagination.

"I've thought a lot about it, and I think the best thing is for Layne to come home with me now. You remember a social worker named Rebecca Sturge? She called yesterday, and I spoke with her at length about it. Isaac, I know you mean well, but I don't think your plan is the best for anyone involved. I've spoken to a friend at the high school, and she said registration is easy, but can't be done until August. Your old school here will transfer any information needed to the new school there. If you come with me now, Layne, you'll have the summer to settle your things into my place and make some new friends before school starts. There are several nice girls your age at the church who also go to that school. I've been meaning to clean out that back bedroom anyway, there's so much junk in there I just don't have a use for any more. You can help me sort through it, and then set the room up however you wish and we can —"

"I'm staying here," I say as soon as I can get the three words lined up in order and enough breath to spit them out. I shove a Cheerio under the milk. It bounces back up with a ripple that spreads away from it to the edges of the bowl.

Aunt Carole sighs with great patience. "Layne, let's be realistic here. I can't pack up and move everything here. My life is there. I can't give up my job."

"Easy, Laynie," Penny reminds me.

"You don't have to." I keep my voice as low and even as I can. Don't yell. Don't freak out. Don't snap. I try to swallow the bile lurching up into my mouth. It burns my throat. I take a deep breath to slow my heart. "I'm not a child. I can stay here." I stare at Zac, pleading for help with my eyes. He puts his toast down and wipes his hands on a piece of paper towel on the table beside him.

"Legally, you *are* a child. And while fifteen may seem very grown-up to you, you're too immature yet to navigate through life alone. It's no fault of your own, you're just too young."

My eyes burn and I blink, blink, blink, trying to keep tears from falling out. Nothing says maturity like a good old-fashioned tantrum. "I can stay here," I say again, and my voice cracks. Zac nods, and the breath I've been holding leaks out of me.

"I'm staying too," he says. "It's already done. I resigned from my job last week and gave notice to my roommates about my apartment." His voice is firm, but he has this way of being decisive without being defiant or defensive. He isn't challenging her, he's telling her his decision.

"Isaac, we've talked about this. I really don't think —" So they had been talking about the What To Do Next while I was figuring out how to get out of bed.

"Aunt Carole, we really appreciate you coming to help us with the funeral and everything over the last couple of weeks, but you're right, you need to get home. I don't know what she said to you, but I already told that social worker that I am going to stay here. We will be fine. We'll work things out together." He looks from her to me, and I'm not sure if he gives me a quick wink or if I imagine it. Let's face it, I am seeing a lot of things that aren't real. Well, a lot of one person at least.

"But your job?"

"Just a job. I can find one here. Mom and Dad wanted me to be Layne and Penny's guardian." His voice catches on her name.

"I know that's what they said. I think it's as foolish today as I thought it was when you turned eighteen. I just never dreamed it would be of any consequence. I don't think they did either." She sighs as if someone has just asked her repeat the simplest of directions for the forty-seventh time. "Isaac, this is all very noble of you, but Layne is a young girl. You don't know the first thing about raising a young girl."

"Neither do you," Penny says.

"Neither do you," I say at the same time, not fully meaning to say it out loud, but I do.

And that stops the argument. Aunt Carole stares at me for a moment, her mouth gaping. I search for words to apologize, but my mind is totally blank. My ears are ringing, and all I can hear is Penny giggling. I try anyway, "Aunt Carole, I ... I ..."

"No, you are quite right, Layne. As I said, it is time for me to go. I will be returning home. I'll have my things packed and be out of your way within the hour. You and Isaac can stay here for now, but I will be working on your move from home." She turns from the table and places her plate in the sink with exaggerated care then sweeps out of the room.

I look at Zac. "Yeah, you could have been a little less cutthroat there," he says, but his lips are turned up on the sides.

I shrug. "Penny's the tactful one."

chapter 7

So Aunt Carole is leaving. Not by marching band or **Star Trek** transporter or magical summons, just in her rented blue Civic. Zac and I stand in the driveway while she loads her suitcase into the car. I don't know how she can lift it up into the trunk and keep her nose in the air at the same time. Zac tried to help. He met her in the hall and tried to take the suitcase from her, but she swatted his hand away and said "Isaac, you've done enough." Whatever that's supposed to mean.

So he and I follow her out of the house and stand on the lawn and watch her fight her suitcase into the trunk with her nose in the air. My throat is locked up so tight it hurts. Guilt swirls around in my stomach. I mean, she is Dad's sister, after all, and she lost her brother. She's sad too. But I keep my mouth shut. I don't feel bad enough to say anything like, "On second thought, Aunt Carole, give me a minute and I'll get some things together and go with." Not nearly that bad.

When she opens her door, she looks at us over the car and says, "I'll be in touch," which sounds more like a threat than anything.

Zac waves his hand and says, "Travel safely," but she has already slammed the door shut. She backs out of the driveway without looking behind her, squeals the tires and takes off down the road.

"Good riddance," Penny says, and I turn to face her, stumble on the edge between the pavement and the grass and grab Zac's arm to keep from falling. Hallucinations have a way of sneaking up on you. She wasn't there a moment ago while we were watching Aunt Carole stuff her suitcase in the trunk. She grins at me — that conspiratorial grin that I must have returned a thousand times in my mirror-image-way when we pranked Zac or shared the last of the ice cream.

"What?" Zac looks at me like I have two heads. Or like I've just been startled by a ghost.

I take my hand back and shrug. "Nothing," I say, but he has already turned to go back in the house. I try to glare at Penny, but the space where she just stood is empty.

I go back into my room and climb back into bed. I pull the covers over my shoulder and inch back a bit so the layers are pinched under my side behind me. I curl my arms together in front, tucking the blankets underneath and my hands under my chin. A tight cocoon. I close my eyes and concentrate on ignoring everything; Zac's voice on the phone, the traffic sounds outside, the lights and shadows flickering around the room, the words in my head. I try to sleep. When I sleep, Penny isn't a figment of my imagination. She's real. We are real together. I drift off, and for a while everything is the way it should be.

There's a knock on the door.

Ignore it. Another knock, and then I hear the door brush open against the carpet on the floor. I squeeze my eyes more shut, hoping he'll get the point, but a moment after the door swooshes over the carpet, I hear Penny's bed sag in front of me.

"Laynie, it's time to get up," he says.

It's even harder to ignore your brother when he's sitting three feet away talking to you than it is to ignore him when he knocks on the door, but I try anyway.

"Laynie." This time when he says my name, he pulls on the blankets and ruins my cocoon. I open one eye to glare at him. "It's time to get up," he says again, so I close my eye. I don't think a one-eyed glare is very effective. "Layne, that social worker called asking questions. Aunt Carole really did talk to her."

"So? You're the guardian, what does she care?"

"She thought Aunt Carole's idea was a good one and thought we agreed to it. She thought you were going with Aunt Carole and wanted to schedule a hearing with the judge to arrange custody this week. She wasn't happy when I said that's not what we're going to do. She wants to come over and see the paperwork. And to go over our options." I try to pull the covers over my head, but he pulls them out of my hands. "Layne, if it doesn't look like we're doing okay, they can petition to have you taken care of."

I laugh. Not appropriate to laugh right now, I know, and it's not a real laugh, more a snarky, sarcastic guffaw, but when I hear "taken care of," I think mob-style. "They'll take care of me? Like kill me?"

"Layne." Apparently he doesn't get the joke. "Like foster-care you," he says. Which so isn't funny.

"They can't," I say, and what I really want to do is pull the covers back around me and ignore him and ignore the social worker and ignore Aunt Carole and ignore the rest of the world. I tug on the blankets, but he's holding them tightly away from my face. I close my eyes instead.

"I'd rather not find out. Listen, get up. Let's clean the house. Let's find the papers we need. Let's get on track and look like we're doing okay. Then when she calls again to schedule the visit, we'll be ready and can show her we can do this." I keep my eyes closed. "Or you can go live with Aunt Carole." I kick at him, but my foot gets caught up in the covers. "Laynie, I meant it when I told her we'd work things out together. I may be the guardian, but I can't do this alone."

I peek at him with one eye, and he is looking at me. His eyes are glistening, glowing green. His lips are pressed together so tightly that they are thin and white. He looks away from me to his hands twisting together in his lap.

"Laynie, get up," Penny whispers. She's sitting right there beside Zac, and he doesn't even know it.

"Okay," I say to her. When he looks up at me I say it again. He smiles, sort of, and pats the blanket covering my knee twice.

FLASHBACK: *Me curled up and eyes red from crying over being cut from the school basketball team. Mom whispered commiserations until I said I felt a little better. She tapped my knee — pat, pat — just before she stood up and left my room. It was her deal closer, The End, the signature at the bottom of the page. Her "you've got this."*

My eyes water, and I bury my face in the pillow. Sobs.

I cry. And cry and cry. Zac sits silently, his hand on my knee. He waits. And then I stop. I wipe my face dry with my blanket, taking deep gulps to slow down my breathing.

"I'll go get started," Zac says and stands up. "Come help me when you're ready." He leaves the room.

I guess What To Do Next starts now.

chapter 8

So since I spent the last couple of weeks mostly in bed, or figuring out how to go back to bed, I'm going to have to work hard to prove to Zac that we can Do This. Maybe prove it to myself too.

Tidying up the house isn't too tough; Aunt Carole must have done a first sweep of it. There's not much out of place. But we have to go into Mom and Dad's room eventually, and no one has been in there yet.

Standing in the hall outside the door to their room, Zac says, "Go ahead." I'm the one with my hand on the doorknob.

"I am," I bark, but I don't move. Zac rests his hand on my shoulder. The weight of it keeps me calm; keeps my breath coming and going at a normal rate, keeps the sob or scream or whatever it is down in the back of my throat.

"Oh my god," Penny whispers, but she doesn't move either. It's not like a hallucination can open doors though. I take a deep breath and turn the knob then push the door open.

They left stuff tossed everywhere. I mean, it's not like they were slobs, but they weren't as anal-tidy as Penny either. Their things lie out of place around the room, like little messages saying "I'll be right back."

Signs They'll Be Right Back

1. A pair of Dad's socks on the floor at the end of the bed.
2. Mom's reading glasses hanging from the power cord of her lamp suspended between the bed and the bedside table.
3. Dad's contact case open on his bureau. Some of the solution has spilled out and dried, leaving a crusty white splatter around the white-circled container.
4. Mom's housecoat tossed over the bed. The bed unmade.

5.   In their ensuite, Dad's toothbrush lying on the counter.

6.   Mom's toothbrush standing in the Dora the Explorer cup with the tube of toothpaste squeezed flat in the middle.

7.   A towel hung over the shower door, another hung crooked on the towel rack.

8.   An almost full toilet paper roll sits perched on the empty roll still on the tp holder.

9.   A laundry basket against one wall, with almost all the clothes all the way in it, some draped over the sides.

10. Dad's *Sports Illustrated* magazine folded open on the table beside his bed, halfway through an article about pro sports salary caps.

It won't take long to erase all their "I'll-be-right-back" memos. At least not the ones left by stuff in their room. Before I pick up each item, I take a mental snapshot. It reminds me of a movie Penny and I watched once where this girl had a huge party while her folks were out, and afterward she had to put her house back together so no one would find out. I try to remember how each out-of-place thing looks before righting it, as if down the road they'll call us and say "Just kidding, we'll be home in a few minutes," and Zac and I will hurry around and put everything back out of place so they think we never gave up on them. Never believed what we were told, never doubted their will to come home to us. But after I store the picture in my mind, I pick up each out-of-place thing anyway.

"Should I wash these?" I ask Penny. We're in the laundry room, and I'm holding a basket of Mom and Dad's clothes, mixed together. They won't be worn again — at least not by them.

"Donate them," she says, which doesn't answer my question.

"Laynie?" Zac calls my name from somewhere else in the house. I find him in the kitchen, standing by the counter pouring a glass of milk. "There," he says and points when I walk in. On the table is one of those brown paper envelopes that's big enough to hold legal-sized documents without folding them. The Papers. "I found them in the safe in their closet. The door wasn't even locked."

"I thought they were at the bank? In the safety deposit box," I say, and my voice cracks with forced enthusiasm.

"Me too. But I think those are it. The will. I saw the lawyer's letterhead when I looked inside." He takes a big swig of milk then sets his cup on the table and leans back against the counter with his arms crossed. He's staring at his feet.

I pick the envelope up from the table. There's a fancy stamp in the return-address corner, and Mom and Dad's names are written in black Sharpie on the front. It's closed, the tab folded into the opening. "Didn't you read it?"

He's still staring at his feet. "What if they changed it? Took me out?" I hadn't thought of that. What if they had? Zac left six months ago. He hadn't come back, hadn't talked to them since. I don't have all the details, all I know is there was a fight while Penny and I were out at a movie.

FLASHBACK: *I followed Penny into the house and bumped into her when she stopped suddenly in the hall. "What are you doing?" I asked, giving her a shove. She stepped forward but kept staring into the living room. Dad's guitar was lying on the coffee table. What was left of it. The neck, with guitar strings twisted and hanging off it. There was wood scattered around the room as if something had exploded. Dad sat in his armchair staring at the remains of the guitar, his fingers curled around a glass with golden liquid and ice. "Your brother left," he said when he saw us standing there. His eyes met each of ours in turn, daring us to ask more. And maybe begging us not to.*

Within a week Zac had moved out, an hour away. He dropped out of his university courses and got some job at an office sorting mail. Six months ago. Whenever I asked Dad what happened, his eyes clouded over and his lips pressed together. Then he'd say in a whisper-growl voice, "I told him that friend of his was trouble," or "He didn't want to hear it. He made his choice." He'd look at me when he answered but not *at* me, more through me like he was focused on something far away. The last time I asked, Dad said "Laynie, just ... don't. Stop asking," and walked out of the room. My jaw hurt, and I realized I was clenching it tightly. I wished Zac could see the pain he'd left behind him.

He talked to Penny and me, mostly by text. Of course, I asked him why he left and why didn't he just come give it a try to make things good again. Each time he'd only reply, "We're not going to talk about this." No matter how many different ways I tried to get information, he never said anything different. Six months ago. He moved on, found a better job in the art gallery, moved in with friends, never looked back. Until ...

So what if they had taken Zac's name out and put someone else's in? Six months is long enough to make a small change in a will. One small step for a legal document, one large step for the rest of my life. What if they had changed the guardianship back to Aunt Carole? Do you appoint guardianship of your two kids to the one kid you don't talk to? Were they mad enough at him to take that back? Did they think Zac was gone forever?

"Open it," Penny whispers beside me. "It's not like *not* opening it will change what's there."

I pull the flap free. It's not as easy as it should be to unfold paper, because the envelope is thick and my fingers are shaking. Also, my nails are bitten down to an all-new level, and my stubby fingertips are clumsy. It tears as I pull it. Finally the envelope is obliterated and I'm able to pull out the documents. The papers are fancy, thick and textured. The words are all formal — incomprehensible legalese — with Mom and Dad's names at the top. Halfway down the first page are my name and Penny's, then Zac's (it's always strange to see Isaac written out in full). The three names are tied together with some legal mumbo-jumbo, but there are the words "appoint as guardian," so we must be in the clear. I look up, and Zac has given up his study of his socked toes and is looking at me.

"Still you," I say.

Zac nods.

Then his eyes get all watery and he says, "'Kay," and leaves the kitchen. I guess I didn't expect a whoop or a cheer. It's not that exciting, but I wasn't expecting tears.

"Should I go talk to him?" I ask Penny. She just shrugs. Some help she is. I take a step toward the door then stop. If he'd wanted to talk about it, he would have stayed and done that. Obviously, if he left the room it was for a reason. Maybe he doesn't want to talk to his new responsibility. I pick up his glass of milk and take a long gulp.

"He probably just wants to be alone," Penny says. Or maybe I say it. Either way, it's likely true.

I finish Zac's milk and put the glass in the dishwasher. It's almost full, so I add some soap and turn it on. I go back and put the load of donation clothes in the wash; they might as well be clean when we drop them off. Then I head to my room. This staying out of bed all day is exhausting. On my way by, I tiptoe to Zac's door and listen for a moment. Silence.

I stand in the doorway of my room — our room — searching for any I'll-be-right-back messages from Penny. Like everything else about us, her space is the opposite of mine. My side of the room is a mess, hers is tidy. Her bed is made, her laundry is put away in the washroom hamper. Her books are arranged on her shelves (and some are on mine, since I don't have many books) with the spines straight up and down. Her bureau drawers are all closed tightly, and I know if I open them her clothes are folded and piled. The top of her bureau has her jewellery box (also neatly closed), a hairbrush and two framed pictures: one of us and Zac when we were little, dressed up and ready for Halloween, and one from grade school of us with Sara. The only thing left out of place is her chemistry book, still open on her desk. I guess the novel left ruined on the road beside the SUV-blob is out of place too. And Penny.

I pick up her guitar and sit at her desk, allowing my motor memory to strum random chords without thinking. It's hard to reach the frets around the cast, and stretching makes my arm ache. But it's not as bad as when I first came home. At least some part of me seems to be healing. When I stop, the plucked notes hover as memory in the silence. I stare at the page Penny had been studying until the black letters shift and blur. I reach out one shaky finger, lift the front cover of the chem book by degrees, and watch the pages on the left flutter over to the right until the hardcover reaches past the vertical and gravity pulls the book closed with a soft *whoomp.*

And all signs of Penny are gone.

Not counting, of course, the persistent hallucination that flops down on the bed behind me at that moment. There are auditory hallucinations, too; people hear voices, so it makes sense that I hear the bedsprings bounce a bit when she lands. I turn to face her. She is lying on her bed with her feet crossed at the ankles and her hands behind her head. "Now what?" she asks.

"Now what." I copy her, but it doesn't sound much a question in my voice. Now what. What To Do Next. Do This. But how? That's the real question.

"I dunno, why don't you tell me?" I ask her. That was a question, and not really nicely put. She just smiles at me from her relaxed pose on the bed, and it makes me mad. I huff breath out of my nose and glare at her for a moment. The edge of the guitar neck cuts into my fingers as they tighten around it. I turn away from her, lying on her bed all casual and carefree like she's not really expecting me to go on without her. As if she's only backed out on our plans to go shopping or go to a movie or go to a party and left me to figure out how to get there myself and if I really wanted to go alone. As if she's not out of everything for good. Now What. Do This. Do what?

My heart is racing. Pounding. I can feel sobs building, threatening to come exploding out.

"Laynie, it's okay," Penny says, which is stupid because it's not.

"Nothing is okay," I hiss at her.

She moves to the end of the bed and sits knee-to-knee to me but doesn't touch me. "I know. I know." Her voice is soothing. "But you need to calm down. Take a breath."

I breathe. I strum a few chords and look up at the shelf of books over her desk to keep the tears back in my eyes. I swallow. Breathe. Strum. Bit by bit, the chords resonate and massage the anxiety away. When I'm in control again, I reach up and pull out a book. It has a blue-grey spine, a single floating feather near the bottom and a dead bird on the cover. She loved this one. Weird. I mean, there's a frigging dead bird on the cover, can't be much of a story. When I try to put it back on the shelf it stops, obstructed, halfway in, and for a moment I get a yucky-gut feeling that she'll catch me messing with her stuff. I take the book back out and look in the space it belongs between two other books. There's a folded paper blocking the book's re-entry. I check over my shoulder, but Penny's bed is empty. I take out the paper and open it, expecting her to hiss at me *put that back,* but her hallucinatory appearances don't seem to match any expected pattern.

At the top of the page, Penny's neat block letters spell out "Summer ToDah!"

A ToDah! List. Compiled all on her own without me. I know because I haven't seen it before. She even drew edges and shadows around the letters to make the title look 3D and coloured them yellow, her favourite.

Summer ToDah!

1. Finish six books from TBR pile. *(Typical Penny.)*
2. Secure employment for the summer. *(Only Penny would write that instead of "get a job.")*
3. Get to 50 push-ups and 5km under 30 mins. *(Ouch.)*
4. Write 30K-word story. *(In case she ran out of reading material?)*

"Geez, Sis, live a little," I whisper out loud. Then I swallow back a surge of stomach bile and blink my eyes until her writing unblurs. I have got to stop saying such mean, stupid stuff.

5. Get to the beach 5 times. Wear red bikini in public. *(Penny looked great in that bikini.)*

She never believed me when I told her so, though. I talked her into buying it, but she only wore it once when we stayed in a hotel on an overnight trip for a hockey tournament. She kept her baggy Acadia T-shirt on over it. Actually swam in the T-shirt, which couldn't have been easy or comfortable.

6. Go on a date (preferably with AP). *(Wait … what?)*

That one is totally un-Penny-like. I can actually imagine her in my mind's eye, scribbling down the first five, then hesitating. She might have even looked around, doubting and rethinking before sneaking the last one in as if she was scared someone would see it and realize her insisting "I'm too busy to date" was a bullshit cover for "What if no one asks me?"

But who is AP? There can't be many boys in our school with names that start with A.

Boys Whose Names Start with A

1.   Asher Phillips — *(AP. Asher Phillips. Are there any other AP's?)*

Other Boys Whose Names Start with A:

1.   Adam Vries.

2.   Antoine Redson.

3.   Adam Lemmi.

4.   Alek Carter.

5.   Aidan Zinck.

6.   Alex Boyd.

7.   Aaron Dickenson.

8.   ...

Nope. Asher's the only one I can think of. My throat tightens, jaw clenches.

I stare at Penny's pretty writing "preferably with AP." *AP.* "Is it Asher?" I ask out loud, but there's no answer. Could it be? My jaw hurts, and I open and close my mouth to relax it. My stomach burns, instantly queasy. Jealous? Of my dead sister? Now there's a new low. "Why didn't you tell me you like him?" No answer. I look over my shoulder, but I'm alone in the room.

It's not like I have a claim on Asher or anything, and I hadn't told her how my stomach fluttered when I talked to him lately. "Penny?" Nothing but silence. Of course.

I carry her paper to my bed and climb in under the blanket. I slip the ToDah! list under my pillow, but I can still see Penny's perfect letters when I close my eyes. This weird Alice-in-Wonderland-feeling starts: the walls are closing in, the room is shrinking. I'm trapped. My cocoon that had felt safe was suddenly tight, imprisoning. I can't ...

Then Zac knocks on the door and opens it. I pull the blanket back to look at him, and he's standing in the doorway, leaning against the frame. His eyes are red-rimmed and his face is puffy, but he's smiling. Or trying to. "I'm sick of casseroles. Do you want pizza?"

With his suggestion I feel an instant need to get out, get away from Penny's list, from our room. From her? Maybe not that far. He's opened the door, and it's my chance to escape. "Yeah, but let's go out," I say.

His eyes widen, and his brows shoot up. If he were a cartoon, they would have left his face altogether and bounced away. But all he says is, "Good plan. I'll be ready in five."

I glance at my sweats and lift the neck of my T-shirt to sniff. "I'll need ten!" I shout after him. I pull Penny's ToDah! list out from under the pillow and slip it back between the dead bird book and one with a basketball on the spine (she didn't even like basketball), shift the books to make sure they are perfectly even and then head to the shower.

"Where to?" Zac asks when we pull the car doors closed twenty minutes later. "Pizza still? Boston Pizza? Freeman's? Salvatore's?"

Each name he suggests evokes a memory of sitting with my parents, with Penny, and the sickening anticipation of running into someone from school. I want out of the house, but I don't want to talk to anyone while we're out.

"Somewhere different," I say, and Zac looks at me for a minute and gives me a small, sad smile that seems to say, *yeah, I know.*

He backs the car out of the driveway. "There's a place I've been wanting to try," he says as he puts the car into drive. The radio is playing a new Taylor Swift song. With the light of the lowering sun and the city scenes flying by the windows, I feel bombarded by sensory input, and the radio sound is one thing too much. I turn it off and we drive in silence.

Zac parks on the street, and I follow him a block until we reach a door on the corner. The restaurant is small and busy, but I don't recognize anyone. Good. The corner opposite the door is filled with a huge tiled oven, fire flickering in the door. A man pushes a pizza into the oven with a long-handled paddle. I take a big sniff in, and my stomach growls at the smells of tangy tomato and cooking bread.

"Okay?" Zac asks.

"Looks awesome," I say. *Penny would have loved this place,* I don't say. We follow the hostess to a table for two by the window and I take the menu she offers. I open the bifold and read the English subtitles under each Italian headline at the top of each side "Red Pizza" and "White Pizza." Items are listed in long, vowel-laden Italian words. I point to one and ask Zac, "What's this mean?"

He shrugs. "Beats me."

A waiter with a black apron and perfectly combed blond hair comes by and puts a glass of water in front of each of us. "Do you have any questions about the menu?"

"What's your favourite?" Zac asks. The waiter smiles bigger and points to one of the entries. I tune him out while he translates the long words and lists the ingredients. Zac orders the waiter's favourite.

When the waiter looks at me, I point to one that has the word "pepperoni." "That one, please," I say, feeling my face flush at my embarrassing lack of confidence to try to say any of the words. The waiter takes our menus and walks toward the prep area around the large oven. Zac watches him go. "Do you know him?" I ask and take a sip of my water.

"Huh?" Zac turns to me. "Oh, nope."

The restaurant is just what I need. Untried and without memories of Mom or Dad or even Penny, who doesn't show. Zac and I bicker over sports stats and song lyrics until the pizza comes, then turn our attention to eating without dripping the delicious melted cheese everywhere. I see no one I know. No one stops to talk to us; even the waiter leaves us alone. When we're stuffed, we ask for the remaining pizza to be boxed up, and Zac pays the bill, leaving a bigger than necessary tip. The walk to the car is cool in the salty waterfront air, but refreshing. The drive home is quiet.

It's not until later, much later, after the pizza and the movie we watched — well, I watched, one of Zac's roommates called halfway through, and he disappeared into his room to talk to him — and I'd done all the bedtime stuff and crawled into bed that I really think about Penny's list. I don't know what makes me think of it just now; I guess just remembering the day. But as I run through her list in my mind, the idea that she wanted me to find it shuffles into my thoughts, and it's hard to ignore. I don't know why it feels like she wanted me to find it; it's not like she left it on her chemistry book, or out on her desk. But when she left that day, she planned to come back. She obviously didn't want me to see it while she expected to be here to do it herself, but once she was gone ...

Maybe that's why she's sticking around, showing up. *She's* the one who asked me "What now?" just before I found the note. That's like some kind of crazy coincidence out of one of her dumb novels. So maybe she's still here to make me find that note and help me do her tasks?

Maybe my Penny hallucinations are more than in my head. I mean, they are still probably hallucinations — no one else can see or hear her, as far as I can tell. I'm not sure I believe in ghosts, but maybe she is making me see and hear and think the hallucinations from wherever she is now.

I mean, I don't know what comes next, after this life, but I can't believe this is it. There's just too much to *us* to imagine that we're totally gone and done with once we're dead. There's got to be some kind of existence after we die. At least I like to think so now, for their sake, Mom and Dad and Penny. I like to think of them out there somewhere watching and thinking of and remembering me. Maybe it's selfish, but it's what I hope anyway. So maybe from wherever she is, she is making me see, hear, feel her *here* for a reason.

Maybe she needs to see the list done before she can go off and chillax wherever dead people hang out.

I hear Penny whisper, "You can do this" and look around the room. She's not here, and the whisper was more in my head than my ears anyway. She needs me to do her Summer ToDah! list. That's it, that's why. It just feels ... *right*.

When I fall asleep, I dream we're at the beach. "We" being all of us: Mom, Dad, Zac, Penny, me and even Aunt Carole. Penny is wearing her red bikini. Aunt Carole says, "You look stunning, Penny!" which seems so weird for Aunt Carole of all people to say that Penny looks at me and laughs, like she is doing in the picture on the wall beside my bed. Then we run to the water and jump in. It's cold, and we shriek and laugh some more. And in that way that dreams work where you see some things and know others, I know that even though I can only see Penny splashing and swimming with me, Zac and Dad are tossing the Frisbee on the beach, and Mom is chatting with Aunt Carole in their beach chairs, and the sun is warm and the sky is blue and everyone is happy.

chapter 9

I wake up and my first thought is: Operation ToDah! starts today. I look at my phone, surprised to see it's only 8:42. It's actually the first morning in two weeks that I've woken up before nine *and* sat up right away instead of pulling the covers over my head again. I sit for a moment with my feet over the bed, my toes digging into the deep threads of the carpet. The house is silent. Maybe Zac is still asleep. Maybe he's out for a run. Maybe he is reading somewhere or whispering on the phone.

I stand up and stretch my arms over my head, relishing the pull from my elbow down my sides. I look around, but I'm alone in the room. Penny's bed is still made, her desk chair pushed in. "Penny?" I mumble, but the silence smothers my whisper. Apparitions don't appear on command. At least not ones of my stubborn sister.

I walk to her desk and pull her ToDah! list out from between the books. I unfold it, press it smooth against her desk and scan it again, looking for the specific details of her exercise goal.

3.   Get to 50 push-ups and 5km under 30 minutes.

"You can do it," Penny says, and I turn to see her sitting at my desk.

"Push-ups? Why did you have to pick push-ups?" I ask her, but she just smiles at me. Crunches, sit-ups, lunges, those I can handle. I lift my arm, heavily encased in the orange cast, up and toward her. There's no way I can do push-ups with my arm broken and casted. Even my healthy but spaghetti-like arm is screaming in protest. "I hate push-ups, and I can't do them with this."

"No pain, no gain," she says.

"Oh, that's original," I spit back.

"You can do an elbow plank with your arm like that." She nods toward my covered arm, and I look down at it. "Five minutes instead of fifty push-ups."

"Five minutes? Are you nuts?" She shrugs and smiles in a way that clearly means *If you don't think you can do it, that's okay, don't bother.* Fine. Challenge accepted. "Move then," I say, and she walks over to her bed.

I shove my desk chair aside and kick some of my clothes out of the way to clear a floor space big enough for the length of my body. I flop down onto my belly. With a deep breath, I raise myself onto my elbows and toes and start the timer on my phone.

"One, two, three," Penny says from behind me. I look down the length of my propped body and see her feet hanging off her bed.

"Screw off," I say, and she laughs, loud at first, and then it fades away. I look back and her feet are gone.

Four … five … six … seven … eight, nine, ten, eleven, twelve thirteen fourteen fifteen sixteen se'teen eighteennineteenTWENTY!

My belly is burning, and my back is clenched and howling: *What the fffff.* If back muscles could howl and swear, that's what mine would be saying. Twenty is a good start. I let myself down and take a minute to catch my breath, my cheek on the rough fibres of the carpet. My stomach growls, so I push myself up, fold Penny's list and slip it into the pocket of my sweats, and then go to find some breakfast.

"Good morning," Zac says when I enter the kitchen. He's sitting at the table with a bowl half filled with milk and his MacBook in front of him.

I grunt something like "hey" and take a bowl out of the cupboard. I turn the Cheerios box over it and a few o's fall out with all the crap-dust from the bottom. I try to glare at Zac, but he won't look up from his screen; he just sits there typing away. "You ate all the Cheerios," I say, pouring milk over the crumbs and dust in my bowl. He doesn't even look up, just shrugs and mutters something about groceries. "Who are you talking to?" I ask.

"My roommate, Sebastian." His roommate. I'm pretty sure he's the friend Dad thought was trouble. I had hoped Zac'd left him behind when he came home. I lean closer to glance at his screen and he looks up, shooting daggers at me, and tips the screen down. "Do you mind?"

"Sorry. Geez," I huff, sitting down and spooning the milk-Cheerios-dust mush out of the bowl. It doesn't taste too bad, but it's slimy and gritty. "Is it serious roommate business? Like who didn't wash the dishes? Who ate all the Cheezies and didn't replace them? Who put the empty milk carton back in the fridge?" That earns me a glance up that is just long enough for him to narrow his eyes at me and give a huge, dramatic, why-must-I-put-up-with-you sigh.

FLASHBACK: *That Exact Look flashed from his side of the breakfast table. I was*

eight, maybe. Nine? Mom fluttered around in the kitchen trying to get us ready, hur-
rying us up and shushing the bickering. She stepped behind me and said, "Laynie this
hair!" as she pressed the bristles of the hairbrush against my head and pulled against
the tangles. "Zac won't give me the peanut butter. He's done with it!" I whined. She
said, "I don't want to hear it," for the third or fourth of the at least fifty times she'd
say it that day. Zac smiled and said, "I'm not done," while he made a concentrated
effort to cover every part of the toast on his plate. "Zac." That's all Mom had to say,
without even breaking stride in the aggressive strokes in my hair. He gave me That
Look and shoved the peanut butter across the table.

I concentrate on my almost cereal and try to block out the soft clicking of his typing. When I shift in my seat, the corner of Penny's folded note pokes my leg from inside my pocket. I take it out and smooth the paper flat on the table beside my bowl.

The plank and running will be easy, even with my stupid broken arm. I mean, not *easy*, but simple to target. An athlete I am not, but everyone knows how to reach fitness goals like that. If I can do twenty seconds of a plank today and twenty-five tomorrow, by the end of the summer I should get up to five min-utes. Three hundred seconds. I hope. The running will be easier. I can already do five kilometres easily, but not in under thirty minutes. Yet. If I start running every day instead of a couple of times a week, I can probably get under thirty by the end of the summer. No better time to start than now. Except tomorrow. Tomorrow would be better.

I only know that "TBR" means "to be read" because I asked Penny about it before. She keeps a note tacked to her desk with "TBR" on the top and a list of book titles written underneath. *Kept.* There's no way I can read six books in two months. None.

Zac says, "Huh?" I look up at him, confused. "You said, 'no way.' 'No way' what?"

"Nothing," I say, laying my hand over Penny's note and trying to look focused on my breakfast.

"That's gross," he says, pointing at my milk-mush. I lock my eyes with his while I scoop a loaded spoonful of wet dust out of the milk and put it in my mouth. Then I open my mouth and stick out my tongue to show the mush on it and throughout my teeth. Cold milk dribbles down onto my chin, and I wipe it before it can trickle to my neck. "You're a child," he says, shaking his head.

"So I'm told," I say through the paste. He closes his laptop, stands and puts his dish in the dishwasher. I hear him step closer to me and then *feel* him hover-ing over my shoulder.

"What's that?" he asks.

"Cheerios dust," I say, trying to will my hand to cover the whole ToDah! list on the table without looking conspicuous.

"No, the paper. What is it?" In my periphery, his hand comes around from behind me toward the list.

In one quick movement I sweep the paper off the table and turn to face him. "Do you mind?" I throw his own cranky words back at him.

He steps back, holding his palms up and open toward me with a lopsided smile. "Sorry. Geez." He repeats my earlier retort and laughs. "Don't run the dishwasher yet, I'm going to take a shower." He turns and walks out of the room, and I imagine throwing my bowl at the middle of his back so that he is covered in the cold, sticky sludge. I'm somewhat surprised, given the recent realization of my imagination, that he escapes unscathed.

"It's not a secret list," Penny says. She's sitting at the table across from me. Where she always sits at breakfast.

I try to glare at her. It's hard to give a nasty look to your dead sister who won't leave you alone. Especially when you'd really rather she *not* leave you all alone and also not be dead, either. "It's mine," I say finally and take my bowl to rinse in the sink. I turn the water on full to hot, and a muffled yell comes from the bathroom. I turn the water off and start counting to sixty.

"It's my list, not yours," she says behind me, but I force my eyes to stay forward, out the window and concentrate on counting — *eight, nine, ten, eleven.* In the backyard a blue jay is hopping across the grass. The grass is long and needs to be mowed. But Dad's not here to do it. How many other jobs are Zac and I forgetting to do? When I reach thirty, I glance over my shoulder. Penny is gone and I'm alone in the kitchen. I let out the breath I didn't realize I was holding and stop counting long enough to whisper, "You left. It's mine now," before resuming *thirty-three, thirty-four, thirty-five.* When I get to sixty I turn the water back on hot. A bellow comes from the bathroom. I can't hear any distinct words, but I'm guessing they're curses.

I'm sitting on my bed strumming Penny's guitar and singing "Here Comes the Sun" to myself. It's my favourite Beatles song. Now it seems less like an affirmation than a soothing promise I need to grasp on to and not let go. My bedroom door swings open in the middle of the "doo doo doo doo" part, and I look up to see Zac standing there with his eyes wide.

"What is it?" I ask. A tight twist of fear clenches me, but really, who else is there to worry about? He's right here; the rest are already gone.

"That Children's Services woman, Rachel Sturge?"

"Rebecca Sturge."

"Whatever. She just called, and she's on her way over to visit. Said she had a cancellation in her schedule and wants to touch base, but I think it's some kind of ambush visit to see how we're really doing." He's wringing his hands as he talks. When he finishes, he sticks them through his hair and laces his fingers behind his neck.

"It's fine, Zac, we found the papers."

"Yeah, but we have to look like we know what we're doing."

"We do," I say, hoping my voice is more convincing than I feel. I'm not sure at all that we know what we're doing. We've tidied the house, found the papers, stayed alive and — bonus — I'm not hiding under the covers in my bed any more. But the overgrown lawn. And have we eaten anything but takeout pizza or casseroles since Aunt Carole left? "Did you get rid of the pizza boxes?"

He frowns, probably trying to figure out where the question came from, having not heard the monologue in my head. "I'm going to clean the kitchen. Get dressed."

"I *am* dressed," I say, looking down at my sweats and T-shirt, but he's already walked out of the room. "I'm dressed!" I repeat to Penny.

"Maybe something a little less top-of-the-pile-on-the-floor?" she says.

"What does my outfit have to do with our capability to survive?" I sniff the shirt. "It's clean. Mostly."

"Maybe just humour us," Penny says. *Us.* The word rings in my ears. The only "us" left is Zac and I. I need to do whatever it takes to keep it. I put on jeans and a clean T-shirt.

The pizza evidence is removed, dishes put away and sink empty by the time the doorbell rings. I'm wiping down the counter with an almost clean cloth. Zac looks at me for a moment then says, "Don't try to be funny," and goes to open the door. That only makes me think of all the inappropriate but funny things I might say that would get us in trouble.

List of Inappropriate Jokes for This Moment

1. Making money dealing drugs is easier than finding a job.
2. We're going to sell the house and move to Vegas.
3. Dropping out of school to hit the road with what was left of our Beatles Tribute Band.
4. I'm seeing my dead sister everywhere I go. *(Wait, that one is true.)*

But when I meet him and Rebecca Sturge in the living room, my mouth is dry and my mind too blank to say anything at all. I freeze in the doorway.

"Hello, Layne," she says.

"Hi," I manage to squeeze out.

"I don't know if Isaac told you or not, but I just wanted to drop in and see how you both are doing. I need to write a recommendation by the end of next week." She says it all so casually, as if she's talking about researching an article for the local paper.

I force a smile. "Yeah, so he said."

"Please, call me 'Zac.' Can I get you a drink?" Zac asks.

"Zac. Right, I'm sorry. A glass of water would be lovely," she says, and Zac leaves the room. "Shall we sit in here?" she says to me, which unfreezes my legs long enough to carry me to the couch, where I sit beside Penny. "How have you been?"

So many people have asked those four words. I'm sure most of them only want to hear me say some version of "good" — minimal and positive to let them off the hook. "Fine," I manage to choke out.

She scribbles something on her pad. It takes too long to write to be f-i-n-e. "I'm sure you're aware that I spoke to your aunt?" I nod. "She is concerned that this arrangement will not be healthy for you or Isaac — Zac. While I am concerned about the impact of this situation on Zac's life, as a minor it is your care that I must prioritize in my recommendation. Your aunt offered to have you live with her." Her tone is even, challenging. She could have asked, *Why don't you just go live with your aunt?* or *Prove to me that that's not the best option.*

I try to smile and look at my hands in my lap. "I just ... I mean, it's ..." It's impossible to find any words that can explain everything. Or something, even. Zac comes in with a glass of water for Ms. Sturge and sits on the couch beside me. Sitting between Zac and Penny, feeling them both here with me, helps me take a deep breath and say, "I want to stay here, go to my school. I only have a few years left. Zac and I can figure it out, we'll help each other."

Zac puts his hand on my knee and squeezes his long fingers. "Yeah, we're a team."

Ms. Sturge writes some more notes. Her face pinches into the middle — brows down, mouth tight and pursed — in a frown. "As a guardian, Is — *Zac*, I'd like to see you claim more of a leadership or care*giver* role than 'we're a team.'"

"Of course, I'll do whatever it takes. Besides, it's what our parents wanted. I found the papers." He picks up the envelope from the table beside him where we'd kept them for easy access. "Here, it says in these that I'm the guardian of Layne and Penny ..." He stops talking, and I can see his jaw working, his Adam's apple rise and fall with a swallow. Then he says, "Well, of Layne," with a whispered, tight voice. He pulls the long legal papers out of the brown envelope and stands to hand them to her. She flips through the pages, not looking at any them with close attention.

"I see," she says, and writes some more. She looks up at us and smiles, but the smile is pinched and artificial. "Zac, Layne, I understand what you want here, but I'm not sure that you understand the long-term implications. While it's only a few years, as you say, Layne, the next few years ahead of you are quite monumental ones. I am not sure that —"

"I am," I mumble.

Zac and Ms. Sturge both speak at the same time.

Zac: "Layne, don't interrupt."

Ms. Sturge: "What did you say?"

I look at Zac and smile then look back at Ms. Sturge, making sure to hold her gaze. "I said 'I am.' I am sure. I'm sure that this is what we need. Both of us. I'm sure that this is what Mom and Dad would've wanted. I've lost my parents and my sister who's … was my best friend —" My voice cracks and I swallow a growing lump of emotion. Swallow again until my throat is clear enough to continue. "I've lost everyone, except Zac. And I don't want to lose any more. Aunt Carole means well, but she's … different from my parents. So different. And her home is far away, and it would mean a new town and a new school and new friends, and I just don't think I can do anything else new. I need Zac. I need my own room with Penny's things. I need to be where I have memories of being with my parents. I need to be here. This is what they wanted and it's what I need."

When I stop talking, the room is silent. Painfully silent, as if a vacuum opened and sucked the sound and the breath and the life out. Ms. Sturge is staring at me as if I'm some specimen, as if she can see through my eyes into my brain to figure out my thoughts and feelings and decipher the truth. I feel stripped and exposed and frightened, and I wrack my brain to say something more to convince her, but I have nothing left to say. Zac's hand tightens on mine in a squeeze.

Ms. Sturge holds up her hand, palm toward me. "It's okay, Layne, I hear you. I still have my reservations, but the paperwork is in order, and I hear what you're telling me. I'm going to advocate that guardianship be transferred to Zac. There will be a list of recommendations that I feel are in your best interest, including that you continue to live in this house, receiving follow-up counselling through my office to ensure your mental health and life skills are sufficient, and some training for Zac in terms of guardianship and parenting. If you're willing to participate with these directions, I'm willing to close this investigation and recommend fulfillment of your parents' plans for you."

"Yes, yes, we can do that," Zac says quickly, standing up and dropping the envelope and other papers he had laid on his lap on the floor. He crosses the living room in wide strides with his hand outstretched. "We can do that," he says again, and she stands to shake his hand.

Ms. Sturge smiles at him and then looks down at me, still sitting on the couch. I'm stunned. Silent and immobile. "Is that acceptable, Layne?"

I nod. My soliloquy took everything I had, and in my relief I've sunk deeper into the couch, unable to respond to her simple question.

"You did it!" Penny cheers.

"Layne?" Zac says, his voice sounding like a plea.

"Earth to Layne!" Penny says beside me, and I barely manage to swallow my laugh of relief. Relief for the social worker's decision. Relief that she can't hear Penny and doesn't know that I can.

"Yes, I can do that," I say finally, pushing myself to stand up as well. "Thank you."

Ms. Sturge smiles then, and I think it's actually a real smile. Her eyes tip up on the sides, and she looks ten years younger. She puts her hand on my shoulder. "You're welcome. I want this to work out for you."

"It will," Zac says. I'm frozen again.

"I will draft my recommendations this week and put them before the court. Depending on the judge, you may have to make an appearance, but it will be a technicality by that point, just a hoop to jump through. Some will do the paperwork without the court time. It all depends on who you draw. I'll be in touch."

She picks up her bag and puts her paper pad inside then shoulders it, walking toward the door. Zac follows her, but I flop back onto the couch. I can hear their voices but don't pay attention to what they're saying. Penny's beside me, grinning. "Phew," I say, "no Aunt Carole's."

"Aw, it wouldn't have been that bad," Penny says, smiling.

"Well, you know what Dad would say," I whisper.

"Over my dead body," we say at the same time. I'm still laughing when Zac reappears in the doorway. He looks at me as if I've lost my mind, which, I'm starting to think, is probably the truth.

"What's so funny?" he asks.

"Nothing. Let's celebrate," I say. "Where's the beer?"

"Ha-ha," Zac says flatly, but he winks at me. "Phew," he says, "no Aunt Carole's." Beside me Penny bursts out laughing again, and I can't help but smile.

chapter 10

When Sara calls me on Thursday, I actually answer the phone. I can tell by her hesitation after I say, "Hey Sara," that she didn't expect me to.

"Oh, hi! I mean, hello, how are you?" She rushes on as if she's worried I'll hang up if she doesn't talk quickly enough.

"Okay," I say. Somehow, it's almost true. I'm in my room but I'm not hiding under the covers. At this moment, at least.

"Really?" Her voice hitches up in surprise.

"Well, I'm getting there, I think," I say. It feels good to be honest, to talk beyond "I'm fine."

She hurries to say, "That's good, that's really good. I'm glad." What do you say next? The quiet on the phone expands until it is pushing painfully against my ear. It's probably only a few seconds, but it feels like ages. I jump when she says, "What are you doing?"

I look guiltily at the computer screen, where I've paused the seventh New Landers video I've watched in a row, catching up on the ones I've missed by ignoring the outside world. "Bingeing on New Landers," I say, and she laughs.

"You must be feeling better. Well, do you want to do something? Grab a coffee or go to the mall or something?"

For some reason those options seem as possible as building a rocket ship and leading a celebrity travel cruise to Mars. I'm not hiding under my covers, but the mundane everyday actions still seem entirely foreign in my existence after the pickup truck. How has it only been nineteen days since I met her for a walk in the park — how is that possible? It's been a lifetime. She left to pick up her mom, and I stayed with Asher at the skatepark. That was an award-winning choice.

"Layne?" I actually forgot she was there.

"You need to get out," Penny says. "It's time."

"Yeah. I do. Let's do that," I hear myself say. It's like I'm watching myself talking to her on the phone, standing away from my body and having no control over the words coming out of my mouth.

"Great!" More surprise in her voice. "I'll pick you up? Half hour?"

"I'll be ready."

I didn't mean to say that either, and when the call ends, I sit there looking at the phone for a moment before Penny says, "You stink, get a shower." She's right, I do. I stand up and go into the washroom to get ready for my first adventure into the Real World of Everyday Things.

After my shower I find clothes that can pass for clean and head down the hall to stand in the kitchen doorway. Zac and Chase are sitting at the kitchen table. Their conversation falls silent when they see me. "I'm headed out," I say.

"I heard," Zac says. I frown and he adds, "Abby's catching a ride over with Sara."

Chase's smile grows. "Abby's coming over now?" He turns his grin on Zac, who seems suddenly to be doing a ninja-good job of avoiding looking at either of us. "She still talks about you, you know," Chase says. Zac dated Sara's sister Abby for almost two years in high school. Sara, Penny and I seemed more bummed about their breakup than either Abby or Zac.

Zac ignores him and asks me, "Going anywhere fun?"

"Not sure yet," I say with a shrug.

"But Abby's coming here?" Chase asks and Zac hits him. Chase smiles at me, and I smile back. It's good to see him sitting in our kitchen again. I didn't realize how much I missed the coming-and-going flock of Zac's friends while he was gone. Chase at our kitchen table is a comfy little bit of the old normal.

Zac mumbles something to Chase that I don't quite catch over the double-beep of a horn outside. "There she is," I say and head to the door. Sara is parked out front in her father's beat-up Civic, talking to Abby as she gets out of the passenger seat. I wave my orange-casted hand at them through the screen door window.

"Laynie, wait," I hear Zac call from behind me while I'm putting on my sneakers by the front door.

I turn back to look, and Penny has appeared beside him, crossing her arms and leaning her shoulder against the wall. "Now that you're home, you could ask Abby out sometime," I say. A blush flares up from his neck into his cheeks and he shakes his head, looking over my shoulder. "Why not?" I ask, probably a little too harshly, driven by a sudden sense of duty and loyalty to my friend.

He looks up at me and his eyebrows are knitted like he's studying my face, and he shakes his head. "It would be weird," he says finally.

"Maybe, maybe not," I say.

"And we've been down that road before," he whispers, digging in his pocket. "*And*, last I heard, she was dating Logan Kennedy." He produces a twenty from his pocket and holds it out to me.

I stuff the bill into my own jeans pocket and say, "It's not that serious, and you're way better for her than him." I finish just as Abby opens the door behind me.

"Hi Layne," she says almost shyly. She slips her arms around me and hugs me. I let her squeeze me and wait for her to step back before saying hi back. "I'm so sorry." There's that word again. I force a smile.

Abby's smile grows for Zac — bigger and more sincere. "Hey you," she says.

"Hey yourself," Zac says and hugs her. Over her shoulder Zac glares at me and I mouth "way better."

"We need milk and bread," Zac says when Abby steps back.

"We may not be going to a grocery store." I hate the whine in my argument, as if I'm negotiating his cooperation with mine. My face warms with embarrassment at my childish behaviour.

"So you'll get groceries only if he'll call Abby?" Penny asks with a laugh. Of course it sounds even more stupid when she puts it that way. I glare at her, and she sticks her tongue out at me.

"Give me back my money, then," Zac says with his hand out.

I slap-five on his open palm. "Milk and bread. Got it." I turn and leave them standing side by side in the entryway.

I yank the Civic door open and slide down into the passenger seat. "Hey."

"Hi! It's so good to see you out," Sara says after studying me a moment too long. I guess she was checking to see if I'm stable.

"It's good to be out," I say. It's not really. My heart is racing, and my palms are clammy. I'd give almost anything to go back to my bed right now. I actually picked up my phone to cancel on Sara four times, but Penny stopped me from calling.

"Where to?"

"How about Coffee Quotes?" I ask and try to ignore the stunned stare she gives me.

Coffee Quotes is the independent answer to the Chapters and Starbucks partnership. It was opened by a retired man after his wife died a couple of years ago. One half is a coffee bar with a counter and stools and a few comfy couches, the other half is lined with bookshelves filled with new and used books. It's Penny's favourite place. *Was.* I've only ever gone there as her hostage. Sara's questioning stare softens into a look that's uncomfortably close to pity. Who knows what conclusion she just came to. Maybe she figures I'm missing Penny so much that I need to go there to be close to her? Or some other after-school-special theory. If she only knew how close Penny actually is these days, without having to go sit in a coffee-scented bookstore.

But item number one: finish six books from TBR pile.

There's no way I can read six books this summer, even if I had a copy of her precious TBR list to choose from. But maybe I can finish *one*. The one she didn't. So by the time Sara slips the Civic into drive and pulls away from the curb, I have a plan in place: to find the red and yellow novel I last saw in the picture on the road in front of the blob-of-an-SUV and read it. For someone who reads a lot, like Penny, that may seem like a pretty lame plan, but I can't remember the last time I read a book. A whole book. But I'll be damned if I can remember the name of the novel she was reading. I've tried closing my eyes and picturing the book, but I can't remember the details. In Sara's car, I try again — try to *see* the cover, the title, the author's name, but it's just blotches of yellow, red and white.

"You okay?" Sara asks. I must look pretty nutty sitting in the car with my eyes squeezed shut. "Oh, I didn't think! Does driving make you nervous now, since ..." Since the pickup.

"No, no, I'm good. I was just trying to remember something." I push to force my voice out, and it sounds tight and strangled.

"Oh." She laughs, but her laugh isn't normal either, more high-pitched. Nervous. I look at my fingers sticking out of the orange fibreglass and wiggle them. The silence after the awkward laugh is thick, heavy and hot, smothering and so very different from the easy stillness we usually share. Used to share? What else did the pickup truck driver take from me? Sara turns the radio up. I glance in the back seat to see Penny sitting there amid a few discarded Tim's cups and a dog's harness and leash. I wonder if Sara's as relieved as I am when she pulls into a parking spot near the Coffee Quotes front door and cuts the engine. "Ready?"

"Ready," Penny says confidently.

I'm not. Nowhere near ready. Not for this shop, for this day, for this life stretched ahead of me. "Yup, let's go," I say.

The door has one of those old-fashioned bells hanging over it that rings when Sara pushes it open. I follow her inside. The smell of coffee is instant. I hate everything coffee — the taste, the smell. I'm not the coffee drinker, Penny is. *Was.* I concentrate on not wrinkling up my nose in disgust while I follow Sara to the counter.

My knees feel wobbly and my hands are shaking. I stuff my hands in my pockets and take a deep breath. Warm coffee smell wafts up my nose.

Smells That Are Warm

1. Coffee (of course).
2. Vanilla.
3. Cinnamon.
4. Gasoline.
5. Skunk.
6. Tomatoes.
7. Leather.

My heart is still racing, but I've run out of odours to add to my list. Cold ones then.

Smells That Are Cold

1. Spearmint.
2. Cucumbers.
3. Rain.

The man behind the counter is rubbing a cloth around the inside of a large, purple mug. He looks up, and when his eyes meet mine his twisting hand stops still, stuffed up in the upside down mug. I try to smile, but it doesn't feel like it worked. He blinks a few times, hurriedly and tightly, like he's trying to shake himself from a daze, then looks away to Sara. "What can I get you?" he asks her. He mostly focuses on her, but his eyes flutter my way once. Twice.

"I'll have a large latte, please, with double milk," Sara says and looks to me. "What do you want? My treat."

He looks at me again, white-faced and blinking fast. "Um, London Fog? Please?" His nervousness makes me uncertain of everything, even my order.

"Sure," he says and turns away with his hands busy at his counter, choosing mugs, pouring, dipping, filling — but every couple of moments he glances over his shoulder. At me. When he turns around with a large mug in each hand, he smiles at me — a twitch and wiggle of his grey moustache. "Here you go. It's on the house."

Sara looks from me to him, frowns as if to argue but then just says, "Thank you."

He nods and looks past her to me, steady now as if he has gathered up some resolve. "You must be Penny's sister, right?"

Ah, that's what his strange looks were about. "Yes," I say on the exhale that flies out as if I've been punched in the gut.

"I thought so. You — you look just like her." That's not really true … even though we're identical twins people can tell us apart. Penny's the pretty one. *Could. Was.* "When I saw you there I thought, just for a moment I thought maybe the news was wrong but then … I remembered she said she had a twin." I force a smile and hope it looks more genuine than it feels. "I am so sorry for your loss and will miss having Penny come in."

"She loved it here," I manage to mutter and then aim my eyes down on my tea, blinking to get the blurred mug to come into focus.

I hear the man clear his throat, but his voice is still gruff. "Well, if there's anything I can help you with, you be sure to lemme know."

"Ask him," Penny says.

"There is one thing." Once again it seems I'm floating away from control of my own actions. My voice is strong and sure, much, much more sure than I feel, wishing I could curl up in a ball and pull something over my head. "Penny was reading a book. She showed it to me, but I can't remember the title or who wrote it or anything about it, really. Except the cover. The cover is yellow, with red and white on the side …" In my mind the image flashes: the newspaper picture of the SUV-blob with the contents splattered about. The yellow book on the road. I try to picture it in Penny's hands instead. "It's probably impossible but …" My voice trails off lamely, and I force myself to look up at the man behind the counter.

"Well, just let me see. If she bought it here, the title should be in this contraption. This thing has to be good for something." His blue eyes flicker away from mine to the screen as he starts pecking the keyboard with his two index fingers. "Phone number?" I rattle off our house number. He taps it in but then frowns, screws up his eyes. "No, no, that's not it …" I recite Penny's cell number, and he enters it. His eyes open out of their studying squint and his moustache pulls back on each side. "Okay. Here's an order, her um, last order," he says and squeezes his mouth shut. His chin bobbles a bit. He clears his throat.

He turns the computer screen so we can see it together, and I step closer to take a look. Beside me, Penny leans closer too. The information doesn't mean much to me. The cursor rests on Penny's cell number, which is followed by our last name then her first (the other half of mine), but when he moves it an inch or two lower and clicks on the mouse, the data shifts to different text and a picture appears on the right hand side. A yellow rectangle, with white letters, red peeking around from the spine.

"That's it!" Penny says, but I already recognized it.

"That's it." I sigh in relief, as if I've just found something important that I thought was missing and gone for good. I didn't realize how much I needed to see that cover again.

"*The Riddle of Ellory*, C.A. Perkins."

"Do you have a copy?" I ask, and he shifts his head up so that he's looking down the length of his nose at the screen to study the computer a moment more.

"Well, according to this we have one. It should be in the fantasy section." He pulls a pen from his breast pocket and scribbles on a scrap piece of paper that he hands to me. I hold it between Sara and I so she can read it as well — the title, author and words "fantasy fiction" are scrawled in chicken scratch. The letters blur and wiggle on the paper, and I blink fast to settle them.

I swallow then say, "Thank you," willing my voice to stay even.

"It's no problem. If you have trouble finding it just shout." I carry my mug in my good hand, the scrap of paper pinched by the fingers sticking out of the cast on my right. Sara follows close behind as we walk over to the aisles of books. It's like a long hallway — two long walls met by a shorter wall in the back making a narrow rectangle of shelves. Both walls are lined with books on shelves that tower up out of my reach to the ceiling. Down the middle between the two walls is another two-sided shelf making the rectangle two aisles of colourful, vertical spines. The books are all different sizes and colours, standing pinched together. I run the pinky of my casted hand along the bumps as I walk, holding the paper between my pointy finger and thumb. Every little distance a paper rectangle of a flag sticks out beyond the books with labels of genres: Biography, Mystery, Cooking, Biology, Romance, YA — what is that? Yoyo Addicts? Yesterday's Actions? Yoga Arts?

"Here's fantasy," Sara says from the other side of the centre shelves. I can see her in the space between the top of the books and the bottom of the shelf at my eye level. She smiles and points. I walk around the end and meet her where a purple rectangle with the word "Fantasy" juts out of the books just above my head. I set my tea down on a small space on a lower shelf, pulling my hand away slowly so as not to tip it, and look back up to where the collection of fantasy books starts. The first book has an author named "Aaron," so I scan through the spines until I get to P: Patterson, Payman, Peabody, Pembly, Perk, *C.A. Perkins*. In bold white letters the name glows on a red spine. I pull the book out with my good hand and lay it flat on my open palm. My vision blurs again. I blink. Blink. Take a deep breath and blink again. The cover is yellow, with a butterfly outlined in simple black lines. White letters with black edging spell out: *The Riddle of Ellory*. I brush the tips of my fingers over the cover. It is matte-soft and cool. Smooth.

I look up, and Penny is grinning. "You'll love it," she says.

"I'll *try* it," I say back.

"Sorry?" Sara asks behind me. I turn to face her, holding up the book. She smiles and asks, "Is that it?" I nod. The silence between us is easy then, as if our shared thoughts fill the space so there's no room for awkwardness. She reaches out and puts her hand on my arm by my elbow. My smile grows. I tuck the book under my arm and pick up my tea, and we head back to settle onto a red pleather couch to sit and chat.

"So Zac's home for good?" Sara cradles her coffee mug in both hands and whispers from behind it.

"Yeah, he moved back home. He's my *guardian*." I try to draw out the word in a mocking way to show how ridiculous it is for me to need one, but I fail miserably. Likely because she knows how relieved I am to have him home. Sara studies me for a minute. I can tell she's trying to decide if she should say something or not. "What?" I ask, forcing her hand.

"Well, I was just wondering … did he ever tell you why he left?" She takes a sip and then waves her hand fast while she swallows and hurries to add, "I know you asked before, but he wouldn't say."

I shrug. "Nope. Nothing more than what I told you already. Dad said they had a fight about some guy Zac was hanging around with. Dad told him he was trouble, and Zac didn't want to listen so he stormed out. Came back the next day and took his stuff, said he found a place to live with some friends."

FLASHBACK: *Guitar pieces spread throughout the living room. Mom on her knees picking up bits and putting them in a clear garbage bag. Crying and pretending not to.*

"That's it?" Sara asks. I shrug again, and she goes on, "I mean, Zac's home now, you could ask him what happened."

"I could, I guess. I mean, when he left I was so mad at him, and I wanted to know what his excuse was and get him to admit that he was picking some rotten troublemaker friends over us. But now …" My voice gets shaky so I stop talking, just shake my head. It's totally not cool to lose it in a coffee shop.

Sara whispers, "It's okay. We don't have to talk about it."

I take a deep breath and go on anyway. Somehow it's soothing to get it out. "But after … everything … it just doesn't matter. I can't be mad anymore." Sara starts to say something then stops and starts and stops again. "What? It's okay, what were you going to ask?"

She shakes her head but says, "I don't know, but your dad not liking Zac's friend? It just seems like a pretty small thing to have such a big fight over."

"I guess. Zac dropped all his classes and got a job at some office in Truro. Dad blamed all of it on his so-called friend. He said he told Zac he didn't want his friend around me and Penny, and he wasn't welcome at the house. He said he warned Zac that the friend was trouble. He said Zac made his choice."

"If it were almost anyone else, I'd think it was drugs or something." Sara blushes when she says that then hurries to say, "But I mean, it couldn't be. Not Zac."

"No, not Zac. But maybe his friend. Dad was so sure he was no good." There's a cold pool swirling in my gut. "I don't know, I mean Dad and Zac are both so stubborn." They are. They were. Are and were.

"Well, I'm glad he's back."

"Me too," I say. The two words are the understatement of the year. Where would I be without him? I shudder at the thought.

"You cold? We could move over there." Sara's already moving to stand up, her finger pointing to a seat further from the air conditioning unit above our head.

I shake my head and put my hand on her arm to pull her back into the couch. "Nope, I'm good. Tell me everything new that I've missed."

She takes a sip of the steaming tan liquid and smiles. "Not much is new, really. I got a job for the summer."

"Yeah? Where?"

"Dexter's, covering vacation shifts and stuff."

"Waiting tables?"

"They say eventually. I have to start out with hostess and bussing, though. That sucks."

"Yeah, you'll have better tips when you're doing the tables." Sara nods. "What about ball?"

"I'm playing on one team — the coed team from last year. We only play Sunday afternoons." Another sip. "You should come out! They're always hurting for girls."

FLASHBACK: *Penny and I played second and shortstop, we practiced every Sunday evening. The coach hit the ball to me, I fielded it cleanly and tossed it to Penny, who threw it to Sara on first. He grinned and shouted, "Watch how Layne and Penny work together to cover second base!" Then he hit it to Penny, and I raced to the bag. She fielded it on her backhand and tossed it to me. I tagged the bag with my toe and zipped it over to Sara. The three of us could turn the fastest double play in the league last summer.*

Penny pulls me back to the bookstore and the stink of coffee by saying, "You should play."

There's no way I could be on the field without her. But I say, "Maybe," because it's easier than explaining. My London Fog has cooled off enough that I can drink it without burning my tongue. Sweet, creamy hot tea slips around my mouth, and I can feel its warm passage right down to my stomach.

"Well, let me know," Sara says, and I nod and pick fluff off my knee, lift it up and let it go, watching it float down out of sight. "What else do you have planned for the summer?" Sara asks. Then she goes on, her voice softer in apology, "I mean, have you made any plans?"

Have you made plans? really means *Have you made* new *plans yet?* and makes me think of Penny's list. My right hand moves to my pocket to pull it out and show Sara, but as my fingertips slip in far enough to touch the paper, the bell jingles by the door as someone walks in.

"You can show her, it's not a secret," Penny says.

But a low voice rumbles a coffee order by the counter, and another group of people is chatting around a table just behind us. Two people browse in the shelves. Their presence pulses against me, pushing and poking until my anxiety stirs. I can't show the list now, here, in this public space. Even to Sara. "Some," I say, opting for vague. "Like I'm going to read this book." I pat the soft cover gently, as if it's a living creature. "And get a job," I add. "Zac and I saw a lawyer last week. There's money for school and the house is paid off, but he said we need to be careful about spending on extra things." Sara nodded as if she understood but she didn't — the real reason for getting a job was Penny's secure employment task, which Sara knew nothing about.

"I can see if Dexter's needs anyone else?"

Waiting tables might be my worst nightmare. So many ways for my clumsiness to interfere with the job getting done.

Ways to Totally Screw Up a Perfectly Good Waitressing Job
1. Crashing into tables.
2. Crashing into people.
3. Dropping food or drinks.
4. Spilling food on myself, or, better yet —
5. Spilling food on the patrons.

"Yeah, I dunno …" my voice says without me, and I resolve to find something else — almost anything else — before she can offer again to get me a job.

The moustached owner shuffles by behind the couch where we sit and stops for a minute, resting his hands on the couch back. "Did you find the book?" he asks. I nod and lift the book up out of my lap to show him. "Good. You take that, my gift to you."

I want to argue, but honestly, I hate that battle to out-polite each other: *I can't really! I insist! Are you sure? Yes of course! Well, if you insist. I really do.* "Thank you," I mutter and hug the book close to my chest. He smiles and puts his hand on my shoulder. It's warm and heavy — not uncomfortable pressure, more like my blanket feels when I hide under it. "Thanks," I say again and mean it.

"You are most welcome," he says. "And if you need anything else from me, you know where to find me." With this he lifts his arms, palms up, and looks around as if showing me the stinky bookstore for the first time.

"Yes, thanks," I say. When I glance away I see Penny sitting in the chair across the table from my spot on the couch. She's smiling again and nodding. She approves.

chapter 11

Someone else is at the house. A small red Mustang is parked beside Mom's car. It makes Mom's Yaris look sad and old. What kind of car does that social worker drive? I can't remember, but I don't think that's it. I would have remembered a Mustang, surely. Maybe it's the lawyer. I hope not, because I just want to go back to bed. When I get to the front door it's locked. Weird. I dig in my bag for my house key, find the single silver charm at the end of my *Glee* lanyard and pull it out. I turn to wave at Sara, who waves back and drives off while I turn the key in the lock. I push the door open.

"Hello?" I call into the quiet house. "Zac? Chase?" Nothing. Maybe they went out with whoever drives the cool car. Good. I'm peopled out. All I want is to climb back into bed, but first I have to put the milk away. I kick off my sneakers and go into the kitchen, put the grocery bag on the counter. I open the fridge and put the carton of milk on the shelf. Something stinks. I bend down to look all the way in to the back of the fridge, searching for the culprit. I move the pickle jar and two jars of jam from one side to the other and finally find a blue cereal bowl in the back covered by Press-n-Seal that's fogged up with condensation bubbles on the inside. I pull it out and stand up.

Something to my left moves. My heart catches in my throat.

"OH!" I jump and drop the bowl on the floor. It cracks into four large pieces — it's very possible that the mouldy, caked-on, dried-out beans held it mostly together, preventing it from shattering.

"Nice," Zac says from the kitchen doorway.

I slam the fridge door. "You scared the shit out of me!"

He raises one eyebrow and nods down to the mess on the floor. "Enough for you to lose your lunch, I see." He grins, a wide smile that announces he's proud of his wit.

"Not funny," I growl.

"It's kinda funny," he argues and hands me the roll of paper towel from the table. I stoop down to pick up the fuzzy beans. He says, "Careful," which only earns him another glare from me.

I pile the dish pieces and the bean-muck on a paper towel and pick the whole package up, turning around to put in the garbage. I wet another piece of paper towel and reach down to wash the spot on the floor. Zac mutters something, and I look up to ask "Huh?"

In the doorway beside Zac stands another guy about his age, maybe a bit older. He has scruff on his face and thick, dark hair. Waves of curls that have ringlet potential if they grow any longer cover his ears and brush along his neck almost to his shoulders. He reaches up and pushes his hair out of his dark eyes.

"Um, hi?" I say and look from him to Zac, who's still grinning at my mess. I raise my eyebrows questioningly, which seems to wake him up.

"Oh, right. Laynie this is Sebastian. Bas, my sister Layne."

I feel my eyes narrow, trained on him, and I try to make them relax, try to smile. But Sebastian. The roommate. The friend.

FLASHBACK: *Dad was sitting in the living room when Penny and I got home from a movie with Sara. The TV was on but I knew he wasn't watching it, because it was tuned to a chick flick he'd never choose. "Where's mom?" I asked.*

"Gone to bed," he said. His fingers were fidgeting with something tucked in his hand. I stepped closer to give him a goodnight kiss and saw it was a tuning peg from his smashed guitar. He saw me looking and smiled a bit, held the peg up, so I took it.

"Why did he go?" I asked. Again. Maybe his offering of the tuning peg, instead of tucking it away in embarrassment, was a sign that he'd offer more information too.

But he didn't. He looked away from me and shook his head slowly. I held out the peg and he took it back, squeezing his fingers around it. He stood and gave me a hug, kissed me on the cheek and whispered, "Goodnight, sleep tight," in my ear as if I was seven years old again. I turned to leave the room and he said, "Laynie?" I stopped and turned around. "That friend of his — Sebastian — he was trouble. Is trouble. He made his choice." I nodded, because he had told me that before, and headed off to my room.

Sebastian offers his hand, and after a moment I hold out my casted arm. He hooks a couple fingers around the ends of mine sticking out of the cast and shakes gently. "Hi, Layne," he says.

"Hello," I say in an even voice, my eyes still fixed on him. He's bigger than me, taller than Zac even, but maybe if I stare hard enough I can intimidate him.

"I'm uh, sorry about your arm. And your folks. And Penny."

"Yeah," I say, even though it's a stupid response. Listed like that it's evident he knows how many things there are to be sorry for. None of *those* are his fault, but the fact that Zac wasn't here for the last six months? *That* I can pin on him. I want to ask, "What are you doing here?" but I stop myself by keeping my mouth clamped painfully shut.

Zac says, "I moved into Sebastian's place when I, uh, left here."

"Yeah, I know," I say with as much apathy as I can dish out. "Dad said." The words are sharp coming out. I'm sure they hurt when they hit their mark.

Zac studies me as if he's consciously avoiding looking anywhere else. His lips are pressed tight and his face starts to redden a bit. His eyebrows pull together. He's mad? He's mad! My knee-jerk instinct is to bark at him: *What do you have to be mad about? You're the one who took off! You chose him over us?* I swallow the words down, and it hurts to force my throat closed over the angry accusations that threaten to spout out. We stand there in silence, the three of us, awkwardly looking at each other, but not long enough for any of us to wonder why we're looking at each other. Well, I'm more glaring than looking really.

I turn away and pick up the two loaves. "I got bread," I announce as if either their eyesight or their intelligence are limited so that they could not draw the conclusion on their own.

"Good, thanks," Zac says evenly. "We were just going to go meet Chase at the park and go for a run."

He looks over his shoulder at Sebastian as if needing his agreement, which is given in a nod. Geez.

It's Sebastian who asks, "Do you want to come?"

Number 3: 5 km under 30 mins but also, no way in hell.

"No, I'm going to put these things away." I wave at the two loaves of bread, two boxes of KD and one jar of blueberry jam as if it should be obvious to them that it'll take me *hours* to put them away, leaving no time for anything else, really.

"Suit yourself," Zac says, turning away and walking past Sebastian, who stands a moment longer looking at me.

"Nice to meet you, finally."

He smiles when he says that, and I make a face that is somewhere between a wince and snarl. I could say "you too" but the word "finally" clogs my brain. "You too" doesn't work because of the "finally." There's no "finally" in my sentiments, because as far as I'm concerned I could've gone my whole life without knowing him. Before I can say something, he turns and leaves the kitchen. I watch him go. He doesn't *look* like the badass influence Dad knew he was, but you know what they say about judging a book by its cover. I obviously don't have the whole story. I don't know everything Dad knew about him, but I'm going to find out.

chapter 12

Back in my room, I change into sweats and crawl under the covers. I take the book out of the grey plastic bag the moustached man gave me. The black outlined butterfly seems to press its wings against the yellow cover, plastering the fluttery, delicate movement into a heavy stillness. Still and quiet. Trapped. I turn over to the back and read praise and reviews then a paragraph describing the mission the heroine Ellory must embark upon: a typical teen must make the choice between a mortal life of love and regular high school drama and a mystic existence protecting the world from lurking evil and fantastical beasts.

"Sounds like a winner," I mutter.

"Give it a chance, it's really good," Penny says. She's standing beside my bed. I shimmy over so there's room, and she stretches out on the bed beside me. Her shoulder is close enough to mine that I should feel her there, but I don't. I look down the bed, where my two feet create bumps under my blanket, her ten bare toes in a line to the right of my foot-bulges. Her toenails are shimmery ice blue.

FLASHBACK: *I sat in Penny's chair, my toes propped curled around the top of her desk. The door swung open and Penny swooped in. "What are you doing?"*

"Mining the Arctic for watermelons," I said, turning back to the nail polish brush just in time to stop a drip from falling from the tip.

Penny flopped down behind me on her bed. "You can't do that at your own desk?"

"The light's better over here," I said then stuck my tongue out in my effort to cover my baby toenail.

"Yeah, that's it. Certainly not the Mount Everest of Crap on yours, right?"

"Right." I twisted the lid on.

"Wait. Do mine," she said, bumming her way to the end of the bed. I spun around

in her chair to face her, careful to keep my wet toes from touching anything. She put a foot on each of my knees, and I started with her left big toe.

Under the blankets, my toenails have chipped blue polish on the ends. Penny's are still neat and shiny. I open the book from the front, flip past the cover pages and that one with all the small print about publishers to the first real page and start to read.

Some movies start with a car race or bombings by airplanes. The action starts right from the beginning. If books were like that, maybe I could read more. But no, the first chapter, or chapters even, spend so much time telling the situation, setting the scene, introducing the characters. It's boring. And so I can't pay attention. I read, my eyes go over the lines and I see the letters and the words, but it's like hearing a conversation in the background — I can hear the voices but have no clue what they're talking about, because I'm busy doing something else. I'll get to the end of the page or the end of the chapter and realize I don't have a sweet clue about what I just read, what happened or even what the story is about. While I'm looking, the page shifts to black and white lines that my eyes are busy scanning while my brain takes off and has its own party with the thoughts and songs and jokes and sarcastic comments I didn't think of at the time swirling around in my head.

So when my phone rings, I'm air-quotes-reading and totally distracted by what I should have said to Sebastian.

Things I Should Have Said to Sebastian

1. Get lost.
2. I'm sure there's somewhere else you should be.
3. I'll find you out.
4. You took his last six months with them, you're not getting any of his time from me.
5. Get lost.

I'm so distracted that I answer the call without checking the caller ID first. "Hello?"

"Layne!" Asher sounds shocked, and the realization that I've answered the phone and am connected to someone trickles into my conscious. I hadn't meant to, but when he says my name there's a familiar twinge of a flutter in my middle.

"Hi, Asher," I say, pressing my hand against my stomach trying to settle the quivering.

"Layne, hi. I didn't think you'd answer." Seems like no one knows what to say, so they say these dumb comments that have no normal response. Or maybe he really didn't think I would because I haven't for a while. For nineteen days.

"I did." Which is true.

"I've texted and called and never heard back …" He stops just short of asking why I've been so rude. I guess he knows.

"I know," I say. "I'm sorry, I just haven't felt like talking to anyone." Truth of the day. Hell, of the whole summer so far.

"Yeah, I get it." And then silence. Just a moment of silence, really, but it feels like it stretches on until eternity, and it leaves me enough time to wonder if awkwardness is banned in Heaven. "How's your arm?" he asks, startling me out of my thoughts.

"It's alright." That's true too. I mean, it aches some, but there are things that hurt worse. A lot worse.

"So, a bunch of us are going out to Crystal Beach on Saturday, do you want to come?"

6.   Get to the beach five times.

For a moment, item number six battles with my need to stay in hibernation and avoid interaction with real people from before. I mean, I survived my Real World Adventure with Sara, but there's a huge difference between a short trip to the coffee shop with one good friend and a horde of people from My Life Before at the beach. Asher knows me enough to interpret my hesitation as reluctance. "Hey, if you don't want to, I get it. I get it, really."

And that just makes me want to laugh. How could he "get it" if *I* have no clue what is going on in my head? What does he know? Somewhere in my muddled, confused brain Asher's assurance that "it's alright" if I don't want to go gets all twisted up with him calling me a chicken on the top of the half-pipe. Even though I know how stupid I was to fall for it the first time, I fall for it again. "No, it's a good idea," I say with that weird out-of-body separation from my smarter, safer self. "What time are you going?"

"Great! Probably 'bout two. Should I pick you up?"

"Maybe. I'll let you know." My brain is catching up with my shooting-off mouth and trying to rein it in.

"Okay then. Let me know. And I'll see you Saturday."

"See you then." I push the red hang-up circle before I can say any more stupid things. I open Messages and flick out a text to Sara pleading with her to join me. She could be a buffer, saving me from uncomfortable interactions with all the Before People and their questions and stares. I could go with her, stay long enough to say we went and escape early. No harm, no foul, and no chicken-shit here. Her response is quick and enthusiastic, with three exclamation marks following the all-capped *YES* then a flurry of questions about logistics: what time, who's going, what should she bring, but I'm already spent from my excess of socializing. I'm not used to people any more. I click the phone on silent, set it on the bedside table and lie down.

When I wake up, I hear unfamiliar voices from the other side of my door. I sit up and listen. It must be the TV. The light coming through the window is evening-dim. I sit up and stretch my arms over my head; the cast is heavy, and my shoulders ache. I tip my head to my shoulder, and my neck crackles. I push myself up, walk over and open the door. The TV voices, instantly louder, grate through me like nails on a chalkboard. I walk down the hall to the living room, where Sebastian is sitting on the end of the couch with his feet stuck out on the coffee table, legs crossed at the ankles. Chase and Corey are sprawled on the floor, and Abby is curled up in the armchair. Dad's chair. The TV light is glowing on their faces. The soundtrack of a car race booms from the speakers.

FLASHBACK: *Mom bustled through the front door as if swept in by the fall wind behind her. "Hi, guys," she said from the hall. I heard the clattering of the closet door, hangers on the rail, shoes against the floor, keys on the hook against the wall and a stream of words she tossed our way as she walked past us from the entry to the kitchen. "Sorry I'm late, traffic was horrid. Any preferences for supper? I'm not even sure what we have, we so need to go shopping. Why is that TV so loud? Get your feet off the coffee table. Did your father call? I texted him but he hasn't written back. I hate stupid texting, I don't even know if he's seen it and is ignoring me or hasn't noticed it yet ..."*

"That's really loud," I say, just a bit less than a shout. Sebastian turns to me with a frown that is somewhere between annoyed and surprised, which pisses me off instantly because man, this is my house, not his. I can ask him to turn it down if I want.

He fumbles with the remote, holds it close to his face in the dark until he finds the right button and points it back at the TV. The volume lowers. I watch the white numbers descend from 53 down to 21 and can almost hear Dad's voice telling us "there's no reason for this to be over 20. Ever." Sebastian turns to me and says, "Huh?" At least he's articulate.

"I said, it's really loud."

"Told you to turn it down," Chase said and then turned to me and added, "I told him to turn it down, Laynie."

Sebastian smiles, if you can call it that. More of a smirk, really, and says, "Yeah, I like to feel it." What is that even supposed to mean?

That's when Zac comes into the room and says, "You woke up."

"I heard voices," I say nodding toward the TV.

"I swear he's deaf," Zac says, and he's smiling too.

Sebastian takes a pillow from the couch and throws it at Zac. His aim sucks. It sails past Zac and hits the framed picture of Mom and Dad on the beach in Jamaica from their twenty-fifth anniversary trip. The frame swings, and for the second it takes me to step toward it, it looks like it's going to crash down. It settles at an angle. Dad's arm is around Mom's shoulders as if he's holding her from sliding off the slanted beach. Sebastian follows up his pillow-toss with a "shut up" to Zac as I straighten the picture. My parents look happy. Relaxed, wide smiles. All was right with the world then, no idea about a pickup truck less than two years later. "Sorry," I whisper to the picture, but I don't know if it's because of the pillow assault or the future they couldn't see.

"Laynie, Bas made spaghetti. We already ate, but there's lots left," Zac says as he steps over Corey and sits on the couch. I bite my jaw tight and my hands fist up. Well, my hand, the one without a cast. The fingers on my right hand curl around the fibreglass and squeeze until a pain shoots up my arm to my elbow. They didn't bother to wait. As if reading my mind, Zac says over his shoulder, "I didn't want to wake you up." I'm pissed but have no idea why.

"No problem," I say, more to myself than to them and walk into the kitchen, careful not to stomp. The noodles are in a pot on the stove, the handle of the spaghetti-serving fork sticking out with its prongs tangled in the starchy strings. I grab a bowl from the cupboard and scoop some into it.

"They're short," I say to no one.

"Sebastian must have broken them up before he put them in the water," Penny says, suddenly beside me, leaning her butt against the counter. The words are tinged with incredulity, as if she just said something more profound like "Sebastian murdered a small child and turned him into noodles." I get it. Long noodles have a solid position in our family traditions. Most spaghetti dinners turned into a noodle-sucking contest — who could draw up the longest noodle without breakage. It was terribly rude and childish and very fun. Mom won the last round. I guess that makes her the indefinite champion. So the breaking of noodles is as atrocious as eating pizza with a knife and fork or leaving the last of the cereal milk in the bowl instead of tipping back the bowl and drinking it out. We have nothing if we don't have class. And Sebastian broke the noodles.

I can hear Dad's voice again, quiet and broken: "That friend of his is no good, Margo."

"They're just noodles," I say. I don't know to whom. Maybe Penny, who shrugs there beside me. Maybe to Dad. Maybe I'm trying to convince myself. I scoop another forkful of noodles and ladle some sauce over them. They're still hot, and steam rises from the chunky red sauce. The smell of tart tomatoes and spices makes my mouth water. I didn't realize I was so hungry.

Penny still stands at the counter, looking at the pots on the stove. "Want some?" I ask. Might as well be polite.

She snickers and shakes her head then says, "I wish." I should have known hallucinations don't eat. I look out into the living room, where the volume of the TV has crept back up. The TV lights up the room, and between it and my spot in the kitchen I can see the silhouettes of two heads on either end of the couch. "Stay in here with me," Penny says from the table, where she's sitting in her usual seat. I don't need much convincing.

I sit across from her in my chair, stick my fork into the side of the bowl and twist it. The noodles are too short to make more than one or two twists around the prongs, so they keep sliding off or flipping straight away. I give up and scoop some noodles and sauce onto the fork like a spoon and manage to get most of it into my mouth. Some slide off at the last minute, running down my chin and splattering on the table beside my bowl. Penny laughs. I try to glare at her, but it's hard to be intimidating with spaghetti sauce dripping off my face.

Sebastian choses then to come into the kitchen, while I'm wiping my face with a paper towel. He looks at me, and I don't care for the snicker before he opens the fridge and takes out two bottles of beer. Dad's beer. "Are you going to come join us?" he asks. "You haven't missed much." Missed much of what? Probably the movie. But I also missed much of Zac's new life. With his new badass friend who breaks noodles too short.

"No," is what I say aloud. I keep the *I'll just sit here and keep my dead sister company* part to myself.

"Suit yourself," he says on his way out. When I look up at Penny's chair again, she's gone. The whole appearing and disappearing act is getting old. I mean, if she's going to stick around to haunt me, the least she could do is stay long enough for me to ask her some questions.

Questions to Ask Penny

1. Why were you in the car?
2. Why are you still here?
3. Are Mom and Dad alright?
4. Where are they?

5. What do you want me to do with your ToDah! list? Finish it? Is that right? Am I right?

6. How do I figure this out on my own?

But she's always gone before I can ask anything. Before I can do anything more than dribble spaghetti down the front of my face. And long before I can figure out any answers.

chapter 13

Later that night, I'm in bed trying to read Penny's book again. Trying to remember how Ellory had gotten lost in the forest and where her so-called friends are that she's there alone. The words run across my eyes, but sentences are interrupted by thoughts of elbow planks and short noodles and finding a job. There's a knock on the door, and before I can respond Zac opens it and sticks his head in the room.

"Can I come in?" he asks.

"You already are," I say, turning back to the book and trying to look very busy reading it. I can't find the place on the page where I had stopped.

"Nope, just my head. Can my feet come in too?"

"Sure, but not your arms," I say, and he laughs. But it's a pity laugh, forced and fake, not a real one. It wasn't that funny a joke.

He comes in and stands by my dresser for a minute, reaching a finger out and touching the frame that holds the picture of Penny and me laughing at our third birthday party. He swallows — his jaw gets tight and his neck muscles raise and lower — then he clears his throat and says, "How was your trip out with Sara?"

I shrug. I should tell him the truth, that I couldn't wait to come home and climb back into bed, but I don't have the energy to go into it. "Alright," I say without commitment.

"I was glad you went. It's time, you know."

Time for what? The clichéd "time to move on"? I call bullshit.

"So, you met Sebastian." He doesn't look at me when he says that, doesn't take his eyes off the picture of Penny and I. Maybe he's not talking to me? Maybe he sees Penny too. I glance around the room, but it's only him and me there now.

When I don't answer right away, he turns to look at me. Studies me. "So is he gone?" is what I say, which isn't very encouraging. And I only say it to get him to stop staring at me like that.

He looks at me a moment more, during which I can see his face shift from questioning and hopeful to angry. Resigned. He nods and says, "Yeah, everyone left," and strides toward the door in two angry-long steps.

My voice stops him. "Sebastian's the friend Dad didn't like, isn't he." I meant it as a question, but it doesn't come out that way.

Zac stops. He doesn't turn around, not right away. He stops walking and stands there with his head down as if he's staring at his feet or his hands or something in front of him. I wish I hadn't said anything at all, but once words come out there's no putting them back. They hang there between us, a reminder of our father's disapproval, the six-month estrangement that didn't end before the pickup and the drunk. When Zac finally turns around his eyes are bright, his face flushed and he's blinking fast. His face is pulled tight with determination, his eyebrows knit together and there's a strong forward set to his jaw, but when his mouth opens, the colour drains out of his face with the intent. He says, just above a whisper, "Dad didn't even know him." His steps are quick as he leaves, and when he closes the door I get the distinct impression he does so with great carefulness not to slam it behind him.

And then I'm alone. More alone than I've felt in the almost three weeks since the accident. I look to her bed, but Penny's nowhere to be seen or heard. Or felt. I know Zac's just in another room, and I stand up to follow him out, but somehow the rest of the house is locked away from my bedroom and I'm trapped by silence and emptiness and isolation that I might never escape.

I need to talk to someone. Somehow. I text Sara *I met Zac's friend* and stare at my phone waiting for her commiserating reply. It doesn't come. I open my text conversation with Asher to tell him the same, but he doesn't know the story, the history behind it, and I'm not in the mood to explain everything. Instead I type *Saturday, what 2 bring?* I stare and wait. Nothing. I put the disloyal phone down.

I pull my blankets up over my shoulders and tuck them in tight around me to keep the shadows away. The silence is a fertile setting for my imagination. The gnawing of what-ifs in my brain is like rats on insulation in the walls.

What-Ifs to Change the Space-Time Continuum

1. What if I'd told Asher to eff off and not gotten on the skateboard?
2. What if Zac had listened to Dad and not stormed out?
3. What if Sebastian's showing up here screws everything up again?
4. What if, if he has to choose, Zac picks him over me? Again?

The questions swirl in my head while I try to hold it together.

FLASHBACK: *I called out and woke myself up out of a nightmare I couldn't remember. Bullies at school or a monster under my bed, nothing as horrific as a drunk in a pickup. The door swung open, and Dad rushed in. He sat on the side of my bed and stroked the hair out of my face until I was calm and lying back on my pillow. Then he picked up my guitar and sang Beatles songs until I fell asleep.*

I swallow down the bulge in my throat and push the blankets off, get up and cross the room to Penny's side. Her guitar rests against the side of her desk. I grip the neck and carry it back to my bed, slip my legs under the covers and cradle the guitar. I pluck the strings and turn the tuning keys until the strings sing out true notes. I strum once, twice and pick until the melody slips out and I sing just above a whisper, "Hey Jude …"

After three verses, the questions are banished from my mind. After four, my heart isn't pounding as violently against my breastbone. By the time I sing some "nah nah nah's" with the melody I'm ready to lie back down. I put Penny's guitar down beside me on my bed and curl around it. I fall asleep.

chapter 14

The next morning I wake up to light blaring in through the window. I check my phone — ten thirty — and feel an unfamiliar urge to get up, get started, get moving, get going. Do something.

I sit up and stretch, relishing the pull of muscles along my ribcage and down into my hips, up through my shoulders into my arms. My casted arm complains with a burn just below the elbow. I tip my head from side to side, stretching my neck and the muscles down into my back.

3.   50 pushups readjusted due to injury to five minutes of elbow plank.

I take my phone to the spot I cleared before and settle down onto my belly, taking a minute to curl my back up into a stretch that goes from my calves to the tips of my shoulders. With the phone in front of me, I push up onto my elbows and toes and tap the start button of the stopwatch. The right-hand numbers fly, but the numbers marking seconds seem to crawl. By the time the count reaches twenty, my back is rigid and my belly on fire. My legs are shaking. At thirty seconds I flop gracelessly back onto the ground, resting my forehead on my arms and sucking air into lungs that had locked closed by my holding my breath. At least thirty seconds is better than twenty.

When my breathing returns to normal and my back stops protesting, I push myself up and go out to the kitchen. The sink is full of dirty dishes, and four empty beer bottles line the back of the counter. Sebastian. I need to find something on him, find out whatever Dad knew and convince Zac that he's no good. I pour a bowl of cereal and sit at the table, thumbing through my phone. I open Safari but stop after typing in S-E-B — I have no idea what his last name is.

"What are you doing?" Penny says.

"Looking up Sebastian."

"Why?" I look up to see if she's sincere. Her eyes are puzzled. Of course. I'm the sarcastic one.

"I'm going to find out what Dad knew." The information didn't make her look less perplexed.

I open FriendSpace instead and scroll through Zac's profile. His wall is full of pictures of friends at parties, at the gym, in our living room, but most of the pictures are older, from before Christmas. The picture of him, Penny and me in front of the tree is still on the first page, him standing between us grinning big and squeezing us close. I pause and stare.

"What? What is it?" Penny asks, leaning closer across the table.

"A picture of us." Maybe the last of the three of us — had there been another? It was only a few days after Christmas that Zac had left. I press my finger on the image and select "save" from the menu.

"It's a good one," Penny whispers.

I scroll back to the top and select Zac's list of friends then enter Sebastian's name into the search field. Nothing. I shorten it back to "Seb" then "Bas" and still nothing. I skip over our mutual friends, Abby, Sara, Chase, Corey, a handful of others, to thumb through the rest of the list, looking for his face. Even among the ones we don't share, I recognize most of the names and faces — some from high school, some from his first year of university. None of them look like the guy I met last night. Then again, lots of the profile pictures aren't of people or may be of different people — I'm pretty sure "William Black" is not a three-year-old girl with pigtails and "Ashley Hickman" is not a Boston Terrier. None of the profiles with un-selfie-ish pictures had names that could be versions of Sebastian.

But then again, how stupid would a drug-dealing criminal be to put his true information on FriendSpace? "Maybe he's using a fake name," I whisper to myself.

"Or maybe he's not on FriendSpace," Penny says, her voice edged with vexation. I study her for a minute. She's sitting across from me in her usual seat, her head in one hand, tracing the lines in the wood of the table with her pointy finger. She doesn't look up when she adds, "Maybe he's not a drug-dealing criminal either."

I look back at my phone. "Dad didn't like him. I've got to find out why and convince Zac before —"

"Before what?" Penny asks. Whose side is she on, anyway?

"Never mind," I say.

"Never mind what?" Zac says, walking into the kitchen. He crosses to the coffee machine, loads in a pod and puts a mug under the dispenser. He pushes the button and the machine whirls into action. "Who are you talking to?" I look up across the table, and Penny raises her eyebrows in a challenge — *go ahead, tell him.*

Cons to Telling Zac about the Penny Hallucination

1.   He'll think I'm nuts.
2.   Probably take me to a shrink.
3.   Maybe send me to live with Aunt Carole after all.

Pros to Telling Zac about the Penny Hallucination

1.   …

"Just talking to myself," I say, and Penny sticks her tongue out at me.

Zac yawns, wide and loud, then covers his hand with his mouth. "Sorry. I stayed up late reading after we watched that movie. You should've joined us, it was a good one." Whatever. I don't care if it won all the Academy Awards, I'm glad I didn't waste my evening sitting in the same room as *him.*

"Yeah, because your evening was full of world-saving productivity," Penny says. It makes sense that a hallucination can read my thoughts, seeing as they originate in the same place. I glare at her and silently tell her to shut up.

"You okay?" Zac asks. I turn to look at him, and he's studying me. "What are you glaring at?" A burn creeps up my neck into my cheeks.

"Really, 'who'?" Penny giggles.

"I'm fine … just thinking."

"Yeah? Looks serious for a Friday morning." Zac brings his coffee to the table and sits down between Penny and I. "Anything I can help with?"

Sure. Why don't you tell me what Sebastian is up to and why you'd choose him over Dad? "No," I say instead.

"Suit yourself." Zac takes a sip of coffee. "Hey, I'm meeting up with Abby and Sebastian to do some touristy stuff down by the waterfront. Want to come with us?"

"No way in hell," I say, but keep the *way in hell* part just in my head. Penny laughs again, and I stare at my cereal to keep from frowning at her. The water cooler beeps, and the fridge hums. Crows scream outside, somewhere a dog barks. Maybe Abby is into Sebastian? How could she go from being interested in Zac to, to *him*? I look up, and this time Zac is staring at me. "What?"

"What did Dad say to you about Sebastian?" Zac asks. His voice is tense, restrained, as if he's using a great deal of effort to speak softly. I shrug to buy myself time. Truth is, Dad didn't say much, but when he did say "he's trouble," his voice was acidic. He knew more than he was willing to tell me, and that was enough. Then. Now I need facts before I have this conversation with Zac. I need to know so Zac can't justify and reason and give excuses, so that he'll see that Dad was right and looking out for him.

I can't talk about this with him now. Now all I have is anger and accusations. Sebastian. Who is he to come waltzing into my parents' home acting like nothing is wrong? He took Zac away from his family for the last six months they had left. He has to know that. If I don't leave right now, those thoughts will take over and I'll be screaming them out loud, and once I start I won't be able to stop. Zac left when Dad said them, what's to stop him from leaving me for the same thing? If I'm going to ferret out the truth and show Zac who Sebastian really is, I need facts.

"Sorry, I have to go. Sara's waiting for me," I say while I check the time on my phone. Lies, all lies, but I have to get out of here.

In my room I text Sara to see if she wants to go for a run, and she's quick to reply with a yes, which is somewhat unfortunate. I would rather she say no so I could use the excuse and stay in my room and do some more Google-sleuthing. But: five kilometres in thirty minutes. So I change into running gear and lace up my sneakers.

There's a knock on the front door as I finish the second knot. I leave my room and head down the hallway, reaching the front hall as Zac opens the door.

It's not Sara. It's Sebastian. Back again.

"Come in," Zac says, "I'm almost ready. I just have to grab my wallet." When he passes me he hisses, "Be nice," so low that I may have imagined it.

"Hey, Laynie," Sebastian says. I wince. "Laynie" is reserved for family and friends. Neither is a category he fits into.

"Say hi," Penny says.

I ignore both of them and stoop to retie my shoe. I want to go hide in my room, but I'll be damned if I'll retreat in my own home.

"You coming with us?" Sebastian persists.

"No," I say to my shoe.

"You should, it's a beautiful day out and we've got a list of places to check out. I think it'll be a fun time."

"I have plans."

"Yeah? What are you up to?" Apparently my short answers don't deter him. He's obviously a socially inept moron on top of whatever criminal occupation he keeps.

"Going for a run," I say through tight teeth, retying my second shoe.

"By yourself? That's no fun. I mean, you can take care of yourself, but it would be more fun to go with someone, you know, get out there and have some company —"

"I am. Going with my friend, Sara," I say evenly. This time I look up from my well-tied sneakers and scowl at him.

"Abby's sister? I met Abby last night. She seems really great, I think she's —" A knock on the door interrupts him, and he turns and opens the door.

"You must be Sara," he says.

"Yes." Sara's voice has that flirty extra melodic note to it. "And that makes you?" I swear she bats her eyelashes at him like some girl out of a chick flick.

"Zac's friend, Sebastian," I say, hoping she caught my emphasis on "friend" and knows which terrible friend he is, but she's still using her flirty eyes with him. I rush between them before he can say anything or fall for her womanly ways. "Are you ready?"

"Yup, let's go," Penny says.

Sara looks over my shoulder a moment longer then says, "Sure," and finally we're out the door and heading down the driveway. "Which way?" she asks when we reach the bottom. Penny's standing beside me, sticking her thumb to her right.

"This way?" I ask her, and she nods.

Sara, not privy to my hallucination, must have thought I was talking to her and says, "Alright" and then starts running. Stunned for a moment, I sprint a few strides to catch up to her then fall into an easy pace. Running is something Penny and I have in common, instead of in contrast, but we approach it totally differently. For Penny running is a challenge. She's always pushing herself to go faster, to go farther. *Was.* For me running is mindless. I don't want to keep track of pace or distance or personal best. I run because when I do my mind stays blank, empty, rested and quiet.

But today I can't find that mindless rhythm.

FLASHBACK: *Penny and I tried to think through what could have happened. We shared snippets of observations with each other, trying to gather enough information to figure it out what happened, why Zac left and hadn't come back:*

"Dad said he was trouble."

"Mom was crying when she was talking on the phone."

"Zac hasn't called all week."

Except it's not a flashback. I hear Penny reciting those lines beside me as we run. I turned toward her to tell her to shut up, but she's looking straight ahead. Penny effortlessly keeps pace beside Sara and me, jogging smoothly and silently. My feet slap-slap on the sidewalk, and the meat on my thighs and butt bounces and jiggles with every footfall. My breath is loud and wheezy. The wind blows loose strands of hair in my face, in my mouth.

"Dad told me he didn't want him around us."

"Zac's living with that guy, the one Dad hates."

I pick up my pace. My feet smack on the ground faster and faster, smacks-macksmack. My arms pump, propelling me forward, and I lean into the run, spurring my legs to cycle faster and faster. Somewhere outside my mind I faintly hear Sara saying my name over and over, but the sound falls behind me, and I push my legs, my arms to move even faster until the sprint is reckless and unbalanced, and I hurtle forward. I glance beside me with a triumphant leer, happy to be rid of Penny's ghost, sure she's fallen back with Sara, but there she is, easily sliding beside me with grace and ease. In my shock the precarious coordination powering my legs disintegrates and I trip. The sidewalk comes up to meet my sprawling hands. Pain shoots up my arms, across my face, through my knees, before the throbbing in my encased arm overtakes the pangs from everywhere else. It pulses with my racing heart, pounding like a jackhammer against the cool cotton lining. I sit up and cradle my arm against my chest and try to will the air back into my lungs.

"Layne! Layne! Are you alright?" Sara's beside me without me hearing her come. She sits and slips her arm around my shoulders. I look past her on my right, around to my left, but Penny is nowhere to be seen. "Are you alright?" Sara asks again.

I nod, and my ponytail flaps against my shoulders. "Yeah, yeah, I'm fine." I take inventory of my aches. My free hand is scraped on the heel. The surface of my cast is scratched and a small crack runs horizontally from one side to the other. Both knees glow red, and angry cuts crisscross across each. Blood oozes and seeps; a line and a drip runs down my right leg. "I'm fine," I say again, more to myself than to Sara.

"I don't have anything," Sara says, patting the sides of her shorts that don't even have pockets.

"I'm fine," comes from me again. Maybe I'm not so fine.

"Look, let's go in there to clean you up." Sara sweeps her hand toward the storefront across the street. Coffee Quotes. Of course.

"I'm fine," I say, this time in protest, but she reaches under my arms and hauls me to my feet.

"Can you walk?" she asks, and I take a step instead of answering her. If I say I'm fine one more time, she'll call the looney truck to take me away. "She must have hit her head," she would say to them, and they'd ask if I was seeing anything strange, and I'd have to ask if dead sisters count.

We walk — well, she walks, I hobble — across the street, and the bell above the door tinkles when she pushes the door open. The air conditioning flushes against my face, cool and refreshing but stinging my cut knees. I follow Sara's nudging and settle into a chair at a table. "Be right back," she says and hurries away to the counter.

I sit still, taking deep breaths, trying to slow my racing heart and my panting lungs. *In through the nose, out through the mouth* echoes in my head in some early phys ed teacher's voice. With each deep sniff my nose prickles with warm, bitter brown smell. Mom and Penny both love the smell of coffee. *Loved.*

FLASHBACK: *Mom and Penny sat at the kitchen table, sniffing the coffee that was too hot to drink. They made this strange quasi-erotic sighing moan, and I told them it was weird. They smiled at me and then looked at each other like I was too simple to understand something secret and special.*

Sara comes back with a wet paper towel. She hands it to me and I swipe at my knees. Not gingerly, like you hear people say, but roughly scrubbing the debris out of the cuts and making the blood flow more. Each rub pushes pain into my knee, up my leg to my core, until I can't smell the coffee anymore.

"I'll get you another," Sara says from somewhere in front of me. I watch a drop of blood build on one cut then trickle down my leg, leaving a narrow, reddish line behind it. I bend over and catch it in its path and wipe it away. Then Sara's handing me two more wet cloths with shaking hands.

"Thanks," I say, looking up at her for the first time. She's frowning. Not an angry frown, but her eyes are narrowed and her brows knitted together. Her face is white. Sheet white. Perplexed is the word Penny would use. She's confused. And worried. I'm freaking her out.

"Do you want me to call Zac?" Her voice is high and shaky.

"I'm fine," I say again before I think of something better, so I rush to add, "Really, I'm good. I just need to clean this up and sit a minute." I try to dab more easily at the scrapes on my knee then press the wet paper towels against the cuts and hold them there. The coolness is soothing. It calms me a bit.

"Yeah?" she asks, sounding unconvinced. I nod. I can actually see her body sigh in relief, her shoulders sag just half an inch or so, her legs lose tension, and she falls into the chair beside me. "Want a drink or something?"

"No, I'm good, really," I say, then add another "really" with feeling. I try to smile at her.

"Laynie, what, what happened back there?" she whispers.

I'm about to say "I tripped," which fits into my typical sarcastic script, but when I look up to answer her, I see her eyes. They are glistening wet. Her hands are still shaking on the table. She blinks. Her lips are pressed together, and she runs a hand through her hair. I owe her more than a flippant remark. "I think … I was trying to outrun her."

Sara blinks a bit faster, but one tear slips out anyway. She swipes her hand at her cheek and nods.

A hand appears and puts a glass of water with ice on the table beside me. I look up to see who the hand is attached too, and the moustached owner is standing there with a second glass that he puts in front of Sara. "Are you okay? I saw you come in but I was taking orders. Do you need me to call someone?"

"No thank you, I'm fine," I say and wince at the words. "Thank you for the water."

"Yes, yes, but if you need anything else, please let me know." He stands there a moment longer as if he doesn't believe me, as if he's waiting for me to show some indication, a sign of impending disaster — medical or otherwise.

"I will," I say instead of arguing and smile at him. He turns and shuffles back to his counter, wiping his hands on his apron as he goes. As he passes the counter to slip behind it, he walks past a red and white sign that reads: NOW HIRING.

    2.   Secure employment for the summer.

Translated out of Penny-speak: Get a job. "They're hiring."

I didn't realize I'd said it out loud until Sara says, "You want to work *here*?"

I smile at her, a real smile. Those are in short supply. I know her surprise has nothing to do with the shop itself and everything to do with the fact that I don't like coffee or books, or know anything about either of them. "Sure, why not?" I shrug and feel my real smile grow bigger.

"I can think of a few reasons," Sara says. "Plus the fact that they'll never hire you."

"And why not?"

"Um, you might have to like coffee and books — or at least one of those — to work here." There's a grin in her voice, and her cheeks are flushed again. Her hands are still.

"You think?" I ask, and Sara laughs because it sounds like a challenge. I am the competitive one, after all. "Okay," I say. Challenge accepted. I stand up, and my knees shake in protest but hold me up. A quick glance down tells me they've stopped bleeding, at least. I take a step toward the counter, then another with more confidence, both in the reliability of my legs and in the successful outcome of my challenge.

I stand at the counter until the moustache man notices me. He hurries over with a concerned look. "Yes, yes, what is it? What do you need?" he asks, running out of breath before he runs out of words.

"Really, I'm good! Just a trip. It's just that I noticed your sign there." I point at the red-lettered sign on the counter.

He turns his head to follow my point and smiles. "You want the job?"

"Well, I was hoping to find something for the summer." I wince a little on the inside at the fib in that statement. I had no desire for summer employment until I found Penny's ToDah! list. While my words are technically true, out loud they sound a little fraudulent, like I'm stealing Penny's words. Penny's wishes. Penny wants a summer job, not me. *Wanted.*

The owner's moustache tips up in a big smile. "Have you worked in a coffee shop before?"

"Um, no."

His smile falters for a minute then grows as he says, "Well, have you worked in a bookstore?"

"No." I can feel Sara watching me, feel a burn in my cheeks growing. I'm about to lose the challenge.

"Well, you must be a reader. I mean, your sister loved to talk about the books she read. We often shared recommendations back and forth. Do you read like her? Really, being a lover of books is more important in a bookstore than having experience."

I could lie. It would be easy to say, *Yes, I love to read,* but I can't step that far into Penny's territory. Penny's the reader, not me. *Was.* "No, I'm sorry. I don't read. I mean, I can, but I just don't. I haven't even finished that book I bought the other day, the one Penny was … I'm sorry to take up your time. I just thought … I mean, I don't know what I was thinking."

I turn to head back to the table with Sara, but behind me he says, "Wait a minute, Layne," just above a whisper. I turn back. He smiles again, his moustache twitching a bit. Of course he knows my name. My sister would have said it at some point, and he was well old enough to know the Beatles song. He smiles at me. "The truth is, I hired your sister for the job."

I take a step back. Open my mouth, but there are no words ready to come out. Of course. It's the perfect job for Penny.

"I hired your sister that morning … of the accident. I called and talked to her. She was going to come in later that afternoon to sign the silly contract my lawyer makes me have and to learn about the machines and stuff." He waves toward the blocks of appliances on the counters behind him. "So if you want the job, it's yours. I'll make sure you get up to speed on everything before I leave you alone. Perhaps you'll end up a reader after all?"

I doubt it. Take Penny's job? Could I do that?

2. Secure employment

I hear Penny whisper, "Don't be silly, why not?"

I manage a smile, a real one, and say, "Okay. When do I start?"

The moustache turns up again. "Excellent. I'm afraid we've not been formally introduced. I'm Winston Forsythe." He wipes his palm on his apron then sticks out his right wrinkly hand over the counter. It is spotted with grey circles, and the blue veins crisscross under his pale skin. I lift my cast, and he laughs and switches his right hand for his left, which is equally as wrinkly, spotted and lined.

"Nice to meet you, Mr. Forsythe." I take his hand. It's warm and dry, softer than I expected. He squeezes, and I wince. The curled ends of his moustache fall into a frown.

"Oh my land, I'm sorry!" he says, releasing the squeeze but keeping my hand in his. He turns it over and looks at the scrapes on the heel. "You need to clean that," he says, his voice low with authority. "And you need to call me Win, every-one else does."

"Okay," I say, stopping short of muttering his nickname. *Win*. It'll take some practice to drop the mister from the name of someone so much older than me.

Mr. Fors — Win lets go of my hand, and his eyes flutter around under the counter. "Let me just take a look at the schedule here to see when would be a good time for you to come and learn the ropes." He moves his hands under the counter, seemingly shifting items in his search. "Ah, here it is," he says, bringing up the binder and setting it on the counter, flicking through the pages. "Lemme see ..."

I glance back at Sara to give her a thumbs-up, and she claps silently. Beside her, Penny beams.

chapter 15

When I get home, my brother is in the kitchen. Thankfully alone. "Hey Zac, back already?" I say as I walk to the cupboard. I take out a glass and run the tap until the water is cold.

"Hey, Laynie," he says. "We didn't go after all. Bas had an emergency come up with work, some fire he had to put out."

"What about Abby?" It would have been a good chance for Zac to spend time *alone* with her.

"Went to the washroom," he answers and turns around. His eyes flicker down over my knees and back up to my face. "What happened to you?"

I shrug. "I tripped." I fill the glass and drink it down.

"How's your arm? Your cast? Should you go —"

"Nope. Arm's fine. I'm fine." I really wish I'd stop saying that. I perch the cast behind my back so he won't see the crack. It's probably too small for him to notice anyway. Time for a topic change: "Guess what?"

"You found a time-travel worm hole?"

I smile. This was Dad's game. When we were little, he used to take "guess what" literally. "Nope."

"You've trained an ancient pterodactyl to deliver your mail?"

"Nope."

"You stole the Hope Diamond from the Smithsonian and traded it for unlimited credits on iTunes?"

That one's lame. "Nope."

"What are you talking about?" Abby asks, coming in the kitchen.

"Not sure yet, Laynie said 'guess what,' so ..."

"Oh! Ummm," Abby smiled and looked back and forth between us, "you and

Sara found a lottery ticket on your run, and when you checked it at the store the guy said it was a winner, but since you're not nineteen you need an adult to come claim it with you and split the winnings?"

Zac started shaking his head halfway through Abby's rambling guess. I laughed and said, "Nope, but you're close."

"You discovered a new flavour of ice cream?" That suggestion comes from behind me. I turn to see Sebastian smiling in the doorway. So he doesn't knock to come in the house any more? "Hey Zac, Abby," he says and waves. With Zac behind me it's safe to frown. Glare even. I think I actually wrinkle my nose at him, that childish preteen look of *OMG you're pathetic*. "Hi, Laynie," he says and just smiles when I shoot daggers from my eyes to his.

"Hey Bas, you're early. I wasn't expecting you until tonight," Zac says from behind me.

Sebastian shrugs in an innocent no-malevolent-plans way. I can see through it, even if Zac can't. "Was able to take care of the work-thing problem a little faster than I expected. I hope I'm not interrupting anything?"

I make sure to transform my face back into a relaxed grin before turning back to Zac to say, "I got a job."

"Yeah?" I know I should not to take his shock personally, but it's written all over his face. Penny is the ambitious job-seeking one. *Was*. I'm more … lazy. There's no better way to say it. "Where?"

If he was surprised by the fact I got a job, the location should knock his socks off. "Coffee Quotes."

"Awesome, Layne, I love that place," Abby says, smiling at me. I smile too, and nod.

"That's great, congrats!" Sebastian says behind me. I ignore him.

"Yeah, congrats. Wow." I give him credit for trying but I can tell: socks violently removed. Zac smiles and then looks past me over my shoulder. I take a step to my left into his line of sight. "I mean, that seems like a great spot for a summer job."

"When do you start?" Sebastian asks, as if it's any of his business.

"He wants me to do a few shifts of training when it's quiet, so the first one is Monday."

"Makes sense," Sebastian says. He had come from behind me to look in the fridge, and his voice is muffled like he's talking into a box. I guess he is — a big, cold, electric box. So he lets himself in without a knock, jumps into our conversations and helps himself to our fridge contents? New Landers would have a solution for this moment, I'm sure.

Suggestions for New Landers Skit Production Team

1. Push him into the fridge and slam it shut.
2. Booby-trap the fridge with one of those boxing gloves that springs out and punches him in the face.
3. Lock the front door.
4. Maybe even move.
5. Plant poisoned beer in the fridge.

I snicker to myself and see Zac's curious frown aimed my way. I turn around so he can't see my face and read what I'm thinking. Sebastian stands up with a beer. Dad's. The four empties are still on the counter. *Drink it all, why don't you.*

"Gotta shower," I manage to squeeze out without yelling. Without screaming. I get out of there as quickly as I can, down the hall to my room and behind the door without slamming it closed. I pick up my pillow and hurl it across the room to Penny's side, where it hits the window and knocks the blinds askew. I feel better. A bit. Breathe.

As the anger seeps out, it's replaced by a feeling like a balloon swelling in my chest, pressing against my lungs and heart. Fear. "What's your problem?" I ask myself out loud.

"He's here," Penny says. She's sitting at her desk. "And we're not."

Somewhere deep in my head that makes sense. In the same deep somewhere that dreams defy logic but make perfect sense while you're asleep. Sebastian being here has nothing to do with their leaving. He wasn't driving the truck. But still … Thoughts chase each other in circles, trying to work out the sense of it all. My head aches, thinking in that somewhere space. I press my fingers to my eyes hard enough that it hurts and ask, "Why does that matter?" But the room is silent. I open my eyes. Penny is gone.

I step into our ensuite, strip off my clothes, wrap my arm in the plastic shopping bag and get in the shower. The scrapes on my knees and hand sting when the hot water runs over them. My right arm throbs from holding the cast over my head, and my left hand works clumsily alone, doing the job of two hands to wash my hair and body. The process is awkward but requires just enough thought and planning to take my mind off other things. For a moment.

Dried off, I get dressed in sweats and tie my damp hair back. My unmade bed looks inviting, soft, warm and covered. I lift the cover and move to climb in.

"Don't," Penny whispers. She's sitting in my desk chair.

"Don't what?"

"Don't go back to bed. Stay up, do something. You have to stop hiding."

I cross my arms. "I did do something. I went for a run. I got a job. That's two somethings." I lift the corner of the covers again.

"Don't," she says.

"Don't what? You don't even know what I'm going to do!" I hiss. Instead of getting in like I'm dying to do, I take the corner of the covers and pull it up over top of the pillow to make the bed. Pull the covers up tight, smooth them out. Prove her wrong.

I can hear Abby's laugh from the living room, and for a second I think maybe I can join them. But Sebastian is there too. I'm better off staying in here. I sit at Penny's desk and smooth her list out flat in front of me. I press the fold creases out with my palm and read over the lines.

Summer ToDah!

1. Finish six books on TBR pile.
2. Secure employment for the summer.
3. Get to 50 pushups and 5km under 30 mins.
4. Write 30K-word story.
5. Get to the beach 5 times. Wear red bikini in public.
6. Go on a date (preferably with AP).

It's still Penny's list, but it's morphing into mine too. I hope she doesn't think I'm cheating with my adjustments. Her six books have been whittled down to the one small novel on my bedside table. I can check off secure employment, and my thirty seconds of plank is ten seconds closer to five minutes than the twenty I did yesterday. I'm headed to the beach on Saturday with Asher. Is that a date?

Asher.

Asher Phillips.

Could she really have meant Asher Phillips? Why didn't she tell me that she was crushing on him? Maybe for the same unknown reason I didn't tell her. I scan through my memory to find a hint, a moment with both of them in it. I remember lots of times Asher and I were together, because we travelled in the same circles at school: conversations in the cafeteria, a few skipped classes for card games, late-night texting. But for all of the videos I can see of him and I talking, each one a bit more flirty than the last, I can't remember one single time seeing him approach Penny while she read somewhere alone, or her saying more than a quick hello to him on the bus in the morning.

My memories tiptoe to that afternoon in the park. Why did I stop? Asher was skating with some friends. His helmet glinted in the sunlight, the chinstrap halves swaying unconnected on either side of his head. He swooped down one slope and up the other, one muscly arm stretched out to the side, the other curved in and down, his hand hovering near the front of the board. When he stopped at the top, he happened to turn my way. He smiled. Even thinking about that smile now makes something in my middle squirm.

FLASHBACK: *Sara tapped me on my shoulder and laughed. "Earth to Laynie, come in Laynie." I remember it was hard to pull my gaze away and look at her. I silently admonished myself, thinking,* Stop being moronic, it's just Asher for heaven's sake. *"You know, we should write to New Landers, ask her what's the best way to get a skater guy to look at you."*

I shoved her with my elbow and hissed, "Shut UP!" She laughed more.

"I have to go and pick up my Mom, you coming?" Sara asked.

But then Asher said, "Hi Layne," and smiled and waved.

So I shook my head.

Why did I shake my head? I should have gone with her.

I turned back to Sara and said, "I'll text you later." She gave me a look. The one she gave when she thought I was being ridiculous and she knew I knew she thought I was being ridiculous.

She rolled her eyes and said, "Okay, later," and walked away down the path.

And I stayed because why? Because he *smiled* at me.

I stood and watched him for a minute while he swooped down one hill and up the other. He moved easily with a grace of a dancer, gliding across a stage instead of rolling over the pressboard half-pipe. When he stopped three turns later, he turned back and grinned at me again. Something in my belly flip-flopped. Not light butterflies, more like pond frogs. The big ones.

"Hey," he said as he walked toward me. His board hung by its front axel on the hooked fingers of his right hand.

"Hey," I said.

"Nice day," he said, and glanced up at the sky as if to be sure it was still sunny and blue.

"Yeah. It's hot," was my contribution to the riveting conversation. And inside my head the voices started yapping at me:

That was a dumb thing to say, is that all you've got?

Say something clever.

Say something funny.

Don't stare.

Don't look away.

Don't slouch.

Don't stand like a priss.

Don't blow it.

None of it made sense; my heart racing, my palms sticky and clammy, my tied-up tongue. We'd spoken a thousand times before, in class, in the cafeteria, on the bus. But never just the two of us at the park.

Say something.

"You're pretty good at that." I even pointed my lame-o finger at his skateboard.

"Thanks. Wanna try?" He held the skateboard out between us on his one finger. The wheels spun slowly.

O. M. G.

I totally knew I shouldn't get on the damn thing. I'm so clumsy, I make up ways to hurt myself. "Nah, I'm good just watching," I said.

He smiled wider then, a bigger smile that made his eyes squint a bit, and laughed a breathy laugh, just one exhale, before he nodded and said, "Oh, I see. You're chicken." He wasn't being mean or nasty or condescending, even, he was teasing. Childish teasing with childish name-calling.

So I should've just admitted to it, said "yes I am" or "so what?" or something witty like "why risk this pretty face?" but in that awkward moment with just the two of us talking not in school or on the bus the most important thing became hide the truth that I am less. I was failing miserably in the heart-to-heart, and perhaps being brazen enough to jump right onto the death trap would make up for my pathetic conversational skills.

And so I got on the skateboard. I actually picked it up, careful to hold it by the axel like he did, and walked to the top of the half-pipe hill.

"Layne, maybe you should start down here," Asher said, which sounded exactly like "You can't do that!" I smiled at him and winked — I thought that was flirty — and put the skateboard down at the top of the hill. "Layne, wait," he said.

I put my right foot on the board, the other beside it and took a deep breath. There was a moment there, a second or part of one, where I knew it was stupid, but when I looked up Asher was smiling at me, and somehow I thought if I could just prove I was cool, fearless, fun — anything but boring — then maybe he'd see I wasn't just one of the boys. So I pushed forward with my left.

I made it down the hill. Fast. Rolled up the other side but couldn't turn around. I slid backward to the middle. I lurched forward and leaned back to rebalance, too far. The skateboard shot out from under me. I fell up — somehow — and while I was suspended in the air, time stopped just long enough for me to think this is gonna hurt *before I came crashing back down, hands first behind me and then flat on my back, my head.*

And I broke my arm and knocked myself out cold. Asher told me he called 911. The ambulance came and took me to emerg. The nurse called them. And they came. They *all* got in the car and headed to the hospital.

Back at Penny's desk, my fingers twitch to clench into a fist, but I'd crumple Penny's list. I force my fingers straight until the knuckles hurt and the urge passes. Perhaps not all of her list needs to be completed. I could leave the last one off — five out of six items is a pretty good success rate. Besides, stealing Penny's crush is in a different universe than stealing her job. So, no. No date with AP then. Even as I decide that's best, there's a pinch of disappointment in my chest, and I can't tell if it's hers or mine.

chapter 16

Saturday morning comes earlier than I want it to. I stand in front of the full-length mirror in Penny's red bikini. It fits. Not great, but it fits. She fills out the top better. *Filled.* The top triangles were round and full on her, but on me they pucker a bit where the material meets the shoulder straps. Where my stomach is scrawny, hers was toned.

"Fat, not toned," Penny whispers. She's wrong.

I watch myself step into my shorts and pull the tank top over my head to cover the bathing suit in a hurry — not self-consciously, the way Penny would have covered it up, but because if I don't rush I'll change my mind and change the suit back to my boringly practical black one-piece.

Penny's list peeks out from between the books on the desk bookshelf, where I put it each night when I take it out of my pocket. My fingers brush along the edge of it, but I leave it there. I don't want it to get lost or damaged by the sand and water. Or seen by the other eyes on the beach. I stuff my towel, sunscreen, glasses and phone in the bag and head to the kitchen.

Sebastian is at the stove frying an egg and says, "Good morning."

"What are you doing here? Where's Zac?" I ask.

His smile falters, and then he pushes it back up. "Had a few too many last night and couldn't drive home, so I slept on the couch. Zac's still sleeping. Want an egg?" He holds the small frying pan toward me. It smells delicious, and my mouth waters.

"No." Better not to owe him anything at all. I get a bowl and fill it with cereal and milk. For a moment while I fish a spoon out of the drawer, I consider taking my breakfast elsewhere to eat it — the living room to watch TV, back to my bedroom — so I don't have to share the space with him, but I'll be damned if

I'm going to be driven out of my own kitchen. I sit at the table and shovel cereal into my mouth while I stare poison darts into his back at the stove.

"Today's your beach day, right?" After a moment he turns to look at me, so I look away quickly and nod, then fill my mouth again. If I hoover my cereal and keep my mouth full, I won't have to talk to him at all. "Right, I thought so. You lucked out with the weather. It's supposed to be hot and sunny all day. Where are you going again?" When I don't answer, he looks back at me again. I point to my full, chewing mouth. "Right. Doesn't matter, you'll have fun wherever you go. Don't forget sunscreen — the UV's off the charts today, I bet. I figure the time when we can actually wear just bathing suits outside in the sun is coming to an end. Soon we'll all need high-tech protective clothing. Not just at the beach or swimming either, but all the time, everywhere we go …"

He rattles on with his monologue, but I tune him out. *Moron.* I can't wait until Zac figures out who he really is.

"He hasn't yet, and it's been over six months," Penny says so I ignore her too.

Dad was smart and an excellent judge of character. I'm sticking with his assessment: if he thought Sebastian was trouble for Zac, I believe him. Sebastian's long-winded sermon on global warming and futuristic fashion isn't the best evidence, but he's probably just playing it cool, manipulating to get me on his side so I don't see what our parents saw. So I don't warn Zac like they did. But Sebastian's not fooling me. And sometime soon he'll slip up, show something about his true self and I'll be able to prove to Zac that Dad was right all along. And Sebastian'll be gone for good.

"Layne?" From somewhere outside the cloud of my thoughts, I hear him say my name. I look up at him standing at the counter with a wet, soapy cloth washing the frying pan.

"That goes in the dishwasher," I say with my mouth full.

He looks at the pan and shrugs. "Just as easy to wash it." Um, no it's not, that's why they invented dishwashers. "You were a million miles away. I asked what your plans were for tonight. Zac and I were thinking of going to a movie, wanna come with?"

No one his age should say "come with." "Can't," I say. He studies me a moment, as if he's trying to see through me. I stare back at him, and he blushes and looks back to the sink of bubbles.

"Layne, I … I mean, can we talk for a minute? I think you might have —"

I jump up from my chair and put my bowl in the sink, dropping it from just high enough that the water splashes up on Sebastian's arm. "I'm late. I gotta go get ready," I say and step away.

His wet fingers close around my arm. I turn and glare at him. "Let go," I hiss.

His grip loosens, but his hand stays on my arm, bubbles dripping from his fingers. "We need to talk. Just for a second?"

Before he can say something else, the doorbell rings and the front door opens. Thank John Lennon. Sara calls from the hallway, "Just me, Laynie. You ready?"

I scowl at Sebastian and swing my arm loose. I actually don't need as much force as I use, but it feels good to swing my arm. I leave him standing there washing the stupid pan and meet Sara in the hall. I've never been so glad to be leaving the house for the day.

The sun is bright through the windshield of Sara's car. Her mom's car, really, but Sara's for the day. There was a time I couldn't wait to be sixteen so I could drive, but that time seems like ages ago. More than three weeks, anyway. Now, I have no interest in ever getting behind the wheel. Riding shotgun is excitement enough for me.

"So what was Sebastian doing there?" Sara asks, breaking my train of thought.

I rub my wrist where his fingers gripped me, not painfully but firm. Thinking about it makes my skin crawl like I can still feel them there. "I don't know," I say. "He said he drank too much to drive home."

"Classy," Sara says.

"Yeah."

"Have you been able to figure out what he's up to?"

"No, I haven't seen anything strange," I admit. "But when he shows up I stay in my room away from him."

"How often has he been there? Where does he work?"

"I don't know. He's been there most nights."

"So where does he get his money? I mean, he has that sweet car, and I've only seen him in expensive clothes." I can see the red Mustang parked in our driveway in my mind's eye.

"I don't know," I say again. "And know what's weird? He always has cash. I mean, he's always giving Zac bills for the pizza guy or groceries."

"That *is* weird. I mean, who carries cash any more?" Sara asks. I shrug. What kind of job lets you miss days but leaves you flush with cash and a red Mustang?

A Shawn Mendes song comes on, and Sara squeals and turns the music up, too loud to talk, which is just as well since I don't feel like talking about it anymore anyway. Today is supposed to be fun. If I can even do fun anymore. Every few minutes I can see Sara glance at me out of the corner of my eye, probably checking to make sure I'm not going to go all kamikaze on her again like when I went running down the hill.

"Maybe she thinks you're going to throw yourself out of the car," Penny says with a laugh.

Not funny, I try to think to her since I can't say it out loud. She smiles and leans against the door, looking out the window, her elbow on the armrest and her hand tucked up under her ear all casual, like it's totally normal to be both headed to the beach and dead at the same time. Her face is tipped up so that the light is shining on her, making her skin glow and her light freckles stand out just a bit. After two glances it hurts too much to look back, so I concentrate on looking out the windshield and singing along with the radio so that Sara thinks I'm enjoying the music, not distracted by my sister.

Crystal Beach isn't far, only forty minutes or so from my door to the gravel parking lot. The lot is pitted with potholes, so Sara drives slowly between the cars parked along the edges. Some of the cars are familiar from the high school parking lot. I try to remember who Asher said would be here, but no names come to mind. Sara pulls in beside a blue pickup that I recognize from the back corner of the school lot. A red string grad tassel hangs from the rear-view mirror. The silver numbers bounce the sunlight into my eyes.

"Coming?" Sara says through her open doorway. The car is off, and she's out, but I haven't moved. I'm not sure I'm going to.

"Yeah," I say and try to look busy gathering up my things in the car: my phone from the console beside me, my flip-flops that I kicked off, my bag between my feet. It doesn't take nearly long enough to pick everything up as I need to be ready, but I take a deep breath and push the door open. Sara is rummaging through the open trunk. She's talking to me, but I can't hear her words. My ears are ringing, buzzing with the other sounds around me: the waves beating the sand out of sight on the other side of the grassy dunes, the occasional seagull screeching or human voice yelling. The wind isn't strong, but there's a faint rustling of the long dune grass.

I walk around to the back of the car and stand beside her. "Here," she says, handing me a folding beach chair, "I brought one for you in case you didn't think of it." Sara knows that Penny is the organized one. *Was.*

"Thanks," I say, relieved my ears are working normally again. Sara lifts a second chair in one hand, shoulders her backpack and pulls out a small cooler in the other hand.

"Can you get that?" She nods at the open trunk, and I feel my face colour at my lack of manners.

"Yeah, sorry." I reach up and slam the trunk down. "Need me to carry something else?"

"I'm balanced." She laughs and starts toward the path to the beach.

I follow, but not before tossing a mumbled "You're no help" over my shoulder to Penny, who falls into line behind me, carrying nothing. Of course, hallucinations can't carry beach gear.

The boardwalk leading to the beach is dusted with sand that crunches under my shuffling feet. Six stairs up, a bridge across the dune and eight stairs down with the last two buried in sand drifts that trip up my flip-flops. The sand slips between my feet and shoes, warm and soft. The gentle breeze smells of salt. I feel my shoulders settle a little lower and my jaw muscles loosen.

"Hey! Sara, Layne! Over here!" Asher's walking toward us, waving his arm over his head. Around him several of the kids from school are lounging on towels and chairs. Two are tossing a football back and forth and a few others are playing volleyball in a makeshift court laid out by shoes marking its corners. Angela Mason, a girl in my English class from last year, holds a dirty white volleyball between her wrist and hip. They stop playing and look our way. *My* way. At me.

Sara turns back to me and raises her eyebrows just a bit, asking me if I'm ready. I haven't talked to many of them since everything happened, my arm, the truck, the funeral. For a second my throat tightens, and I think my breakfast might make a reappearance, but then Sara smiles and nudges my arm with her elbow. Behind me Penny whispers what Sara says without words, "C'mon, you can do this. You have to do it sometime. Might as well be now." I smile at Sara and nod.

When Asher reaches us, he takes the chairs from us and smiles. "I'm glad you came," he says, looking from me to Sara and back again. His eyes linger on mine, and I feel heat in my cheeks that isn't from the sun. I look down at my feet and kick my flips off, stoop to pick them up and stare at them in my hands instead of looking back at him. "We're set up over here," he says, as if we didn't see the entire tenth grade and all their beach toys behind him.

I watch Sara's feet as they start moving away, waiting for Asher's feet to follow, but they stand still with sand scooped up on top of his toes. He's waiting for me. My soles are burning hot in the sand. I stare at my feet, willing one or the other to take a step forward. Finally Right gets the message. I watch my toes kick sand up ahead of me and Asher's feet move along beside mine. "I'm glad you came," he says again softly. I try to stomp out the quiver in my stomach because: Penny's list, Penny's bikini, Penny's date, Penny's AP. Not mine.

Sara and I open her beach chairs and add them to the edge of the camp of towels and chairs our classmates have laid out. She sets the cooler between us and says, "Help yourself."

"Thanks," I say, though the thought of eating or drinking anything right now makes me feel pukey. Nerves. I drop my bag and shoes at the foot of the chair, stretch my towel over the rough mesh and sit down. I can't look up. I can feel everyone's eyes, if not blatantly staring, sneaking glances my way. Do I look different? *I* may not look different myself, but I'm sure they think it's strange to see me without Penny. Half of us is missing. Half of me. It makes me almost wish they could see her there, where she's sitting in the sand beside my chair, silently smiling into the sun.

Sara puts her hand on my shoulder. "I'm going to go play volleyball. You good?"

I smile, hoping it doesn't look like the cringe I feel. I hate that I seem fragile enough, pathetic enough, to warrant a babysitter. "Yeah, of course," I say quickly. Over my left shoulder, I watch her walk away and catch the ball tossed her way. Sand peppers my right arm, and for a second I wonder if figments of imagination can toss physical items if they're small and light enough.

Asher stands where Penny had been. "Oh sorry," he says and reaches out to brush the sand off my arm. I brace myself for his touch, coaching myself not to flinch, but when his hand reaches my arm, it's surprisingly warm and soft and soothing. "Sorry," he says again, more seriously. I smile. He lays out his towel beside me. Penny is nowhere to be seen. "You okay?"

I open my mouth to say *I'm fine*, but "I feel like everyone's watching" comes out instead.

His smile is quick and light but looks a little sad somehow. "Then let's go for a walk," he says, and then he's standing, reaching down and helping me up before I can protest. We walk in silence down to where the water has packed the sand into a cooler, harder surface. I glance around, but Penny hasn't followed us. I watch my feet, sometimes his, and sometimes look up at the horizon where the dunes and rocks curve in to meet the water. Before long the sound of the breeze and the waves is between us and the screeching voices of our classmates. "Better?" he asks, startling me.

"Yeah, this is … better. Thanks," I say and realize I actually mean it.

"They're just worried about you," he says as he stoops to pick up a shell. He tosses it toward the water, and it slices through the top of an incoming wave.

"I just want everything to go back to normal." It sounds so simple in words, not the grand impossibility it really is. The horizon blurs, and I blink quickly until it is clear again. Asher says nothing, which is a relief from the ever-so-helpful platitudes I've been deleting off my phone. My favourite: *You'll find a new normal.* I don't want new — the old one had been working just fine.

"I heard Zac's back for good. How is he?" he asks after a few more steps. So he and Sara have been sharing notes.

It feels good to answer a question that isn't about me, but I don't want to talk about the drama around Sebastian's visits. "He's doing okay too," I finally say, which is mostly true.

We're nearing the end of the beach, where the sand and grassy dunes gave way to large grey rocks with flimsy trees growing between them. Asher stops and reaches down to pick up a pebble. He turns it in his fingers and tosses it sidearm into the water. "Dammit," he mutters.

"You can't skip stones on the waves," I say.

"Wanna bet?" He looks around his feet for a moment, bends over and picks up three rocks in one hand. He holds one up pinched in his thumb and finger between his grinning face and me. *Watch me*, he says with his eyes. He turns and stares out at the ocean for a minute, pulls his right arm back and swings it forward, releasing a spinning stone. It slices into the face of a wave and disappears under the water.

I laugh. It feels good to laugh. He turns back toward me and glares as if it was my ridicule that sabotaged his efforts. I press my lips together in an attempt to contain my laughter, and he faces the ocean again, waits, pulls his arm back and lets loose another stone. The projectile flies through the air, over the top of a cresting wave and falls out of sight on the other side. My laugh splits through its restraints and tumbles out. He doesn't bother to look back, but I see his shoulders rise and then set, evenly and solid. He stands stone-still for a moment, and then his arm pulls back and swings forward. The rock leaves his hand and moves toward the water as if hovering. It meets the water once, leaves a light splash and skips back out — twice — before cutting into the base of the wave.

"YES!" Asher yells, pumping his fist and spinning around to face me. He raises his finger up and points at me. "Ah-HA!" he says, laughing. He puts both arms straight out from his sides with his palms up and yells into the sky, "Let the doubters see the mastery of my skill!"

I laugh again.

"Here, try," Asher says, handing me some stones he selected. I doubt I can do it, but it's easier to toss the stones than to argue with him. We stand side by side, sidearming stones into the waves for several minutes until my arm aches in my cast. He manages to skip a few, but mine all crash ineptly into the waves. I sit back on a rock and watch him toss rocks in while I try to come up with a metaphor about the rocks, the waves, my life and my lack of skipping. Bouncing back.

It could be a song about trying and trying and trying and sinking anyway. While the concept makes sense in my brain, the words and connections are all muddled and tangled together. I can't come up with a way to explain it to anyone else. Except maybe Penny, who always understood me. But she's not here to hear it.

"You cold?" Asher asks when he turns his back on the ocean and comes to sit on the rock beside me.

The breeze has picked up a bit, but the air is still warm. I suspect his question is more an effort at small talk than a true evaluation of my wellbeing. "I'm good," I say. He sits close beside me on the rock, his arm brushing against mine. He picks up a shell and turns it over and over in his hand, studying it. I watch it turn in his hands too. The iridescent shine shifts across the surface as he tips it one way then the other. "It's pretty," I say.

"Yeah, beautiful," he says, his voice lower than normal and a little husky. Huh? I look up from his hands to his face, which is much closer to mine than it should be. His half closed gaze rests on my face. He smiles a little and starts to lean toward me.

There's a moment (like a fraction of a second unless time actually stopped) that I almost just close my eyes and let him kiss me. It must have been fleeting, because he was very close, and that moment of wavering happened between the time he starts to lean in and the time I stop him by saying, "Penny's here."

He leans back as slowly as he leaned in and smiles at me. "She is?" he says, and I can't tell if he's making fun of me. I stand up and stride toward the water, not knowing how far I'll go. Or if I'll stop. When the Atlantic covers my feet, my ankles, halfway up my calves, I hear splashing behind me. He touches my shoulder, and I pause. The cold bites at my skin, making my submerged skin pain and then go numb. "Tell me about it," he says, a whisper above the sound of the water.

I had sworn to myself not tell anyone. Not Zac or Sara. There are so many reasons not to, top of the list are:

1.   Everyone would think I belong in a looney bin

and

2.   Before the pickup, I shared Penny with everyone. Now she's all mine.

And yet after he ran, splashing through the water and stood there beside me and said, "Tell me about it," it all comes out.

"She's here. I can see her. Not just in my mind or that stupid 'always in your heart' thing people say — I actually *see* her. Not all the time, either, just sometimes, and I can't figure out the pattern to it. It's not when I need her or when I want her; in fact, sometimes I wish she'd go away and then I feel … rotten for thinking that way. Mostly I'm glad she's there. And I hear her too. She talks to me, we talk together. But she won't answer questions. I've asked. I've begged her to tell me things like why was she in the car? She won't tell me the why about *anything* …" And I run out of air. When I take a deep gulp in, it's wet and salty and makes me cough.

"Maybe she doesn't know why," Asher says beside me. I look at him — scrutinize him, really — analyzing his eyes, his mouth, each line and muscle of his face to see if he's joking or setting me up or humouring me or patronizing me. Pitying me. But he stands there in the cold water and says, "Maybe she just doesn't know." His eyebrows raise with a sad smile.

"You believe me?" A tear escapes out of the corner of my eye. I swipe at my cheek, adding cold salt water to the side of my face instead of drying the tear.

"Sure."

"Why? I think I'm whacked."

"Maybe a little." He laughs a bit. "But if you weren't a bit crazy after all that happened … you'd be in trouble." Which makes a weird sort of sense. I feel his fingers land one at a time until his hand is resting on my shoulder, warm. "Is she here now?" And I don't have to look at him to tell he isn't messing with me. It's an honest question.

After a second I glance around us in the water and turn back to see the rocks where we had been sitting. "No, I can't see her." I look down and watch my feet shimmy under the cold water. They aren't moving, but my eyes see them shift and wiggle from side to side. I can't feel them, numb from the cold, but my brain senses movement. Sometimes opposite truths can be real. I look up at Asher. His face is set in a serious concentration. "Aren't your feet cold?" I ask.

He groans, as if he'd been holding it in for hours. "Freezing! Oh my GAWD it's cold in here!" He lifts his right foot, then left, and stomps around as if trying to pull them out of the water. He kicks up the water, splashing both of us in the process.

I scream in a girlie squeal that I've never heard myself make before and turn to run, casted arm held up to avoid the water, to the rocks on the beach. He follows, splashing as he goes. Out of the water, we stand and laugh that laugh that falls out when nothing is funny, but all you can do to ward off tears and reality is laugh loud enough to hide the fear. When the laughs settle into chuckles and then to smiles, he looks at me, steadily holding my gaze. "Do me a favour? Tell me when you see her," he whispers. I chew on my salty lip and think for a minute before I nod. "Want to go back?" he asks, and I nod again.

We start walking back, this time seeing the beach spread from the narrow point to a wider stretch on the horizon. Far ahead, small figures are moving and jumping, the football sailing in the air, a Frisbee sliding out into the water. Asher's fingers slip between my fingers and curl, his palm presses against mine. He squeezes. If I'd anticipated his gesture, I'd have pulled away out of reach, but much to my surprise my fingers squeeze back without thought.

When Asher and I reach the group, Sara calls me over to join in their volleyball game, and for a while I'm too distracted avoiding injury from the hurtling white sphere to worry about where Penny is. The afternoon grows hot. When they announce the game is finally over, I beg out of the tie-breaker to cool off with a careful wade in the ocean, splashing water on my legs and middle while keeping my cast dry, and then lounge in Sara's beach chair in the sun. I pull Penny's novel from my bag and open it to the dog-eared page, smoothing the folded corner flat. (Funny, she hasn't said anything about me folding the pages like that. She would have killed me before.) I scan the page for recognizable text, trying to figure out where I stopped reading. None of it is familiar. I flip a page back, then another, start again at the beginning of chapter three. My eyes scan the text, but my mind follows the voices and snippets of conversation around me. Laughs and squeals and curses and shouts meld into noise that only makes enough sense to divert my attention from the words on the page. As long as I'm busy "reading," the owners of the voices will leave me alone. So I hide behind the book. Every so often I glance over the pages to where Asher is tossing a Frisbee with some other guys, or to Sara playing volleyball. I'm content to watch and listen from the outside until Sara comes over and picks up her towel.

"I have to go, Layne, gotta get ready for my game tonight. I'm sure someone else can give you a ride if you want to stay longer?"

I close the book and stuff it in my bag. "No, I'm good to go too," I say, standing, stretching and then bending to pick up the towel, shake the sand off and roll it up to fit in my duffel bag. We fold our chairs, close the cooler and pack our bags in silence.

"You headed out?" Asher says, suddenly behind me.

"Yeah. My ride." I nod to Sara, who shrugs in apology.

He doesn't look at me, just glances at Sara then around us. "I could take you home later," he says. "If you want to stay."

"Thanks, but I should get home anyway," I say, feeling a twist in my stomach. I don't want to lie, especially after telling him so much truth earlier, but I don't know how to explain how tiring it has been to hang out in the old normal, the normal from before the truck. He glances up at me and smiles. Maybe he knows somehow.

"I'll walk you out," he says, picking up the cooler and taking the chair from Sara.

"Thanks," Sara and I say at the same time. We walk in silence to Sara's car, where she makes herself scarce packing the trunk, setting her things in the back seat and folding into the driver's seat, examining the radio dials with great scrutiny.

Asher hovers near the car, waiting. I smile at him. "Thanks for the chat," I say, trying to keep my voice light, my words casual, hoping the burning in my cheeks isn't as red as it feels.

"Anytime. I mean it," he says. "So, if I were to call you …?"

"I'll answer." I nod as I say it. I hope I can follow through.

Chapter 17

Monday morning I'm awake before my alarm goes off, staring at the light and shadow playing on the ceiling. Nerves about the job. The shadows shift shapes, growing dark in one area then sliding across the white to another corner. When we were little, Penny and I were terrified of the shadows, convinced they were monsters growing and changing and readying to swoop down off the ceiling to … I don't even remember what we thought they'd do. Perhaps steal us away? Or eat us? What were the worst nightmares we could imagine back then?

FLASHBACK: *My father came in and settled down on my bed. He waved Penny over and we lay on either side of him, our heads on each of his shoulders. We weren't frightened of the dark so long as he was there. "The shadows are from the streetlight behind the leaves outside. Look how the tree is moving, the shadows move too," he whispered. I raised my head from his shoulder, resting my chin on his chest to see out the window. Just as he said, the shadows moved with the tree as it swayed in the wind. My neck started to ache with the angle, so I rested my head back on his shoulder as he pointed to the ceiling. "Do you see that dinosaur shape? Look how big his spines are. And there! I think that's a fiddle, with a bow going back and forth."*

Late into many nights, Penny and I would lie in our beds and look upward, as if we were in some field watching the clouds float. Monday morning the leaf-shadows roll over the ceiling, and I lay in bed labelling the shapes out loud. "Sheep … giraffe …"

"Mickey Mouse head …" Penny says, lying in her bed. I look at her and she glances at me, smiles, then turns her eyes back to the ceiling.

"Spoon …"

"Truck …" she says, and I see the shadow she means. The boxy front with round, light-filled openings in the shadow where the headlights would be. It grows, spreads across the ceiling in the pickup shape, as if it's coming closer, closer, taking over. I turn my face from the ceiling into my pillow, squeezing my eyes shut. Silence. After a moment I peek with one eye. The pickup shadow is gone, broken back up into swaying dappling of light and dark. Penny's bed is empty. I pull myself out of bed and make myself reach forty-five seconds in my plank.

Showered and dressed, I slip into the kitchen, hoping not to wake Zac, but he is sitting at the table dressed in a suit, his tie tossed over his shoulder.

"Where are you going looking like that?" I ask too quickly to keep the incredulity out of my voice.

"Job interview, remember?" he says between bites of Cheerios. Somewhere in my brain a memory of a conversation pricked, an interview for a job in town.

"Right," I say and reach for an apple out of the bowl on the counter. I crunch a big bite and wipe an errant trail of apple juice off my chin with the back of my hand.

"You have your job thing today too, right?"

"Orientation."

"Yeah, orientation. You nervous?"

"No," I lie. "It's at a coffee shop, how hard could it be?" Zac smiles at me over his spoon. I'm not fooling him. "What's your interview for?"

Zac shrugs and sips the last of the milk from his bowl. "Just an office thing," he says with his mouth full. A twinge of guilt pricks in my chest. Zac isn't an office-type guy. He's a free spirit, a musician, an artist. He left a great job working at the art gallery giving tours, hosting workshops to move home and work in an office. My face must have flinched or something, because he puts his hand on my arm and says, "It's just temporary, Laynie. To get by for now." I nod but don't feel much better about it. "Want a ride?"

"Yeah, that'd be great."

"Alright, I'm leaving in five." He stands and puts his bowl in the dishwasher then leaves the kitchen. I sit for a moment, staring at the tooth marks in my apple. These are moments when reality seems absurd. Zac working in an office, me working in a coffee shop, Mom, Dad and Penny ... gone. I lay my hand against the outside of my jeans pocket and feel the folded edges of Penny's ToDah! list through the material. Secure employment. I probably should add "And not screw it up" after.

We're getting in the car when Zac's phone rings. He puts the keys in the ignition but answers the phone instead of starting the car. "Hello?" he says. He looks at me and mouths, "Gimme a sec," and stands back out of the car, leaving me watching through his window. He paces with his hand in his pocket, watching his feet.

"Who was that?" I ask when Zac sits back in the car and shuts the door.

"Sebastian," he says as he shifts the car in reverse and backs to the end of the driveway. Stops to wait for a red car to go past.

"What did he want?"

He shrugs. "He was just wishing me good luck with the interview."

"What does he do? I mean, that car he drives sure is pretty, and he shows up any time of day. Does he even have a job?" Zac looks at me a moment too long. His eyes are steady, studying, as if he's trying to figure out the motive behind my comment. I thought it was pretty clear.

He looks away, checks over both shoulders and eases into the road before answering evenly, "You don't have to worry about that."

"I do, though, because you said it yourself: 'We're in this together.' Or didn't you mean that? You're off to a job interview for some stupid office. I'm working at a coffee shop. He just shows up all the time and tries to blow out the speakers on the TV, drinks Dad's beer, crashes on the couch and eats our food." My voice spins higher and higher until I stop in a squeak. I wish for once I could have a normal argument like a grown-up.

"Of course I mean it. But I'm telling you that you don't have to worry about it. He has money. He's been helping out. Like, *he* bought the groceries the other day."

I feel scolded for a minute and realize my crossed arms and turned-away face likely look like a childish pout. I can hear Dad saying Zac's friend was trouble. If he has a legit job, why is Zac dodging the question? Maybe Sebastian *is* selling drugs or something just as illegal. Or dangerous. That must have been what Dad meant all along. Could Zac be involved too?

"You need to lay off him." Zac's words snake over to me from the driver's side, smacking me in the face. My eyes water as if I've actually been slapped. I was so sure I'd been covert in my Sebastian Sucks mission that I wasn't expecting Zac to comment on it. I chance a look at him. His eyes are locked on the road, his hands white-knuckled at ten and two as if he's concentrating not so much on the road as on *not* looking at me.

I replay the nasty looks I've tossed at Sebastian in my mind. Zac never saw, I was careful. Wimp must've ratted me out. "What did he say?"

"Nothing. But I've heard you. And I've heard him trying and you just …" He pulls to the curb outside Coffee Quotes, takes a deep breath and finally turns to look at me. "Look. I need you two to get along."

"He's trouble, and you picked him over us," I hear Penny say, but when I glance over my shoulder she isn't in the back seat. Come to think of it, the voice was a lot closer than the back seat, like right in my head. And actually, it sounded more like my voice than hers.

"Fine," I say, but there's no way I'm giving up on finding out the truth about Sebastian. I'll just have to be more furtive about driving him away. I push the door open, but Zac grips my left arm and stops me.

"Laynie." He looks at me. There's something urgent about his gaze.

"What?"

It's one of those moments that are impossible to measure. Maybe a second, a heartbeat, a breath, maybe a year or a lifetime. He stares at me with his frantic, desperate eyes, his mouth open as if he is choking on the words.

Then, finally, "Nothing. Good luck with the orientation." He lets go and looks back out of the window.

For a second I don't move. Can't move. I stare at Zac, stone still except for his rapidly blinking eyes looking out the window. I want to ask, "What?" again, but I'm certain, somehow, that if I push him now he'll crack and break and fall apart.

"Layne," he says, his voice ragged.

"Yeah?" I ask on my inhale. I hold my breath, not sure if I want to hear what he has to say.

"I'm going to be late." Just his mouth moves to talk. Then he clamps his mouth shut and his jaw squeezes.

"Good luck," I say and step out onto the curb. I wave, but he doesn't wave back as he drives away.

chapter 18

The bell over the door jingles as I push it open, and Winston Forsythe smiles at me from behind his moustache and the counter.

"Layne! Hello! Come in, come in, come right around here." His smile is natural, pressing up into his eyes, which makes him seem genuinely excited to see me. I'm pretty sure he has no idea how inadequate his new employee promises to be.

"Hi," I say, hoping my smile doesn't reveal how anxious I am. "Thank you." I'm not really sure what I'm thanking him for — the welcome? The job? The invitation behind the counter, from where I can single-handedly destroy his small business? But it feels like the right thing to say. I walk around the end of the counter and behind it. There are shelves under the counters, on the wall and the island, all tidily lined with plates, mugs, tall glasses, napkins and boxes with labels.

"Come, come, here." He holds out a dark green apron by the neck. "This is for you."

"Thank you," I say again and take the apron, hang it around my neck and tie the straps around the back. I look down at the outlined book, open with a teacup balancing on its pages on my chest, and smooth the apron flat.

"There, you look the part." He smiles. "Now tell me, what do you know?"

I glance around at the machines on the back counter, large, shiny boxes with buttons and spouts and levers and lights. What do I know? I know nothing. Literally. I feel heat rising up my neck into my face. "Um ..." Useless trivia knowledge — like the fact that a human head weighs eight pounds — pops into my head like flashcards, but I'm pretty sure none of that is quite what he's looking for.

"No worries, we will start at the beginning." He points to a machine that has a spaceship-shaped part on top. "This is our espresso machine. It makes everything: lattes, cappuccinos, macchiatos, anything that has an espresso shot or hot milk in it."

In rapid order, Win points to items on the counters and in cupboards and on shelves under and above the counters, labelling things as he goes. My head starts to spin a bit, and his words blur together to make one long sequence of sounds that has no meaning. The bell over the door rings, and a woman in a blue suit walks in. She beelines for the counter, her high heels clicking on the floor, and says "Large decaf soy latte." No "hi," no "please."

But Win smiles at her and says, "For here or to go?"

"To go."

"Will that be all?"

"Yes," she says without looking up from her fingers digging in her wallet.

"Layne, come see, I'll show you how this contraption works." I step closer to the cash register and watches as he pushes in selections of each menu on the screen. "I used to have a regular old register, but my son wanted me to upgrade to this computer thing. I won't admit it to him, but it's quite a bit easier this way. Don't tell him I said that, though." His fingers slide over the touch screen choosing "decaf coffee," "large," "soy" from about a billion icons. When he pushes the green rectangle at the bottom of the screen, the screen shifts to black with her order listed and the price. "That'll be four seventy-five, please."

The woman curls her fingers into her wallet and pinches some coins between her first finger and her thumb. She drops them into Win's open hand. "Thank you," he says with his genuine smile. She ignores him.

"Come watch," Win says, and I step closer to him by the espresso machine. He picks up a large paper cup from a stack to the right of the machine and puts it under the spout. He pushes two buttons and turns the lever and waves his wand and clicks his heels and hands the steaming tan drink to the lady by the counter with a friendly, "Here you go!" He turns to me. "See? Easy."

Anything but easy.

The customer takes the cup without looking up at Win and snaps a lid onto the top, turns and click-clacks out of the shop. "Are they all so ... friendly?" I ask.

Win laughs, a gruff, low, huffing sound that wiggles his shoulders. "Sadly, no, some are less friendly." He shakes his head as if thinking more about the comment to himself. "But most people are lovely, you'll see." I'm not convinced I will. "I've shown you the coffee half, let's have a go at the books."

I follow him out from behind the counter to the two aisles of books. He starts his labelling again, listing authors' names and types of books interchangeably. It's like he's speaking another language, and I follow along, picking up infrequent words that are familiar. He turns and smiles at me. "Perhaps it's best if I just give you time to peruse the books." Perhaps. Sure.

The bell rings again, and a guy my age walks in. He's wearing a red East Coast hoodie with the hood up, gym shorts and boots. Boots. Like lace-up hiking books that aren't laced up. "Hi, Zander," Win says. So Boot Boy is a regular.

"Hey, Win," the guy says without looking up. Very regular, I guess. Zander steps toward the counter, but Win stays by the fantasy section, shifting and rearranging books to make them even and straight. He catches me watching him and smiles, winking one chocolate eye at me. Maybe he wants me to show some initiative, jump in with both feet. Sink or swim.

I walk toward the counter and take a deep breath to steady my nerves. "Can I help you?"

Zander looks up, startled. I guess he didn't see me standing with Win in the books. When he looks at my face, I actually see the colour drain out of his own, like in the cartoons when the pinky-red falls from the forehead to the chin like a bathtub being drained, leaving pasty white skin.

"Oh," he says and freezes on the spot. How could I have screwed up already?

Win hustles over behind Boot Boy. "Zander, this is Layne. I've hired her to help with our summer rush." The words "summer rush" in the awkward silence and empty coffee-slash-book shop make me want to laugh, but I bite the inside of my mouth to stop the giggle from coming out. "Layne, this is Zander. He's worked with me for a few years now. He can help you with anything you need to know." Oooooh.

"Hi," I say. "Sorry, I didn't realize —"

"Me either," he rushes to say over my words. But he's still staring at me. It's getting creepy.

Something on my face? Breakfast? Boogers? I reach up and touch the corners of my mouth with my fingers, brush my nose with as much discretion as I can muster under his studious gaze. "Do I have something ..."

That breaks the spell, and he looks away and takes a big gulp, making his Adam's apple pull up and drop down in this neck. "Sorry, I just ... you remind me of someone."

Penny. Of course. She comes here all the time. *Came.* If Zander works here, they must have crossed paths. "My sister," I say and curse the crack in my voice.

"Penny," he whispers. "I'm sorry."

"Thanks," I say, wishing for an earthquake to strike or a tornado to touch down and sweep me away. I had hoped I'd be safe from these conversations here.

Win shuffles past Zander to stand between us, puts a hand on each of our shoulders. For an uncomfortable moment we stand there, the three of us connected by Win's age-spotted hands as if we were having a moment of silence. Forget earthquake or tornado, I'll even take aliens. Beam me up, Scotty.

"Okay, Zander, I'll leave you to show Layne the ropes. I've introduced her to our gadgets back there, and she met Ms. Walker already —"

"Lucky her," Zander says, suddenly easy and casual. His face is a normal colour again.

"Yes, quite. I have some paperwork to complete in the office. Holler if you need help, but Layne, you're in capable hands." He taps Zander's shoulder twice, as if making sure I knew whose hands he was leaving me in, then shuffles past the counter through a door in the wall panelling that I hadn't even noticed was there.

Zander steps around the counter, takes off his hoodie and hangs it on a coat hook at the end, then replaces it with a green apron that matches mine. He picks up a cloth by the faucet of the sink, runs the water and rinses it, squeezing and twisting the water out of it, then wipes it over the counter. That I can do.

"There seems to be a lot to learn," I say.

He looks up and smiles. "Yeah." He glances to the secret panel door and back at me before he goes back to wiping the counter, digging his finger in the edges where machine or display meets the laminate.

Great. A conversationalist. I swallow a sigh so that he won't hear it and start thinking of topics I could introduce that won't result in a single word response or pitying looks.

Conversation Starters for Non-conversationalists

1. Strange food aversions.
2. International politics and foreign policies.
3. Armchair sports.
4. Tarantino movies.

"Here, I have something to show you," he says, interrupting the list in my head. He stands still but his hands are rummaging under the counter. With one more peek over his shoulder at the office door, he pulls a folder up from under the counter and lays it flat then pushes it toward me.

"What is it?"

"Cheats." It's one of those pocket folders that holds three-hole punched papers. The lower corner is worn and bent, curling back up stubbornly when I push it down flat. I open it up, and inside there are loose-leaf pages with neat handwriting on the lines. Penny's handwriting.

"What is it?" I ask again.

Zander looks at me for a minute. His face is sort of pinched and tight. "Penny was going to work here."

"Yeah, Win told me."

"She was nervous to apply for the job, said she didn't know enough. So I got her to meet me after work a few times and showed her some things. She insisted on writing them down. She didn't want Win to know, thought he'd have less faith in her."

"Such a nerd," I mutter, not meaning to say it out loud.

Zander gives a nervous high-pitched giggle that doesn't fit his size and quickly says, "You said it, not me." I couldn't help it, I laugh too.

I flip through Penny's secret notes. What a rebel.

FLASHBACK: *I asked Penny, "Why are you rewriting those? Just study the handouts."*

Penny looked up from her typed physics notes and corresponding handwritten notes. "I remember it better when I write it out myself."

I run my finger along a line of her precise letters. Her handwriting. It could have been Pulitzer-winning poetry and it wouldn't have a bigger impact. Just seeing her handwriting reaches into me and tightens my throat. Of course, it isn't poetry. Each page has the name of a drink on the top followed by the machine that make the drink and point-form directions. On the last page is a list of coffee guru shorthand definitions translated into English: double double, skinny, half-caf … I'll never know it all. "Can I take this home?"

Zander nodded and smiled a slow hook to one side. "Yeah, I guess it's yours now," he says. He looks sad. Not with the usual pity or unease about me and my grief standing there beside him. Just sad.

"Thanks," I say, turning back to the pages with Penny's tidy letters linked in lines. For several moments he seems to bustle about nearby while I study Penny's notes. They're straightforward and clear, and I start to visualize the steps in my head. I read the directions then look up and try to follow along in my mind while I watch her walk me through each step, demonstrating it for me. Hallucinations can be helpful at times, I guess.

"It's usually really slow on Mondays," Zander says from the other end of the counter. Startled, I turn to look at him then back to where Penny had been showing me how to make a cafe misto, whatever the heck that was. She's gone.

"It's probably why Win told me to come today." Zander opens his mouth as if he's going to say something but shuts it and turns away. I should let it go, since he's obviously uncomfortable saying whatever he was just thinking, but Penny is the respectful one, not me. *Was*. "What?" I ask, my voice a bit louder than it should be.

"Oh, nothing, I just …" He fiddles with the paper-wrapped straws, pushing them around in the blue and green glass where they stand.

Try again, less hostile maybe. "It's okay, really. What is it?"

He looks at his hands for a minute, rubbing his right thumb against the back of his left hand as if trying to remove some smudge of dirt. Just as my patience is ebbing away he says, "Your parents were in the car too?" It's a statement and a question all rolled up in one — like he knows the answer, but it's too vehement a statement to make.

"Yeah," I say, the word falling out on the sigh that escaped when I started breathing again. I didn't even realize I was holding my breath, waiting for him to come out with it already.

He looks up at me. "So who are you living with?"

"My brother. He's older and out of school and is getting a job and everything."

Zander's eyes flicker with recognition. "Oh right, I remember Penny talking about a brother — he moved out a while ago, right?"

Okay, enough with the questions. They're creeping closer and closer to way too personal. There's no way I'm getting into the whole story of my brother taking off and not looking back, of ignoring my parents' warnings and choosing some miscreant friend over his own family. Even *thinking* about it makes me grind my teeth. He's home, and before too long he'll see the truth about Sebastian too, and it will all be in the past. "He's back," I say, adding just enough snark to make him realize I'm not talking about it with him, even if he *was* Penny's friend. I stare him down until he looks away, and I turn back to Penny's notes. But I can't read them — every time I try to concentrate on the words, my brain starts off on some wild goose chase trying to think up the last line of the new Taylor Swift song or to remember random groceries I need to get.

With a squeak, the hidden door pulls open and Win comes through, twisting his apron around his hands, wiping them off. Instinctively, I close the folder and slip it under the counter. I don't know why it has to stay secret; it's a dumb secret to keep in the first place. But it's Penny's secret. *Was*.

"How are you two making out here?" he asks, smiling at both of us from behind his moustache.

"Great," Zander says first. "We went over some types of orders, and the restocking of supplies is done." So that's what he was doing with all the cups.

Just when Win nods and says, "Excellent!" the bell by the door jingles and all three of us look up. Sara and Asher are standing in the doorway, grinning widely at me. My face burns. Win says, "Welcome! Come in, come in out of that heat — has it started to rain yet?" I'm not sure why he asked them, since the whole front of the store is one giant window, and we can clearly see it's not raining.

"Not yet," Sara says. The two of them are standing in the doorway like grinning halfwits as if they don't know what to do now that they're inside.

Zander clears his throat, and it works, because I look at him. He nods with his eyebrows up. Subtle.

I repress the sigh that threatens to come up and ask, saccharine-sweet, "What can I get for you?" *Shoot me now.*

As if they're a four-legged, two-headed creature, they move together to the counter, still grinning foolishly. They look up at the chalkboard menu behind me. "What's good here?" Asher asks. His eyes are actually twinkling. I know it sounds cliché, but I swear a spark of light flashes.

Coffee, I want to say, but because Win is watching, "The lattes are nice." A real fancy-named drink. And one I know how to make, thanks to Penny's notes.

Sara smiles and says, "Great, that's what I'll have, please."

I take the milk carton out of the fridge and pour some in the steamer, turn it on and pull a large paper cup out of the dispenser. I pour steaming coffee into the cup, trying to hold my breath while it pours so as not to smell the bitter odour. The milk steamer beeps and I pour the hot white foam on top of the black, swirling it into a light tan. I take a second to smile to myself, then turn back to the front counter and hand it to Sara. "Thanks!" she says. "It smells great!" To each their own, I guess.

I look at Asher, trying not to let him see how proud I am of the drink. He winks. Or did he? It was so quick, I may have imagined it. And he's already rattling off a long list of random words.

"Um, sorry ... What was that?" I ask.

He smiles too-sweetly, as if he's trying desperately not to laugh and repeats super slowly, "Can I have a large — non-fat — half-caf — caramel — macchiato, please?" I could hit him.

"Sure," I say and try to repeat the drink to myself low enough that they can't hear me: "Large, caramel, caf-half ..." I stare unfocussed at the counter, trying to visualize a page from Penny's binder to help me. If only I could take a sneak-peek. There's movement to my left. I turn to see Zander stepping in with a large paper cup in his hand. He hands it to Asher and then tips his head to the computer.

"Right," I say then study the computer screen, trying to remember where Win had started with the order earlier in the morning. All the icons look the same, and the lettering underneath is way too small to read.

"I'll show you," Zander says softly enough that maybe only I hear it and points to the screen, the icon for "large." I push that and follow his prompts until both drinks are entered and the total rung up.

"That's nine dollars, fifty cents please," I say. Phew, no shake. That's got to be the first time in a long time my voice cooperated.

"I've got it," Asher says and hands me a ten-dollar bill before Sara can find her wallet in her purse. When I hand him his change, he winks again. I think. I could have sworn I was one of those girls who would get pissed off if some guy winked at me. Condescending or what! Turns out if the fluttering in my stomach means anything, the "or what" is closer to the truth.

They give me a wave, small enough to be appropriate between customer and coffee barista, and head out the door. I wipe the counter where their drinks left small wet rings. My phone vibrates in my back pocket, so I pull it out and read a text from Asher: *Tks 4 the coffee, coffee grl* and a smiley face. Apparently I'm a sucker for smiley faces too.

"Layne," Win says from the books, "I'm afraid I'm old school. No phones behind the counter."

"Oh, of course! I'm sorry!" I slip it back in my pocket as it vibrates again. My fingers itch to pull it out, but I'd rather not get fired on my first day.

The rest of the morning goes quickly. I explore the shop, trying to familiarize myself with the tools and utensils and materials behind the counter then the books on the shelves. Zander doesn't talk much. Every now and then he'll blurt out some weird fact or ask a question that has nothing to do with anything, but he has a strange way of knowing exactly what I'm wondering about in the shop and impeccable timing for stepping in and helping me out. Customers continue to trickle in over my shift. Each time one does, Zander nudges me to do a little more of the process by myself so that the last order just after 1:00 p.m. is filled, rung up and completed entirely by me. As the customer takes his coffee to a table by the window, Zander holds out his palm for a subtle low-five behind the counter.

chapter 19

When that first shift is over, I untie my apron and hang it on the hook where Zander points. "Thanks for the help," I say, meaning it.

"Yeah, no problem," he says. A kind of faraway, sad look slips over his face for a moment, but then he smiles and it's gone. Maybe I imagined it. After all, I *have* been seeing a lot of things that aren't really there. Well, one persistent thing a lot of the time. His smile and gaze linger on me. Too long, Boot Boy. He finally looks away when Win fumbles out of the back room.

"There now, that wasn't so bad, was it?" Win says, pulling his moustache up at the ends.

"I managed alright."

"She did great," Zander says behind me.

"I've done up a rough schedule. Just have it on paper here, you know, the old way works, why fix it?" I can think of a hundred reasons why he should use an app but don't suggest any. He lays the paper on the counter, and I look at the table. My name is written in small swirly letters inside seven of the fourteen boxes. "I've just done up the next couple of weeks. Feel free to trade with the other staff if you can't do a shift. The final copy will be posted in the staff room by tomorrow afternoon."

I take a picture of the table with my phone. "Thank you, I'm sure they'll be fine." What else do I have to do, really?

"You can take a coffee to go. Did I say that before? Two free coffees per shift." He looks at me with his eyebrows pulled up and his moustache turned down. I swear it's a test, one final exam of the orientation to see if I'm worthy of the job.

"Thanks," I say again and fill a medium to-go cup with hot black liquid. I add some milk for good measure. Zac can drink it. I hurry to collect my bag and head out the door, hoping Zander will give me a passing report on my first shift.

The bell jingles as I opened the door, and I'm hit by the hot, sticky air before I even step out onto the sidewalk. Too hot to walk. I'm so glad Zac is picking me up. Glancing left, then right, I see Mom's car parked on the side of the street facing away from me. As I pass the back of the car, I see Penny sitting in the back seat. She gives a little wave, and I wave back. I pull the front door open and toss my bag onto the floor. "I got you a coffee," I say.

"Thanks, but I don't drink coffee. Vile stuff." What the — Not Zac. Sebastian. What is he even doing here? I stoop and look in, and my surprise must be painted all over my poker face.

"Yeah, Zac got called in last minute for another interview, but this was on empty, so he took my car and asked if I'd pick you up."

"But why are you here?"

"To pick you up."

I don't mean *here* here, I mean *there* here, like at our house. Again.

"Oh," I say, only because I can't be bothered with asking more questions.

Sebastian turns the car on, flashes his blinker and checks over his left shoulder then pulls out onto the road. "How was the first day?"

"Fine."

"Yeah? That's good. I worked in a Tim's when I was in high school. It can be crazy busy." He stops talking to laugh for a moment. I stare straight ahead, watching the lines on the asphalt slip under the front of the car. I want to look around to see if Penny's still in the back seat, but I don't want Sebastian to think I'm looking at him. Surly and childish? Yes, but also necessary. He's still talking. "I used to say, 'You know how people always warn you about talking to them before their morning coffee? Well, I served them their morning coffee after they waited in line for ten minutes.' Talk about mood. Can you imagine?"

From the corner of my eye I see him turn to look at me with the last three words. I guess it's not a rhetorical question. I shrug without looking, and he turns back to the road. "Zac's interview started a half hour ago. He said he'd text when he was done. I have some errands to run ..." I can't help but envision him in some dark alley, his hood up and his hands in his pockets meeting some criminal for a drug deal. He's looking at me again.

"Huh?" I say intelligently.

"I asked do you want to come with? Or should I drop you off at home first?"

My toes actually curl when he says "home." *Home? My home and Zac's. Penny's and Mom's and Dad's. So, so not yours.* "My home," I say.

"Alright." His voice sounds a little gravely, a little hesitant. There's a twinge in my chest, that ugly heavy-sick feeling of guilt that I get when I know I've hurt someone's feelings. This whole interaction feels very middle-school-ish. I could've walked. I should've walked. Silence, finally. But it's stiff and uneasy, and I don't know which is worse — his rambling or this. He pulls into our driveway. "There you go," he says, slipping the gear to park. "Do you have your key?"

"Yeah," I say, hurrying out of the car. The strap of my bag gets caught up in my feet, and my rush only works to snarl it further. I swallow the growl that wants to come out, take a deep breath and meticulously detangle myself. Penny giggles behind me on the sidewalk, and I swear at her under my breath.

"Sorry? I didn't hear you?" Sebastian says, looking up at me, hopeful and attentive, as if I'd just whispered the secret of life but he missed it.

"Nothing, just talking to myself." It's basically true.

"Okay, see you in a bit."

Can't wait. "Yup," I say before I swing the door shut. "Jerk." The growl finally slips out as I step toward the house.

"He doesn't seem all that bad," Penny says beside me.

I stop and stare at her. Realizing that Sebastian is still in the driveway watching me, I force my feet to start moving again. The last thing I need is him getting the upper hand by reporting to Zac that I'm looney tunes, talking to ghosts. "Whose side are you on, anyway?" I snap without looking at her. "He's bad news — Dad knew that. And now that Dad's gone he's always around." I reach the door and dig in my pocket for the key. The car is still idling in the driveway. I put the key in the lock and turn it and push the door open. "Besides ..." I say, turning back toward Penny, but she's disappeared again. The car honks, and I resist the reflex to look at it. The engine revs a bit, and I hear the wheels roll backward. Good riddance to both of them. I slam the door shut behind me.

In my room I take the time to reply to the texts I've gotten while I was under the phone ban at work. Four from Sara, two from girls I haven't talked to since school let out — more pity texts. They wouldn't have texted me before, but I've learned family tragedy makes people reach out. Not in a good way, though. Three from Asher. My middle flutters. The last one: *Howd it go?* I send him a series of emoticons that demonstrate the progression of the day: shocked, scared, overwhelmed, thinking, excited, happy, exhausted. My phone shakes immediately with a reply:

Asher: (three extra-smiley faces and some clapping hands.)

Asher: *Wanna do sumthin 2nite?*

My stomach twists. I don't want to keep talking about butterflies, because that's corny, but there's a reason someone made that saying up.

Me: *Sure*

Asher: (more smiley faces)

We thumb out a plan — he'll pick me up for an early movie and a stop at the dessert place by the theatre. My fingers are twitching with energy. Anticipation. Anxiety. Then — guilt, heavy and sick. "It's not a date. We can still be friends," I tell Penny. Or myself? The room is silent and still. "We're just friends," I repeat, but my stomach still hurts. I throw my phone on the bed and step over to the plank-sized bare spot on my floor and force myself to do two planks for forty-five seconds each before collapsing on the floor.

chapter 20

I'm trying to read page thirty-seven in my copy of Penny's book for the third time when someone knocks on my door. I heard Zac and Sebastian come in the front door but decided to ignore them in protest of Zac's choice to send Sebastian to pick me up. And in Sebastian's choice to be here at all. I ignore the knock too.

The door opens anyway. Zac sticks his head in. "What are you up to?"

I lift the book to show him how obviously stupid his question is. "Reading."

He raises his eyebrows and mouths "oh," but he has the good grace to suppress the sound that goes with. Instead he asks, "Is it good?"

"Meh," I say, tossing the book and my pretence of being annoyed aside. "How'd the interviews go?"

"Meh," he says with a laugh. He steps in and leans against the doorframe, looking at his feet. His toe digs at the edge of the rug.

"Is he gone?" I don't quite manage to keep my voice casual.

He stares at me a minute. Hard. I feel my cheeks burn. "Yeah, he's gone. I just came in to tell you supper's almost ready. Made spaghetti for supper. Again. Sorry, I'll have to figure out how to cook, I guess." His voice is even. Angry but controlled.

"Cool it," Penny says, and I think she's talking to me, not him, even though he's the one who's heated.

"I like spaghetti," I say, which is true. As long as the noodles are the right length. "But I'm going out tonight."

"Yeah? To do what?"

"A movie then dessert."

"Great. With who?"

There's something different about his voice, like it's suddenly more an inter-rogation and less a question of interest. Not only does his frown look like Dad's, but now he sounds like Dad too. Part of me knows why he's asking and that this is his new role, but none of me likes it. At all. I go with vague. "Just a few people," I say. There'll be a few people there, I'm sure; doesn't matter if I know them or not. He studies me as if he's trying to see inside my brain. He's going to ask more questions — I'm not sure I can handle anymore of Dad's voice coming out of him without losing it on him. "I won't be out late," I add.

"Sure," he says with a nod. He slips back out the door and closes it behind him.

My phone sounds. It's a text from Asher: *Almost there. 3mins.*

I texted back: *Will b ready.* I grab my bag and jacket to get out of the house before he comes to the door. Zac's sitting on the end of the couch watching TV, balancing a plate of spaghetti on his lap. Alone. "See ya," I say as I rush past him, ignoring the clench of guilt. Why should I feel guilty?

"Laynie, wait!" Zac says, and I stop but didn't turn around. "What time do you think you'll be back?"

More Dad-speak. Geez, who died and made him boss? Oh, right.

I really want to say something rude like "what's it to you?" but it's not him I'm angry with; he's just the only one left to direct it at. I turn to face him, and he smiles. The anger dissolves into more guilt: a sharp, solid spear slipping into a bubbling vat of molten steel, raising the top to the overflow line. It's not like he asked to be the boss. He doesn't even want to be here — he made his choice, moved away. "I dunno, maybe eleven? Okay?" I say to make up for my surly attitude.

He smiles and nods, seemingly relieved. "Have fun," he says and turns back to his movie. I slip out before my guilt can say anymore.

I stop on the step for a minute to take a deep breath. Asher's already there, sitting in the car looking at his phone. His shaggy hair falls to obscure most of his face. The stupid winged creatures are awake again in my middle. Penny's there, standing beside me, smiling. "Have fun," she echoes Zac's words, and my guilt expands in my chest.

Have fun. I can see her ToDah! list in my mind, with her last hesitant addi-tion, "Go on a date (preferably with AP)." I stole her job. I stole her date. "It's not a date," I say, but my voice is weak and unconvincing. I'm stealing her life. All this time I thought I was completing her ToDah! list for her, but is that really the truth? Who am I doing the list for? And what right do I have?

I should go back into the house, have spaghetti with Zac. Except I can't.

Reasons Why Not to Just Turn Around and Go Back Inside

1. Zac's still on the couch. He seemed relieved that I was heading out. If I go back now, he'll ask why, and the answers lead too directly to the Penny hallucination.

2. Asher looks up and smiles, and the smile kind of chases away my thoughts for a minute.

3. It's not a date. He's just a friend.

I walk down the driveway to the car and open the passenger seat.

"Hi," he says through his smile. Chick flick cliché, I know, but it is crooked to the right side.

"Hi." I turn my head to look for my seatbelt and see Penny standing on the step. I should get out, go back, apologize to her for stealing her date, for stealing her list, for being in the hospital so that she got in the car. I put my hand on the handle to push the door open, but she smiles and waves. It seems like an endorsement. An absolution. She doesn't look mad, but then I shouldn't be surprised; Penny's the magnanimous one. *Was.*

And Asher is saying something I can't make out. The car pulls away from the curb, and I watch Penny disappear behind us.

We walk to the restaurant across the parking lot after the movie. The movie was funny. I laughed more than I have in weeks. But when I realized I was relaxed — happy even — I felt a point of thick pain in my throat and in my chest. Shame. I tried to swallow it down, but it caught, painfully sharp, and lodged in my throat. I tried to stop thinking after that and in a while was laughing at the characters' antics on the screen again. When Asher slips his fingers between mine and squeezes, I smile at him but slide my hand free a moment later under the pretence of checking my phone. It seems the butterflies are raging a war against the cold spear of guilt in my chest. They flutter their wings faster, harder, trying to melt the ice.

The restaurant is dimly lit, with small tables and chairs scattered around the left side and a long counter with glass display on the right. We look at all the cakes and pies in the display case. I order a piece of double chocolate cake and he choses a slice of lemon meringue pie, and then we find a table for two by the window. The butterflies are winning.

"Who's your favourite band?" Asher asks out of the blue.

"Tough one," I stall. The truth is not a popular one; I mean, everyone appreciates the Beatles, but they're not necessarily on the cool list for our generation. But it feels strange to lie to Asher about something so trivial when I already told him the whole truth of Penny's stalking me from beyond the grave. "The Beatles."

"They're cool," he says, and I let my breath escape. "I want to hold your hand."

"Huh?" What? He tried to hold my hand a couple of times already and had done so without awkwardly asking my permission. I guess I'll have to spell it out. Not. A. Date. I need to convince myself first.

"That's my favourite Beatles song, 'I Want to Hold Your Hand.'" He looks like he's trying not to laugh. "What's yours?"

My cheeks burn, and I'm glad for the redirection. "That's impossible," I say. "I refuse to answer. Who's your favourite? Band, I mean."

Asher reaches across the table and pulls my hand toward him, turns it over, palm up, and counts on my fingers, "Phillip Phillips is great, Maroon 5, Twenty One Pilots, Justin Bieber —"

"Bieber?" I snatch my hand back and cross my arms. "*Bieber?* Are you serious?"

"Yeah, his new stuff is good." I make a face, and he laughs. "I mean, he's no John Lennon, but ..."

"No, he's not," I say in my snarkiest voice.

Asher looks up behind me and says, "Ah, saved by the cake!" A waiter comes to the table and puts our plates down in front of us. We sit in silence while we take the first few bites. The chocolate is heavenly, rich and creamy icing, soft melt-in-your-mouth cake. I suppress a groan, too weird a sound to make, even on this Not a Date.

"Good?" Asher asks after a couple of moments.

"So good," I say through the bite. I push my plate a couple of inches closer to him. "Want to try it?"

"Of course," he says. He takes a small piece of cake with his fork and puts it in his mouth, keeping his eyes locked on mine. He smiles before he chews. His eyes close, and he groans the groan I was too embarrassed to let out. It does sound foolish, so I laugh. "Yeah, it's good," he says, laughing with me. He pushes his plate toward me. "Here try mine."

I do, a small bit. "No, not as good as mine," I say, returning my attention to the dark brown half-piece left.

"No, not as good," he echoes, reaching toward my plate with his fork. I pull the plate back closer to me and stab his hand with my fork. "Ow!" I laugh. He watches me, his eyes shining with the light in the room. I feel my face flush and look away. Now is the time for the Not a Date conversation.

"How are you?" he asks before I can say anything. His voice is serious, and I know it's not the flippant question most people ask when they want to hear "good" or "fine" instead of the truth.

"Okay," I say. It's true. "But I don't want to talk about it tonight," I add without realizing it's coming out. The butterflies lose some ground as the cold guilt cuts through my middle. Asher's the one person who knows about Penny, who knows how messed up I am, and he seems to actually *really* care when he asks. I'm rude to be so short, but it's the first night I've laughed and felt relaxed, I don't want to undo all that by talking about Ghost Penny or Stupid Sebastian. Also: Not. A. Date.

"Got it," he says, and I look up to see if he is hurt or rueful at my rebuke. He doesn't seem to be. He gives me a small, sad smile and reaches across to lay his fingers on my hand. I smile back and resist the playful urge to stab him again. Probably wouldn't be as funny the second time anyway. "How was the rest of your shift at work?" he asks instead, and his hand stays on mine unaccosted. I leave it for now.

"Not bad," I say. "That guy that was there, Zander? He showed me a lot, and he had this folder that Penny made that had instructions and recipes for everything. By the end of it I had a lot figured out." A slight exaggeration. "Are you getting a summer job?"

"I have one at the golf course," he says before putting a big bite of pie into his mouth. A bit of meringue catches on the corner of his mouth. His tongue slips out to lick his lips clean, and the butterflies take over the battle.

"What do you do?"

He shrugs. "A bit of everything, really. I do some landscaping and some caddying. The shifts are really early, so I'm off early in the afternoon. Sometimes I stay to play a round."

I wrinkle up my nose. "Ugh, I hate golf."

"Have you tried it?"

"Yes!" I say, with little effort to hide my incredulity. "Well, once. I was very bad, so I hate it."

He laughs. "Yeah, it's not a try-it-one-time sport."

"It's not a sport!" I say, and he glares at me. The corner of his mouth twitches, but his eyes are steady. "It's a game, maybe, but not a sport."

"You're out of your tree," he says evenly.

"Golf. You drive around in a little buggy and hit a ball with a stick. How is that athletic?" He shakes his head and puts another forkful of dessert into his mouth. He shakes his head again. "Well?" I push him to answer.

"I'm not even going to dignify that with a response," he says, still shaking his head.

"Not a sport," I mutter.

"Tell you what. You come with me for a round. Eighteen holes. Hell, *nine* holes, and I'll change your mind."

"Golf is miserable," I say, feeling my bravado slip away as I'm backed into the corner. Echoes of him calling me chicken on the half-pipe bounce in my mind.

A smile curls one side of his mouth. "So you've said. I dare you. Nine holes." His smile is relaxed, but his eyes are locked on mine.

I lift my casted arm and my eyebrows. "I'm afraid I can't."

His smile drops, instantly, and he turns a little white. He shakes his head again and whispers, "Right. I'm sorry, I …"

His guilty face crushes me. "Fine. When my cast is off and my arm is better, I'll try a round."

He studies me a minute, maybe to see if I'm lying or saying it when I don't really mean it. "Okay," he says softly, and the deal is done.

I click the button on my phone; it's after eleven. "I should get home," I say, hoping I don't sound too lame. "I told my brother …" Loser, nerd, baby, goody-two-shoes — the labels slip around in my brain.

But he doesn't make fun of me for being anxious to go home. "Yeah, I didn't realize it was so late," he says. He smiles and sighs like he's reluctant to go. I hope I'm not imagining it. "Let's go." He picks up both plates and sets them on the counter, turns and waits for me to gather my bag and jacket and catch up to him.

The car ride to my place is quiet. He reaches across and slips his long fingers around my hand in my lap. I smile at him, but it's obvious he has the wrong idea. I tried to keep it all cool, but somehow I've led him on. Can't two friends go to a movie? I pull my hand loose to use both hands to redo my ponytail then slip both under my thighs on the seat out of reach. I have to tell him. Not. A. Date. The silence gets tense, charged with thoughts and words that aren't said. I search my brain for something witty or interesting or anything, really, to say that isn't dull or stupid or about Penny, but it's otherwise blank. He keeps his eyes on the road. He pulls up to the curb in front of the house. Escape is imminent, but first A Conversation. I stare at the house so I don't see Asher. Try to find words. The light in the living room is on. I wonder if Zac is waiting up for me.

Asher's fingers land on my arm, and I turn to look at him. It's dark, except for a streetlight a few feet away, so it's hard to read his face. His eyes flit back and forth between mine. "I had a great time," he says, and I almost puke because isn't that what everyone says at the end of a date?

Number six: Go on a date (preferably with AP).

Penny's list. Penny's date. Not a Date.

"Yeah," I say, suddenly finding it hard to breathe. I glance into the back seat to see if Penny has slipped in unnoticed. It's empty. I can't look at him; he might smile or something, and I'll lose my nerve. I stare at my hands. "I did too, but — "

"Layne," Asher says, his voice so soft and thick it breaks my resolve. I put my hand on the door handle and pull it. The door opens. "Layne?" he says again, his voice higher and unsure. I freeze, staring at the triangle of pavement I can see between the door and the floor of the car.

I shake my head. I can't look back at him. If I do I'll be caught, trapped. "Goodnight," I say quickly and push my way out of the car. I think he says my name once more, but I can't be sure because my heart is pounding too loudly in my ears. I hurry up the driveway and fling the door open, shut it carefully so not to slam it, and lean against it, trying to catch my breath.

"Layne? Is that you?" Zac calls from the living room. Who else would it be?

"Yeah, I'm home. Going to bed. Good night." Before he can say anything more, I hurry down the hall to my room. I don't slam that door either — small victories. I sit on my bed, trying to stop the spinning in my head.

"What's wrong?" Penny asks from her desk chair. Her chemistry book is still on the desk, but it's closed like I left it. I don't know why I'm surprised to see it closed; hallucinations really have no need to study, or the ability to open a heavy textbook.

"Nothing," I say, then laugh manically because (being *from inside* my head and all) I'm sure she can see my mind to know that isn't true. "He was going to kiss me," I whisper. I look to see her reaction — is she angry that I stole her date? The desk chair is empty. I throw my pillow at it and bury my head under the other one on the bed.

A knock at the door. "Go away," I whisper, knowing he won't hear me. If Zac finds me hiding under my pillow, he'll ask stupid questions to figure out what's wrong. I sit up and say, "Yeah, come in."

"Hey," he says gently, "you okay?"

"Yeah," I say, getting up and retrieving the pillow. I look anywhere but at him to figure out how to look busy.

"Did you have a good night?"

"Yeah," I say and add "great" in the hopes it sounds convincing.

"What did you see?"

I tell him the name of the movie, and he nods. I add, "Sorry, Zac, I'm just really tired. I'm going to go to bed."

He nods again but stands there a moment longer. Then says, "Alright, I'll leave you to it. Have a good sleep."

"Thanks, good night," I say as he pulls the door closed. The butterflies are gone, all killed off by the cold guilt spear in my chest. I slip off my jeans and climb into bed in my T-shirt, suddenly too tired to even change into my pyjamas. I pull the covers up over my shoulders and try to fall asleep before the tears come. I'm not nearly fast enough.

chapter 21

The next morning my alarm goes off early. My second shift at the coffee shop. I force myself to wait a painful fifty seconds in a plank before getting up and shuffling to my bathroom. I stand at the sink, watching my eyes open from a squint as I get used to the light. My lids are puffy, and the whites of my eyes are rimmed red. I look terrible. I run my fingers through my hair, smoothing the waves back away from my face, then rub my cheeks and eyes hard. I linger in the shower too long so that when I emerge glowing red and hot I don't have enough time for breakfast. I dress quickly and shoulder my bag, slip down the hall and out of the door unheard.

Maybe walking to work will indicate I don't need any pickups from work — especially if Zac is busy. I keep a quick pace. The morning air is already warm, but wet with the mist of dew rising off the grass. My brain starts to swirl with thoughts of last night: the easy laughter at the restaurant followed by the edgy silence in the car and my abrupt bailout. My phone has texts from Sara and Asher.

Sara's:
Having fun?
Where R U now?
Home yet?
How was the nite?
Waiting for deets.
Srsly. Ur killing me.
I give up. G'nite.
Asher's:
R U OK?

I wince and suck air in through my teeth, making a high-pitched sound. I reply to Sara — *GR8 nite. Off 2 work* — enough to satisfy her, hopefully, and noncommittal enough to be true. I hover over Asher's conversation. Stuck. I should have been more up-front, more straightforward. Told him from the start that we can't … I can't. He seemed to listen and tried to understand before, so maybe … But …

I don't know what comes after the "but." I just know that whatever happened last night can't happen again. I touch Penny's list in my pocket. Whatever feeling he had in the car, *I* had in the car, but it's not fair to Penny. I can't. And so it's not fair to him. I close the text conversation without replying. I open iTunes and stuff my earbuds in my ears, hoping the music will drown out the thoughts. When the phone rings — twice — I ignore it. Whoever it is, it's not someone I want to talk to right now, since my list of living people that I want to talk to this minute is very, very short. As in none.

When I arrive at the coffee shop, I'm met by a dark-haired girl behind the counter. "What can I get you?" she asks as I step closer. She doesn't look up from her task of arranging mugs off the dishwasher tray onto the shelf.

"Nothing, I'm Layne. I just started working here yesterday." I step behind the counter and try to stow my bag in the space Win had shown me. Another bag is there, camo green with silver studs around it. I push it over to make room for mine and see her staring at me out of the corner of my eye. I stand up to face her, and she grimaces. I think it's supposed to be a smile.

"Tracy." She drops her effortful smile and turns away from me to wipe down the counter. I take down the apron I hung up yesterday and tie it around me. "You can unload the rest of the mugs and wipe that table down," she says from the other end of the counter, where she's rearranging the muffins on the display plate.

"Sure," I say. Geez. I wish Zander was here instead of her.

I open the dishwasher and move the hot mugs to the shelf where clean ones are kept, making sure to turn all the handles out for easy access, as Zander suggested. When that's done, I fish a clean cloth out of the drawer by the sink and run it under the hot water. The whole time, I can see Tracy moving about at the end of the counter, glaring up at me every so often. What's her problem? I concentrate on not looking her way, avoiding eye contact at all cost. It's not even five minutes into the shift. It's going to be a long one.

I'm wiping the third dirty table when the bell over the door jingles. I look up, ready to welcome a customer, but see Asher standing there, his hands in his hoodie front pocket. His eyes are on me, but his head is tipped forward. Some strange instinct tells me to go hug him, but I hold on to the edge of the table I'm cleaning and scrub harder at a dark brown spot instead.

"Hey," he says.

"Hey," I echo without looking up.

"I tried to text and call you ..." His voice trails off, sounding strange.

"We're not allowed to use phones here."

"Ah," he says. "Can we talk?"

"I just started, and we're busy." Even without looking at him, I can see him in my periphery looking around at the empty tables before looking back at me.

"I can wait or come back. When's your break?"

"I don't know," I say then turn to see Tracy striding toward us. Her gaze is locked on Asher, intent and determined and not very friendly. At all.

"Can I get you something?" she asks with forced civility.

Asher frowns, looks back and forth between us and then steadies a scowl on her. "Actually, I just came in to talk to Layne for a minute."

"We're busy," Tracy says. The same strange hunch that had nudged me to hug him pushes me again to say something, anything, in his defence. I bite the inside of my cheek to stay quiet.

Asher looks once more at me, waits a moment — probably for me to step in — then gives me a small nod and turns and leaves. *Don't.* I concentrate to keep my feet locked to the floor instead of going after him. "You're welcome," Tracy says behind me. I turn to look at her, hoping my face doesn't display the bewilderment I feel. "We get all sorts of creeps in here. You just got to be firm with them."

"He's not a creep," I say a little too loudly. At least my voice didn't shake as I said it.

"Ah." Tracy turns and looks at me, her smile smug as if she just figured everything out. "We're here to work, not flirt. Boyfriends aren't allowed either. "

"He's not my boyfriend," I say, my voice just barely more than a whisper.

Her smug smile grows. "Ex-boyfriends are even worse. Keep the drama somewhere else." She turns and walks away before I can figure out what to say.

I should quit. Right here. Right now. I'm going to.

"Not worth it, Laynie," Penny says. She's beside me, glaring at Tracy's back. I wish she were some kind of malignant poltergeist instead of a benign hallucination. She could throw mugs and plates and muffins at Tracy, just to scare the crap out of her.

I return to wiping the tables and straightening the chairs around them. Throughout the shift, several customers come and go. I'm able to dodge most of the serving to avoid having to ask for Tracy's help. It's hard work keeping busy enough that I don't get within five feet of her. The bookshelf has probably never been so straight.

"My shift is over," Tracy announces out of the blue. She turns the tip mug over on the counter and makes a big show of splitting the tips into three portions. She takes two and says, "Training fee."

"Tell Win," Penny says, standing with me behind the counter as we watch Tracy hang up her apron and skip out of the door.

But I let it go. "Not worth it, Penny," I say, using her words. Seven dollars and fifteen cents isn't enough to be called a rat. I sneak my phone out to peek at the picture of the schedule to see how many shifts I'm paired with her. I'll trade shifts to stay away from her. I don't care what anyone thinks. The home screen glows. It's one.

I knock on Win's door and hear him shuffling inside before he calls out, "Come in!" I step into his office, a small space under some stairs that's lined with crammed bookshelves. A desk is buried under papers and several mugs in the middle of the room. "Ah, Layne! How is your second day going? I'm sorry I have not made an appearance today, I'm working on some paperwork." He waves his hand at the piles of sheets on the desk.

"Good, but I think I'm done?" I say. Maybe I shouldn't have interrupted him. Maybe I should've just kept working until he came out to relieve me.

His mouth pops open, and he looks at his watch. "That time already! How the day gets away from me! I'm coming out."

"Do you need me to stay?" my voice asks without my permission.

"No, no, you must be tired! It's quitting time for you. A lesson for life: work hard, but stop work at quitting time and leave the job behind." Somehow I don't think he follows his own advice. He comes to the door, and I back out to let him pass. He grabs his apron from his door and ties it on. "Hurry on, now, I'm sure you have somewhere better to be." I wonder if he'd be offended to know that my only "somewhere better to be" is my bed at home.

"Thank you," I say reflexively and put my bag over my shoulder.

"Good night!" he calls out after me, even though it's only midafternoon. I pull my phone from my bag and check the messages. Smiley faces from Sara, Zac asking if I want a ride home. Nothing from Asher. Relieved or disappointed? I don't know. I send a smiley back to Sara and assure Zac I'm fine to walk, turn on the music and try to get lost in it on my way home.

When I get home I head straight to the kitchen to find something to eat.

Sebastian's there sitting at the table, pecking away at a laptop. Of course. Why wouldn't he be here, alone, in the middle of the day?

"Hey, you're home," he says.

"Yup," I say from inside the fridge.

"How was work?"

"Fine," I say, taking the milk out and closing the fridge door. "Where's Zac? What are you doing here?"

He doesn't answer either question. Instead he says, "Layne," his voice low and even. I hear the click of his laptop closing. Apparently he means business.

"Yeah?" I open the cupboard and take out a tall orange glass. Pour the milk. By the way the silence behind me swells, I know he's glaring at me. I can feel his eyes boring a hole into my back. Somewhere in my mind I snicker at a mental image of the two of us in a standoff at the O.K. Corral. When I can't stand the quiet any longer, I turn around to glare back at him.

He's looking at me, but not glaring like I thought he would be. His eyes are open and soft, not frowning, and when my eyes meet his, he smiles. "You don't like me much," he says. It's not a question, not even an accusation. It's a statement made with a calm voice.

I take a moment to weigh my options.

WWNLD (What Would New Landers Do?)

1. Lie — "Of course I do, I'm just cranky. Always. It's not you, it's me, blah blah blah."
2. Avoid, abort, escape — "Do you hear a kitten crying? Maybe it's a baby?"
3. Tell the truth — "Nope," or maybe, "Hell no."

Number three it is.

"No I don't. Dad said you were trouble." I can actually see the words hit him; his encouraging smile falters. He blinks once slowly, as if he has to order his eyelids back up and his eyes to look at me.

"I know he did," he whispers. I expected relief and triumph when I dropped my charade and let him see I'm onto him. But all I feel is a tight clenching cold in my ribs.

"Layne, back off," Penny whispers, sitting at the table beside him. You've got to be kidding me.

I steel myself against the icky feeling dripping in my chest. I push my shoulders back and make my head tip up straight. "You're the reason Zac left."

Mission complete. He puts his hand to his face, rubs his eyes with his thumb and finger then pinches the top of his nose before looking back up at me with another smile. "You need to talk to him," he says. He stands up and takes a step forward and smiles at me again so that, for a moment, I get the weird feeling he's going to try to hug me. I can't back up, the counter's right behind me. I cross my arms. He shrugs. "Zac'll be back soon. Tell him I went home and I'll call him later," he says, then "Talk to him." He leaves the room.

All the air goes out with him.

chapter 22

I hear the front door open and close. His Mustang engine revs and fades out. I head to my room. It's empty. I put the glass of milk on my desk and sink into the desk chair, pick up Penny's guitar and fiddle with the strings. My stomach is spinning too much to drink the milk now. The encounter in the kitchen went so very different than the confrontation I had planned. I had hoped to find some incriminating evidence of his dubious activities and present the proof to him. He was supposed to act surprised at my cleverness and embarrassed at being caught red-handed. Maybe a little mad to be thwarted. But definitely not sad. And he wasn't supposed to say "talk to Zac." In fact, he was supposed to beg, "Please, don't tell Zac." Plead, even threaten. I was ready for all that. Not "talk to Zac" with a sad puppy dog face. Worst of all, my face-off with Sebastian was supposed to end with him leaving for good — on his own or with Zac's shoe print on his butt. Not with "I'll call him later." Trying to figure out where it all went wrong makes my thinking spin and twist and turn over so that I can't follow my own train of thought. Instant headache. I strum a couple of C-chords to drown out the sounds in my head.

My hand works up and down on the strings. The vibration moving from the strings through the pick, my fingers and up into my cast is soothing. As I slip further into the music, my left-hand fingers start to dance over the frets, and I stop thinking about the notes as they fall one after the other into melody.

"You should write a song," Penny says. I look up from the guitar. She's sitting on my bed. I smile at her, and she smiles back. I strum some twangy chords and sing:

"Alone I sit and write this song

I'm seeing things, I must be wrong

There's no way that you're here with me

Hallucination you must be."

"That's terrible," Penny says, but she's laughing. It's good to hear her laugh, even if it's not real.

I look down at the strings for a minute, and when I look back up she's gone. Only my twisted sheets and two pillows are on my bed — there isn't even a dent in the mattress where she was sitting. Hallucinations don't leave a trace you can see.

There's a noise from outside my room. I jump in my chair. Without the guitar and bad singing, I can hear Zac's voice. He's not really shouting, but that strange in-between volume of people trying hard not to yell and not quite succeeding. I go out into the hall. He's in his room. Zac's voice, then silence, then more angry voice. Back and forth. He must be on the phone. A fight, but I can't make out the words. With who? The turns are short. Zac's volume rises incrementally then falls to an even growl, only to rise up again. I stop by the door to try and hear more, but the words are lost and muffled. I feel a pang of guilt for listening in, but ...

Maybe my confrontation with Sebastian *did* work.

I wait for relief to seep into me and wash out the tight guilt in my chest, but it doesn't come. After one more shout, Zac falls silent.

I stand outside Zac's room and the silence grows thicker, like smoke from an undetected smouldering fire. I stand there paralyzed until the silence starts to soak into my lungs and suffocate me. Penny stands beside me, her face worried, eyes wide. I tip my head toward Zac's door, asking silently "should I knock?"

She shrugs. "He probably wants to be left alone," she whispers. I don't know why she's whispering; no one else can hear her. My hand reaches out and knocks on the door without my meaning to. "Zac? Who was that?" I say, just loud enough to get my voice through the door. No answer. "Zac?"

"Not now, Laynie," Zac says, his voice thick and low.

"Was it Aunt Carole?" I know it wasn't. But he'll correct me.

More silence, then I heard his feet shuffle to the door. It opens a crack, enough to see his face, angular and tight. "No. It was Sebastian."

He's the one who opened the door, but suddenly I feel like I'm the one who's too close, intruding. "I just ... are you okay?" I ask, resting my fingertips on his arm as if that might help show my intent.

He forces a smile and says, "I'm fine. Later, okay?"

I nod, but he's already shutting the door. I say, "Sure," as casually as I can manage. I tiptoe down the hall and close my door softly, though I don't need to; there's no one left to disturb.

I lie on the bed, trying to figure out where all the pieces went. Maybe he finally figured out what Sebastian was up to, realized Dad was right. Finally? Finally.

But I can't find happiness in me. Or relief. Or accomplishment. Just a cold shaft of guilt and regret that I don't understand. He's trouble. Maybe he's gone. How hard can that be to understand? But it doesn't feel right.

"Is he gone?" I ask Penny. There's no answer.

I text Sara: *I think he's gone.*

Sara: *Zac left again? OMG*

Me: *No, Sebastian. Big fight.*

Sara: *The drug dealer friend?*

Me: *Yeah.*

Sara: *Good.*

Me: *Yeah.*

But it doesn't feel good. I spend the rest of the afternoon restlessly pacing between my room and the kitchen, past Zac's closed door. I wait for it to crack open to pounce on him and make him realize how he's better off without a friend like that. I text with Sara, even send Asher a casual just-friends-like message. I watch New Landers, play the guitar and try to read Penny's book. I make frozen chicken strips and fries for supper and leave a plate covered in cling wrap in the fridge for Zac. I try to watch a movie, but I can't keep my eyes on the screen. Zac's door stays closed.

Finally, I shuffle off to my room and close my own door, change into my 's and crawl into bed. I pull the terrible book out from under my pillow and try to read the next page four times before I give up and fall asleep.

chapter 23

I don't know what woke me up, but I'm instantly wide awake, sitting upright in my bed. My ears buzz, stretching to hear what shook me alert. Shuffling, voices not much more than a whisper.

My thoughts start running: what if Sebastian came over to confront Zac? What if he's not alone, what if he brought others to ... my imagination breaks free, and in my mind the possibilities for Sebastian's retribution are endless. If he is dealing drugs, his friends are probably dangerous.

911?

I reach for my phone, but it's not on the bedside table. I texted Sara in the living room while I wasn't watching the movie. *Crap.* Left it there. I push the covers back and step out of bed, open my door a bit and peek out. The hall is empty and quiet, but at the end I can see movement, shadows shifting in the entryway. Someone's in the house. I have to warn Zac.

I creep down the hall slowly but steadily forward, intent on making it to Zac's door without the sources of the voices and shadows hearing me. I'll slip into his room and wake him up. We can use his phone to call the police. I won't let him go out to deal with it himself. I can't risk it.

I get to Zac's door, put my hand on the knob —

Wait ...

That's *his* voice. Zac's. Not through his door, from inside his room, but at the end of the hall. A word or two whispered, then silence. Could they have already gotten to him? I stop to listen, but there's nothing more. I sneak down the hall and look around the corner careful to stay out of sight as much as possible.

There's no gang of drug-dealing thugs.

There *is* Sebastian. And Zac.

Zac's back is to me. Sebastian's hands are up on Zac's jaw, his fingers curled around the sides of his head so that Zac's bed-head hair sticks out in tufts between each one. They're not fighting. They're kissing.

I gasp, turn and run back to my room, but I can hear them talking again, not in whispers but in soft, anxious voices. "Laynie?" Zac calls after me just before I close my bedroom door. Through the door I hear his footsteps come quickly down the hall, more muffled whispers between him and Sebastian and finally a knock. "Layne, can I come in?"

I don't answer. He opens the door anyway.

His hair is messed and his eyes green, red-rimmed and swollen.

FLASHBACK: *The hospital, waking up to find Zac sitting by my bed.*

He looks the same. He steps in and sinks into my desk chair, smooths his hair back with both hands and weaves his fingers, clasped together in front of his mouth, elbows on his knees. "So ..." he says, studying me.

"So?" I echo. Was this why he ran away? To keep this a secret? But why? We stare at each other for a minute, and I try to read his mind. His eyes are flitting over my face; he's probably trying to do the same. The silence is a tangible barrier between us, pushing against me. Questions stack one on the other in the silence like bricks building a wall, up and up and up closing him from me. "Is that why you left? Why the secret?" I ask finally, hoping to keep a window open in the wall forming between us.

He slumps back into the chair, presses his hands against his mouth as if he's trying to keep his words in. "I never wanted it ... me ... to be secret," he says finally. His eyes are steady on me. Almost pleading. The last of my anger drips away.

"So why didn't you tell us? Did you think we'd care? You just took off!" My voice breaks at the end, and he blinks as if I'd slapped him.

He doesn't move for a moment, just looks at me, then his eyes shift and he looks past me, through me, as if seeing something or someone else in the room. Penny? Can he see her? I look over my shoulder, expecting to see her sitting on her bed, but she's not there. "I told Dad. That night ..." I can barely hear him. "I didn't think he would ... But when I told him ..." I see the living room as it looked that night I came home with Penny. The smashed guitar. The tight set to my father's jaw, challenging me to ask something, anything, after he said "Zac left."

"You told Dad? He knew?"

"Yeah. The night he ... I mean the night I left, I told him and he, he freaked out."

"Well, I'm sure he just was surprised." Zac starts shaking his head, so I keep talking to keep him from arguing. "You didn't stick around to work it out. You just ran away and —"

"Christ, Layne, stop being so naive!" His curse shocks me silent. I blink back sudden unbidden tears. "He kicked me out," he says softly, as if the words hurt to push out. He spoke so quiet, I must have misheard him.

"What?"

"He kicked me out." This time louder. More sure.

"No," I whisper above the roaring in my ears.

"Yes," Zac says in a soothing voice, as if he's speaking to a frightened child.

No. There's no way our father would do that.

FLASHBACK: *Dad watching us the first time we got through the Beatles' "Yesterday" without mistakes, pride wetting his eyes.*

FLASHBACK: *Dad and Zac chirping at each other in the driveway, shooting hoops. They came in for a drink, sweaty and laughing, Dad's arm around Zac's shoulders.*

FLASHBACK: *Dad standing at the fence on the ball field cheering. He yelled "good eye!" for the ball, "nice swing!" for a swing and miss. "Next time!" for the eventual strike out.*

FLASHBACK: *Dad sitting at the dinner table drilling us in turn about school: "What was funny today?" "What was interesting today?" "What was frustrating today?" "How'd that math test go?" "Did you finish reading your novel?"*

FLASHBACK: *Dad sitting on my bed, rubbing my knee as I sat and cried over some reprimand I can't remember now. "I'm disappointed in you, Laynie, but I still love you so much."*

I squeeze my eyes shut against Zac's words.

FLASHBACK after FLASHBACK after FLASHBACK: Dad laughing with us, watching us, cheering for us, touching our heads, our hands, giving us hugs and praise and encouragement ... and love. Each image blazes on my eyelids as if my brain is presenting a slide show of proof against what Zac just said.

"No," I say again and then "NO" more loudly.

"Yes," Zac says softly.

I shake my head, but he keeps talking. "He did, Layne. I told him about, about me and about Sebastian, and at first he was really quiet for a moment, and he smiled. He *smiled*. I thought it was going to be fine, but then his face changed and ... and his voice — it was something I'd never heard before." Zac stops, swallows and blinks and presses his hands against his head as if trying to keep something from coming out. "I — I won't tell you the details, I've tried hard to leave it, to forget the yelling, forget everything he said about sin and God and ... and he gave me a choice, so I guess it really was me who left but ... it wasn't a choice I could make, Laynie." I hear him breathe loudly in and out and in and out. In and out.

I keep shaking my head, as if the gesture is enough to ward off his words.

"He kicked me out," Zac says, his voice steady. "And we didn't talk, for a long time. Then a few weeks ago, he called. We talked for a bit and he — he was trying. But by then ... I just, I didn't want you to know. I mean, I wanted to tell you the truth about me and Sebastian, but I didn't want you to know all of it. About Dad. And there was no way to tell you half of the truth."

Of course.

His words start to fall out of him faster and faster, as if he's rushing through a plea to be heard before I can form judgement. "And maybe that's just an excuse. I mean, I hoped you'd be okay with it, but if I'm honest, I guess I was, I don't know, gun-shy? I mean, I never expected Dad to react that way. And you're all I have left. You and Sebastian." The last words are spoken on a whisper as he runs out of air. He looks at me for a moment and winces. "In the past six months I've learned having Sebastian is not enough."

"He's trouble." I didn't mean to say it. Really. I need the argument, and the proof to back it up. But once it's out there, I might as well keep going.

"Laynie, he —"

"No, Zac, listen. Dad *knew* he was trouble. Don't you see? That's why he acted like that. It wasn't about you at all. Like where does he get all his money? I mean, he shows up here all times of day. He doesn't work, and yet he has that car and all that cash all the time? How does he get it? I've been thinking about it, and I think he's actually dealing drugs or something. He's trouble, Zac, Dad knew, he knew —"

"Layne!"

"Zac, I'm sure that was it. You must have misunderstood. Dad knew there was something wrong. He didn't care that you're gay, why would he? He just didn't want you getting involved in Sebastian's life — into drugs and stuff. And you must have misund —" Zac stands up and closes the distance between us in two wide steps. His hands come down heavy on my shoulders, his long fingers pinching the hollows under my collarbones. A shake. My jaw clacks together. I swing my arms up between his, pushing him off me and standing up in one forward shove.

He looks at me, his eyes wild and open wide. Then he rubs his face with his palms and falls back into the chair with his head in his hands, elbows on his knees. I sink back onto the bed. He starts talking, words dripping out of his mouth toward the floor. I close my eyes but can't block out what he's saying. Sebastian isn't involved in drugs or anything else illegal. He makes his money producing webcasts. He has a website that spoofs on advice columns. He reads and choses the letters, writes the scripts, hires the actors. It started off small but took off, millions of views and thousands of dollars in advertising.

"Oh," I whisper. Not a drug dealer. I was wrong about … everything.

Silence then. Outside my brain, at least. Inside my mind buzzes.

I open my eyes, and my father is in front of me, an image standing strong and smiling. And he starts to crumble bit by bit, like a sandcastle we might've made together on the beach. Slowly at first, the top of his head ,his face and shoulders collapse, trickle down, faster and faster he gives way, crumpling inward on himself until a shadow stands in his place.

A shadow I don't know. Really, never knew.

"What about Mom?" I whisper, terrified of the answer. Is she going to be taken from me again, too? Not by a drunk in a truck, though, but by words and anger. Their words. Their hateful anger.

Zac drops his hands and looks up at me to offer a small, sad smile. "I think she tried," he says with a shrug. "She called me a lot. And I think it was her that finally convinced Dad to call, to start talking to me again. But she was worried about you and Penny, and she wanted me to wait to tell you anything. She didn't want you to know about Dad and our fight. She said it would work out, and everything would be fine, and you'd never have to know what really happened."

"I thought you left," I whisper, more to myself than to him. All those months I thought he had chosen to be gone, choosing some no-good friends over family. Them over us. Over me. It wasn't *his* choice at all.

He smiles, just a small one. "I didn't want to." He sits up straight in the chair again, brushes his sweatpants flat with the palms of his hands. "I agreed to give Mom her time but then … we ran out. And I didn't want you to know what Dad said, because he's not here to … I knew I had to tell you and I tried, but it felt wrong. Every time."

"So Mom's no better. She let you leave, let him kick you out. Let us think all along that you were the one —"

"Laynie, stop. I was so angry. So angry at both of them but … they were trying. They really were. Dad was working through it. I mean, think about it — everything he was ever taught! He really was trying to figure out how to accept it, accept me. We were talking again. And really, what good does it do to be angry now? They're gone."

They're gone, alright. They were never here to begin with — not how I knew them at least. "And Sebastian ..." I say. I've treated him terribly. My face flushes warm, and my stomach churns, cold and sharp.

"Of course Dad blamed him, at first." Zac's voice has an edge of resentment. "But that was changing too. Dad met us for lunch the week before the accident. He even managed to argue with Bas about baseball." Zac's light laugh dissolved into a sigh. "Actually, Sebastian's the reason I've gotten through everything, leaving home and then when the accident happened ... I know I shouldn't have brought him here without the full explanation, but I convinced myself it'd be worth it because you'd eventually realize he's a good guy." He looks at me, his eyes pleading. "I need you to know that."

"Now I know," I say. But know what? I know the truth. And I know he needs me to be okay with it. With all of it. My head feels like it might explode.

"Now you know," Zac says with a soft, genuine smile. "So ..."

"So," I echo. Our conversation has spun right back to the beginning. I'm dizzy. We sit in silence, and as the moments slip away the tension ebbs.

Finally, Zac stands. "It's late." He reaches out to me as he passes the bed. I reach up and brush the tips of my fingers against his. "We'll talk more tomorrow?" I nod, and he steps out the door and closes it behind him. Murmured voices slip under my door, but instead of threatening they're reassuring. Safe. My thoughts are spinning so fast, I'll never sleep.

chapter 24

I wake up slowly, rising gradually from a strange dream about a castle maze to the sound of rain hitting the roof. Time? I reach blindly for my phone on the bedside table. Not there? Oh right, I left it in the living room. And then it all comes back: the frightening awareness of voices in the house, my silent sneak down the hall and discovery of Zac's secret. Our talk. The truth.

And by truth I mean the whole truth — about Zac, about Sebastian. About Dad. He loved and supported and cheered unconditionally — how could he …

FLASHBACK: *Dad with his set jaw and with his angry eyes, his frown tight with disparaging disappointment when I asked about Zac. "He made his choice," he said.*

"You didn't give him a choice," I snap and knead my eyes viciously with my knuckles to rub out the image.

I sit up and see Penny sitting at her desk, hunched over, writing something. "Did you know?" I ask her. "How could he?"

"I don't know," Penny says.

"How do you not know?" I barely keep my voice under a shout. What good is it having access to my sister from the other side of death if she doesn't come with answers?

I throw the covers off, go to my cleared space of floor and let myself down roughly. With a deep breath I push my body up into a plank and concentrate on breathing in and out instead of holding my breath locked in my lungs and counting fifty-two Mississippis. Fifty-two seconds. I lie on the floor for a moment, willing my heart to stop racing then push back up again. Sixty seconds. A minute. A new benchmark. Again. Fifty-seven. Again. Forty-three. Again. Twenty-two Mississippis and I collapse on the rug. My arms ache, my shoulders are throbbing. My face is wet with sweat and tears, and I think maybe I'll never get up.

But I do get up and pad into the bathroom, turn the shower on hot and stand in front of the mirror watching the steam fog it up as the water runs. The edges and shapes of my flushed face blur with the condensation, the details that make me *me* grow foggy in the droplets, blending into shapes and colours until there's no human face there, just blotches of colours that match my face, my hair, my T-shirt. I raise my hand and press my palm against the cool wet glass. A couple of drops collect by my thumb and traipse down the mirror, increasing in size and speed and leaving jagged trails. I wipe my hand across the mirror over my reflection, and for a moment the cloud is gone. I can see all the details of my face — my swollen eyes, each freckle and the faint scar on my chin that nobody else notices. If only it were that easy to make things clear again.

After my shower I dress in yoga pants and a T-shirt. I tiptoe down the hall to the kitchen in an effort not to wake Zac and Sebastian. I didn't need to bother, because they're sitting in the kitchen eating eggs and holding hands. I sigh as loudly as I can and say, "Can we keep the kitchen a PDA-free zone?" They look up, and I make a performance of rolling my eyes.

"She lives!" Zac bellows in his scary voice.

I flash him a single-finger salute and check the frying pan for more eggs. Empty.

"I'll make you some more," Sebastian says, shifting to stand up.

"No, it's fine," I say then wince at my habitually sharp response. I'll have to work on that. I turn and smile, hoping it doesn't look as forced as it feels. "Really, I'd rather have cereal anyway."

"You sure?" Sebastian asks, but he sits back down at least.

"Yup," I say with extra sunshine and shake the box of Cheerios. I'll really work on it.

"Hey," Zac says, and I turn from pouring the cereal into a bowl to see him pointing at the counter. "I plugged in your phone."

"Thanks."

"Lots of texts," he says through a mouthful of eggs. I bring my cereal to the table and sit down across from the lovebirds. Pour the milk. "What's with Asher texting you a bazillion times?" Zac asks.

I glare at him. "Don't read my phone!"

He puts his hands up, palms forward in surrender, and laughs. "Whoa there! I didn't. It was beeping like crazy — that's how I found it in the couch. In the time it took to plug it in, three texts came through."

Priority number one: make sure my body and face and voice don't give away how desperately I want to go to the phone and read all the texts right away.

Priority number two: re-establish my expectation of privacy.

"And then you read them," I say. Just because he gave up his big secret doesn't mean he has the right to go snooping in my private life.

"Not really," he says with a shrug. "I'm just curious. Are you two …?"

"He's just a friend," I mutter and know it's the wrong thing to say as soon as the words are out. Isn't that what everyone says?

He nods at me, his eyebrows all pulled up, smirking. "Bas and I are going to the market downtown, do you want to come?"

As fine as I am with my new understanding of their relationship, I don't particularly want to spend the morning as a third wheel watching them canoodle at the market. And while I know in my head that my previous resentment and loathing for Sebastian was unjustified, it's not like it's attached to a switch I can flick to "off." I'm not up for a prolonged period of being nice. "No, thanks," I say. "I've got plans with Sara." Which will be true eventually, because I have plans to *make* plans with Sara.

"Alright, I'll bring you back something." Zac clears his dish and Sebastian's and rinses them in the sink.

"Zac, five minutes then?" Sebastian says.

"Yeah, that's good with me." He smiles. I watch him watch Sebastian leave the room. His eyes are soft, and he's somehow far away. He looks like Dad.

FLASHBACK: *Mom laughed and left the room. Dad watched her go, his eyes dreamy and his smile relaxed, before he turned back to me and said, "Sorry, did you say something?"*

My throat is tight with guilt for having gotten everything so wrong. Once Sebastian is out of the room, Zac turns to me, his smile gone as well. "Hey," he says gently. "You okay? Want me to stay home?"

Okay? This must be a new low benchmark for okay. I shake my head a little too eagerly, a little too quickly. "I'm fine, I'm fine," I say, trying to convince him. My phone beeps, thanks to some mystic power of the universe that knows I need backup. "That's probably Sara!" Again a little too eager.

"Or Asher again," he says and laughs when I hit him on the arm. He studies me a moment longer before he says, "Alright, but if you change your mind, call me." He puts the dishes in the dishwasher and washes his hands then dries them on his pants. "Promise?"

I nod and smile to prove I'm fine. He leaves the kitchen, yelling out to Sebastian about which car they're going to take. I blink back tears and reach for my phone.

Eight texts from last night:

Asher: *Hey L.*

Asher: *U there?*

Asher: *Can we talk?*

Sara: *This movie is so boring! Lame.*

Asher: *Want 2 do s'thing tmrw?*

Asher: *Sk8 park? Ha ha.*

Asher: *Sry. 2 soon.*

Sara: *Cant sleep. U up?*

Asher: *Im good w wtv. But lets talk, k?*

And five from this morning:

Asher: *GM. U up?*

Sara: *Wanna go to the mall?*

Asher: *U awake yet? Txt me.*

Asher: *Creepy me again. Sry. Got2 wrk til 3. Will txt l8er.*

Sara: *I'm coming 2 wake U up.*

And literally as I'm reading that, the doorbell rings. I hurry to open the door and let Sara in from the rain.

"Phew, it's wet out there!" she says, slipping out of her jacket and hanging it on the hook on the wall. I never understood why people say that, it's the most useless observation.

"I just got your text," I say over my shoulder as we head to the kitchen. "I was going to call you."

"Sure you were," she says with a laugh.

"Want some breakfast?"

She shakes her head. "No, I already ate. I saw this sweet shirt at the mall last week, but I didn't have enough. Got paid yesterday, and I want to see if it's still —" She stops talking and looks at me. I feel my face heat under her scrutinizing look. "What happened?"

I feel my control slip away. My eyes fill with tears, and I cover my face with my hands, trying to hold the sobs in, press them back down. A chair scrapes across the floor, and Sara's arms tighten around my shoulders. "What is it?" she whispers.

Through halting speech and gasps I ramble off the events of the previous night, from waking in fear of the voices to racing back to my room after discovering Zac and Sebastian and their kiss.

"Kissing?" she asks when I get to that part. I nod. "Oooh," she says with a face full of sudden realization.

"What?" I ask.

"It's just something Abby said. She was moping about, and I said something dumb about her calling Zac, and she told me to stop, that it was never going to work out, and I didn't know anything. She was so defensive, I didn't get it. Now I get it." I take a deep breath, rub my stinging eyes. "So Zac's not just friends with this drug dealer, he's actually *with* him."

"He's not a drug dealer."

Sara frowns. "So what does he do then? You said he doesn't work. Is his family rich or something?"

I sigh. Processing everything last night was exhausting, but explaining it to Sara is somehow more gruelling. I feel like puking and push the cereal bowl away from me. "New Landers," I say. "He's the head guy of it. Owner? Producer? I don't know what his title is, but he came up with it and writes the sketches. Zac said he makes good money on the advertising." I watch her face. It's like slow motion as each muscle twitches to let her jaw fall open and her eyes widen.

"No."

"Yeah."

"So he's *not* a drug dealer, and he's rich and successful. How could your dad think he's trouble?"

Wasn't that the question of the day? I tear up again, swallow the lump in my throat and stumble through a brief summary of the rest of my conversation with Zac.

She whispers, "They kicked him out?"

"Apparently," I say. My throat hurts from being tight. "Well, at least my father did. Zac said Mom tried to help but ..." How do you justify any "but" in that situation? Sara nods, and I don't have to finish. "Zac said he and Dad were working it out, but then ..." She nods again.

"Brutal," Sara mumbles. "I never would have thought *your* dad would be ..."

Be what? So many words have tumbled through my mind since Zac's revelations: stupid, homophobic, hypocritical, backward, prejudiced, dishonest, hateful, judgemental, evangelical, fanatical, extreme. None of them fit my father as I knew him, and yet the truth is there in a list of angry words. And no matter what labels surface, the one that keeps coming back is "sad."

We sit in dejected silence. I fiddle with the string of my hoodie, then with the folded edges of Penny's ToDah! list in my pocket. I steal glances at Sara, who sits studying her hands. It seems neither of us feels comfortable changing the subject. *Well that's a bummer, let's go to the mall* seems somewhat inappropriate. Sara says softly, "I'm sorry." I shake my head against that word again. She's not the one who needs to apologize. It's too late for that.

I blink fast and take a deep breath, determined not to cry again. I force a smile and say, "Anyways. Topic change, please."

Sara's smile isn't forced. "Did Asher text you?"

By the way she asks, I know she knew he has. I consider lying for a moment; what will she say if I deny the collection of messages I just found? But I'm spent from crying. "Yeah."

She looks at me just long enough for my cheeks to burn a bit. "He texted me and asked if you were okay. Said you'd had fun the other night, but you haven't said much to him since. And he said he went by the store yesterday …" My stomach twists a bit in guilt. Everything seems screwed up.

I want to explain to Sara how great it felt being with Asher and how awful it felt stealing Penny's crush. But that makes no sense, because Penny is gone, even though she's sitting at the kitchen table with us. I steal a glance her way, quick enough that Sara won't notice, and she makes a face that says *yeah, can't help you with that*. "I've just been busy," I say, knowing how lame it sounds. "I didn't reply to your texts either." That sounds better and comes out with more of a take-that confidence. "I left my phone in the living room last night, anyway, and it died. Didn't see any of them until just now."

She frowns like she doesn't believe me. Probably because she doesn't. "You should text him back," she says simply. I nod. Agreeing is easier than arguing or explaining or convincing.

My head hurts. My eyes hurt. I want to go back to bed. "You can't," Penny says. "Sara's here. Go out and do something." I want to argue with her, but Sara's studying me again.

"Let's do something," Sara says.

I wince. "I think I may just go back to bed." Penny glares at me. What does she know? She's not here trying to figure everything out.

"Laynie, let's go out, get out of the house. You'll feel better." I doubt it. But Penny is nodding at what Sara just said, and I feel outnumbered. Agreeing is easier than arguing or explaining or convincing. "Let's go to the mall. I got my first paycheque from Dexter's. We can get ice cream." She smiles. "The Layne I know never says no to ice cream."

I think the Layne she knew is gone, along with everyone else. But again it's easier to agree. "Okay," I say, defeated.

I shuffle down the hall to my room. Empty. Once inside I pull my phone from my pocket and scan Asher's texts. The truth hurts. Zac's truth hurt Dad. Dad's truth hurt him, hurt me. But keeping a secret lets it fester. If I'd known what really happened, what could I have said? What could I have done?

No more secrets. If this has shown me anything, it's the necessity of being honest and straightforward. I owe it to Asher to tell him the truth: as much as I may like him, there's no way I can steal him from my hallucination of a sister. We need to talk. I hit reply and thumb out a message, Yes, let's talk. What time? I take a deep breath and touch "send."

I'm pulling on my shoes when my phone beeps with a text-reply from Asher: *Pick u up at 6*? I type *yes* and a happy face and hope it isn't flirty.

chapter 25

I'm ready to leave by five thirty and wander into the kitchen to find a snack while I wait for Asher. I steal a couple of cookies from a crumpled bag in the pantry and sit at the table. I shouldn't eat them; I'm not hungry. Nerves. Nerves make me munchie. I eat the cookies, but they don't help. My palms are still clammy and my ears are buzzing.

"Why so nervous?" Penny asks from across the table.

"I don't know what to say, how to tell him."

"Just tell him the truth," she says, and it sounds so simple.

I flinch. "Yeah. Just like that."

"Just like what?" Zac says from the door, where he and Sebastian are standing, looking quizzically at me. Penny laughs. I shake my head at him and mutter something incoherent. The doorbell rings and saves me. I jump up, knocking the chair over behind me. Zac blocks the door and looks down at me with studious eyes. "I wonder who it is that drives my sister to such animated behaviour?"

"Let me past, jerk!" I try to sound angry.

"You should go see, Zac. Out of custodial duty, and all." I train my death stare on Sebastian as he walks past me to the fridge.

"Yes, I think I will," Zac says while I'm looking away, and so he's two steps ahead of me to the door. I catch up to him as he swings the door open. "Oh, it's you."

"Um, yeah. It's me," I hear Asher say. "Is Layne here?"

"Yes, I'm here." I push past Zac, elbowing him in the gut as I go by. "Please ignore my stupid brother." Asher looks from one to the other of us, his eyes round. "Let's go," I say, grabbing his sleeve as I walk past and tugging him away from the door.

"Eight thirty curfew!" Zac shouts after us. I ignore him.

In his car Asher puts on his seat belt and turns the engine on before asking, "What was that about?"

I shake my head and try to squelch the smile pulling at the corners of my mouth. "I dunno, he was just being dumb."

"You look great," he says earnestly. I look down at the casual jeans and T-shirt I'd chosen specifically not to send mixed messages. This is not a date. I didn't mean to look "great."

"Um, thanks," I say and laugh in spite of myself. A familiar fluttery tugging starts to shift in my middle. I press my hand against my belly to stifle it and remind myself it is not a date. He pulls away from the curb, and I stare straight out of the windshield, gathering courage.

"I need to tell you something."

We both say it at the same time. Then we laugh. His seems to be natural, but mine is tight and nervous and painful in my throat. "You first," he says.

No more secrets. Tell the truth. And if I don't speak up now, I'll lose my nerve. All my built up courage will dissipate and leave me speechless, or worse, blubbering nonsense. I jump into the middle of the story from where there'll be no turning back. "Penny likes — liked you."

He looks like it was the last thing he expected to hear. "O-kaaaaaay," he says slowly.

"No, I mean *liked* you, liked you. She wanted to … I mean, she left this list. Not for me, for her, but I found it and it was all the stuff she wanted to do this summer and on it she wrote that she wanted to go out with you." I run out of breath, inhale deeply and hold it, waiting to see what he'll say.

"Is she here? Now?" he asks, and I'm not sure if it's a joke or not. I check the back seat and shake my head. "I mean, I liked Penny and everything, she was a nice girl, but she was not really my type." We pull up to a stoplight, and he stares straight ahead.

His rejection of Penny cuts through to the fluttering winged creatures in my middle and slays them all in one swipe. "Not your type? Not your *type*? Why do guys say that? What does that even mean?" My voice is high-pitched, squeaky and breaking.

"Whoa, Layne, I mean —"

"No, I get it. Not your type. By that I suspect you mean she was too smart? Or maybe too classy? Too funny? Talented? Or how about too mature? That must be it."

"Layne, I never said —"

"Never mind. That's all I had to tell you. I mean, I thought maybe I had to tell you that I couldn't betray her by dating the guy she liked, even though maybe *I* liked you too, but now I realize now that *you're* not *my* type. That's closer to the truth." The light turns green, and he lurches forward, wheels squealing. I sneak a glance and see his jaw muscles working under the skin. His eyes are still focused out front. His stony silence makes my chest hurt.

"Maybe I should just take you home," he says evenly.

It's a good plan, since I think I'm going to throw up. Puking in his car is pretty much the only way this situation could get worse. "Fine," I say and glare out the window. He takes a couple of sharp rights to lead us back the way we came. We ride in hostile silence. My face is burning and my stomach is twisted. My eyes sting.

When we pull into my driveway, my hand is already clenched around the handle of the car. I push the door open even before he comes to a full stop. "Layne," he says beside me, low and even. I stop with one foot on the ground but don't turn around. "I liked Penny. She was quiet, but always nice to me. I know she was smart and funny, but it was always *you* I was interested in. That's all I meant to say."

I swallow hard and push the door farther out. Stepping out, I close it behind me. I watch him back out without looking up at me and speed off down the road a little too fast. "Smooth," Penny says from beside me, where she's suddenly appeared.

"Shut up," I say and walk past her, knowing there's no way I can leave her behind.

I needn't have worried about how to ward off questions from Zac. Once inside, I barely reach the bathroom in time to aim my retching at the toilet. He knocks lightly and asks, "Layne? You okay? Need anything?"

FLASHBACK: *Mom rested one hand on my forehead and handed me a glass of ginger ale with the other. "This'll help," she said gently. She knew what worked.*

I need my mom.

I wipe my mouth and manage to say, "I'm sick. I'm just going to go to bed."

"Sounds like a good idea," he says. "Let me know if you need anything." He seems to hover there for a moment before I hear his footsteps go back down the hall to the living room. I sneak out and hurry to my room, change into sweats and an old T-shirt and climb into bed. Thoughts are hammering around inside my head. Pictures and words and sounds that won't join into comprehensible ideas but ricochet against each other: pickup truck, broken guitar, hateful slurs, the ToDah! list, Win Forsythe, incoherent shouts and whispers, skateboards, butterflies and

Penny. Penny is always there. I reach for the book on my bedside table. I scan the page with the dog-eared corner, but none of it is familiar. I clench my teeth in painful frustration and flip the pages all the way back to the beginning: *Many stories do not start in the dark of a stormy night ...*

chapter 26

I read until the thoughts quiet in my mind. I read through the muted voices in my head and the blaring ones coming from the TV in the living room. I read through the burning in my eyes. And by three in the morning I turn the last page of the book and close it. I press the book between my two palms. "How did it end?" Penny asks from her bed, where she's curled up on top of the covers.

"The ending was sad," I whisper, lying back on my side to face her. My body mirrors hers in position, my right hand tucked under my chin, my legs pulled up to my middle.

"Yeah, I thought it might be," she says.

"The girl —"

"Ellory?"

"Yeah, Ellory. She moved to New York, even though her family wanted her to stay and take over the job as the caretaker of the forest."

"That's not so sad then."

"But she left everyone behind. And everything. Everything he'd done and worked for, she just let it go to go off and figure out her own dreams."

Penny smiles at me. A soft, gentle smile that Mom used when we were being unreasonable. "Sounds like a plan. You should try it."

I push myself up onto my elbow. "What? So you're saying I should just take off? Move away?" Right. That's an excellent plan. I'm sure I can convince Zac I'm capable. I'll just tell him Penny said so.

She matches my movement, turns and pushes up to face me. Her smile grows and she shakes her head. "No, of course not. I just think you should write your own list," she says.

"I don't need a list," I say.

"You do," she says. "You have to figure out what you need, what you want. Not what I want or Zac or even Mom and Dad. You need to let go of before and figure out now. A list will help with that."

"I don't need a list," I say again, tears pricking at my eyes, catching in my throat. I don't need a list; I have hers. I have her. "I need you," I whisper.

"You'll always have me. I'm part of you now. But you need to keep going. Make your own list, move on. It's time to let go."

She smiles a happy, relaxed, confident smile, wiggles her fingers in a small wave and whispers, "Goodbye, Laynie." And then … she's gone. She didn't vanish slowly, like ghosts do in the movies, sparkling or shimmering or growing more and more transparent until all you can see is their floating eyes. She went all at once: she was there smiling at me and the next breath I'm alone in my dark room.

"Penny?" I whisper, then say again as loudly as I dare, "Penny?" No answer, of course, and no reappearance. There's an emptiness in the room, in me. And I know as sure as I knew she was there that she's not anymore. That's it. She's said what she stuck around to say. She's gone. Gone. They're all gone. I roll onto my back and stare at the ceiling. Tears slip down, cold, into my ears. Across the ceiling, the shadows shimmy. I search the shapes for her hair, her profile, her legs, feet, hands, eyes, but they're just black blotches and blobs, not meaningful images. I turn, bury my face in my pillow and cry.

I lie still, spent. My stomach is hollow — empty — and growls in protest. I push myself up and tiptoe to the kitchen, make a sandwich and sit at the table, reluctant to go back to my empty room. The house is quiet. Too quiet. I want to scream and fill it with sound, fight back against the silence. I don't.

I hear Sebastian's footsteps a moment before he walks into the kitchen.

"Hi," he says, opening the fridge and taking out a bottle of beer. Dad's beer. No it's not. The label is blue instead of red.

"Hi," I say back. My ears feel warm. My mind is blank. For the life of me I can't figure out what to say next.

But he speaks first. "Can't sleep?" I shake my head. "Me either. My mind won't shut off." I know how that feels. He spins the bottle on its base. "You okay?"

Zac's words sound strange echoed in Sebastian's voice. "I don't know," I say, and mean it. Then on an impulse I add, "How about you?"

He smiles, and it's nice not to feel any hostility building. "I'm great, actually. Really great." He brings his beer over to the table and sits down across from me. "I want to say I'm sorry."

"For what?" Only hours ago, all I wanted was for him to acknowledge his evil ways and get lost. Now his apology confuses me. With everything that has happened and everyone involved in this mess, he seems like the last person who needs to apologize. Of course, the first person on the list is not able. And if we're making a list, I'm probably somewhere near the top.

"There's lots I'm sorry for. For splintering your family, for pulling Zac away, for showing up here and not explaining why, for being in your space, for how you found out about us. All of that and probably more."

I start shaking my head before he's finished talking. "No, I know now. You didn't pull Zac away. My father, my parents —" My voice cracks, and I stop talking. Hostility might be waning, but my guard isn't lowered enough to lose it in front of someone who was the enemy a day ago.

He nods. "I know. I know what it feels like to realize someone is different than you thought." There's a flicker of remembrance in his eyes before he blinks quickly. "You'll find a way to work through it and figure out again who they really were."

"I'm not sure I want to." One tear betrays me, slips out of my eye and trickles down my cheek. I swat it away.

"You will. He's still your dad. They're still your parents. They loved you. They loved Zac too." He studies me a moment, as if trying to decide what else to say. I'm biting the inside of my cheek, trying not to cry. "You'll figure it out. Sometimes it takes a while," he says finally. Maybe forever.

"I'm sorry I've been so horrible," I manage to say, my voice gravely and unsteady.

"You? Horrible? Nah." He laughs, a low relaxed sound. "Is this a truce?"

I nod, blinking furiously. It's like some helium balloons have lifted the weights off my shoulders, then keep on lifting until my back is pulled up straight and my lungs are full. "Truce," I say. We even shake on it; he curls his long fingers around mine sticking out of my cast.

And that's when Zac walks in, his eyes bleary and half closed. He stops and stares at our clasped hands, and a smile creeps across his face and up into his eyes. It might be the best smile I've ever seen.

"Told you I'd win her over," Sebastian says with a cocky head tilt. I take my hand back and swat his shoulder with it.

"Laynie, you feeling okay?" Zac asks. I'd like to know what this "okay" is that everyone talks about.

My eyes sting and my face feels puffy when I smile. "Maybe someday," I say with a hoarse voice. He nods. He gets it. "For now, I need to sleep." I stand up and turn to Sebastian. "Thanks," I say, and he winks at me. I slip past Zac and head back to my room.

Still empty.

I climb into bed and pull the covers up to my chin. "Write your own list" echoes in my mind. It's in her voice, but in my head; she's not here in the room anymore.

I reach for Penny's folded ToDah! list on the bedside table and find a pen in the drawer. I open her sheet of paper and smooth it over the cover of the yellow and black book. Penny's list takes up the first third of the page. I leave three lines and then write "Layne's ToDah!" underneath.

Layne's ToDah!

1. Finish reading a whole book.
2. Get a job.
3. Do 5 minutes of plank and run 5km in under 40 mins.
4. Make things right with Sebastian.
5. Write a song.
6. Fix it with AP.

I add small checkmarks beside number one and two and hover my pen over number four before leaving it unchecked. There's still work to do. Numbers three and five are works in progress as well, but there's lots of summer left. Number six? I'd better start on that soon. No time like the present. I pick up my phone and text Asher. My hands shake so that I have to backspace four times over the short message to get it right: *Sry 4 freaking out.* I feel better once it's sent and hope he won't ignore it in the morning, but I'm not expecting a reply to come immediately. *Im sry 2. I picked dumb words 2 say.* I send a smile back.

Me: *I didn't know she liked u.*

Asher: *Me either.*

Me: *But its 2 weird. I just cant.*

Asher: *I know. Its ok.*

I send another smile, and he sends some weird face that I think is supposed to be sleeping. *G'night,* I text and hold the phone a minute. Nothing comes. I put it aside and study the list again. My hand shakes, and my fingers pinch the pen painfully tight.

7. Forgive.

Some will be easier to check off than others. Maybe it's not just a Summer ToDah! list after all. I wiggle down into the bed and slip our lists under my pillow. Penny's bed is empty. The leaf shadows on the ceiling sway, and I watch them as I fall asleep, but they're just black shapes.

chapter 27

I wake up to a knock at my door and then Zac's voice. "Laynie? Layne? Shouldn't you be up?" he says from the doorway.

I sit up and rub my eyes, trying to figure out what day it is. "What time is it?"

"It's eight thirty. Didn't you say you're working at nine? Are you feeling okay to go?"

Working? Nine? I shake my head to try and clear the fog that's between me and comprehension of the who and where and what of right now. Next shift, Thursday at nine in the morning. Today. "Shit!" I say and vault out of bed.

Zac laughs. "Get ready, I can drive you."

It's the fastest shower ever. I get dressed and tie my wet hair back, kick on my shoes and arrive in the hall in less than fifteen minutes. "Can we go?" I ask Zac, who's standing in the kitchen with Sebastian.

"Yeah, let's go," he says and turns to peck a quick kiss on Sebastian's mouth.

"Gross!" I say. Sebastian winks at me, and I smile and then smile bigger when I realize it's a real one. "Come ON!" I say for good measure.

I arrive at Coffee Quotes three minutes after my start time, cursing the bell over the door that announces my arrival when I had hoped to slip in quietly and not draw attention to my late arrival.

"Don't worry, Win stepped out for a bit," Zander says from behind the counter. "He'll never know."

"Never know what?" I say with a wink, thanking my lucky stars my shift partner is him and not Tracy. I walk behind the counter and stash my bag, slip the apron off its hook and drop it around my neck.

"Nothing, nothing at all," Zander laughs. "But you do need to earn my silence." He holds up a chore list pinched onto a clipboard. "I've saved the best for you — bathroom."

I scrunch up my nose. "I haven't been trained."

"I have faith in your natural talent," he says. "Mop's in the closet in the bathroom."

The bathroom is small and cleaned daily, so it doesn't take long to scrub it. By the time I join Zander out in the coffee shop, a couple of tables have filled with customers. I jump in to help him serve the few people waiting in line and busy myself wiping tables as people leave. The dishwasher is a constant beast, demanding to be loaded and run again as soon as it's finished. And the business keeps my mind on mugs and coffee and books and tables and far away from everything else. Zander takes a break during a lull when no customers are in, and I spend that half hour in the bookshelves, putting books in their places and straightening spines.

When he returns it's my turn to squirrel away in the small staff room-slash-stock room in the back. I'm reluctant to leave the distraction of the coffee shop and be alone in the quiet room. "I don't need a break," I say.

"You will, better take it now while you can," Zander says knowingly. My feet do hurt a bit.

I sit quietly at the bistro table, flipping through a catalogue someone left behind, trying to keep my brain distracted. The final shift calendar is pinned to the wall, and I look to see who I'm working with next. It's been tidied since the version Win showed us, and the scrawled names have been replaced by tiny evenly printed names. Along the bottom Win added: *If you can't make your shift, please attempt to rearrange a switch yourself,* and then a list of our names and phone numbers. Tracy Bauer, Andrea Ford, Alexander Page, Layne Wheeler (added at the bottom). Was Penny's name originally on that list? The question sneaks in, and I push it out of my mind. I open a note on my phone, title it *CQ Staff,* and thumb-type in the names and numbers.

Face-palm. Literally. There it is staring me right in the face. Penny's last ToDoh! item glows in my mind while the conversations I've had with Zander about Penny drop like jigsaw puzzle pieces into place. Zander's name is Alexander Page. AP. *AP.*

"Zander?" I ask Penny, but of course there's no answer. I'm still alone in the room.

Zander pushes the door open and says, "Hey, you got your wish. Break's over, I'm getting slammed out here."

"Yeah! Right now!" I say, stuffing my phone into my pocket and following him out the door.

I'm totally distracted for the first thirty minutes back on the floor. Like two creams instead of two milk, dark roast, not light, kind of distracted. Zander sends me more than a few glares as he mollifies irate customers and fixes my mistakes. "What's wrong with you?" he hisses when he walks past me to dump a third mug of coffee in the sink. I think that one may have salt in it instead of sugar.

"Sorry … my head's somewhere else."

He looks at me as if he's trying to decide if he should be angrier or give it up and laugh. "Well, kindly bring it back," he says finally. I nod and force myself to concentrate.

When the rush slows down again, I take a cloth to wipe the already clean spot of the counter near where Zander is restocking mugs on the shelf. "I was just looking at the schedule," I start. "Copied the names and numbers at the bottom into my phone." I scrub extra hard at a swirl in the wood pattern.

Zander stops to look at me a moment. He seems confused. "Yeah? That's genius," he says with a snicker.

"I noticed your name is Alexander." I stop scrubbing and look at him.

He blushes. "Yeah, no one but my mom calls me that, though." His embarrassed laugh settles into a sigh. He studies his hands. "Well, now at least."

"Now?"

"Yeah, now." He chews his lower lip and studies me then looks away as if he's trying to decide whether to share what he's thinking. I hold my breath, afraid that if I make the slightest move, the slightest sound, whatever thought he's thinking might scurry back into secret. "Penny used to call me that. It started as a mistake — she heard my mother use it, and I didn't know how to correct her without embarrassing her, and then, by the time she heard Win call me 'Zander,' well, by then I kind of liked it. It didn't sound as lame when she used it, you know?"

I nod. "She was like that," I say quietly.

He nods too and says, "She was really great," so quietly I almost miss it. He wipes his cheek, and we stand there for a moment, not looking at each other. When he whispers, "I'm sorry," it doesn't sound dumb or insincere or awkward. I know he is, and he knows I am too. Sorry for her AP.

When he turns back to the mugs, I pull my phone out of my back pocket and open the texting app.

"Win's just in his office," Zander says as a warning.

"I'll be two seconds," I rush to say, thumbs flying over the phone. I text Asher's phone: *Off @ 3. Can u pick me up?* My chest tightens a bit. Of course I feel guilty, asking him for a favour after being so nasty less than twenty-four hours ago. I stare at my phone for a moment but no reply comes.

"Layne, really, he hates phones. He fired someone last summer just for —"

"Done," I say, stuffing the phone in my back pocket and swatting him with the wet cloth. "Goody-two-shoes," I add for good measure. Penny was the rule follower, not me.

chapter 28

B y the time Andrea and Tracy arrive to relieve us at three, my hidden phone still has not vibrated. Disappointed, I dawdle getting ready to leave — hang up my apron, sign out on the shift chart and gather my bag from under the counter — to put off looking at the blank phone. I open the door, the bell rings and I step out of the shop, walking with my head down over my flicking thumbs, texting Zac to ask for a ride. Not looking where I'm going, I walk right into someone "Oh sorry!" I say, trying to sidestep out of the way without showing my face. A burning blush rushes to my cheeks.

"No worries," he says.

My eyes are a half second ahead of my thoughts, and my face tips up to see Asher's. He smiles, and the slaughtered butterflies are instantly resurrected. "Sorry, I didn't have a chance to text back. I left my phone in the car. You still need a ride?"

I nod. My face seems to be frozen in a goofy wide-eyed grin.

"Okay, um, let's go," Asher says, obviously creeped out by my pea-brained expression. He turns toward his car.

"She doesn't like you," I blurt out. Smooth.

He stops, turns back and walks back to me, shaking his head with a nervous laugh. "What? Who?" His brown eyes narrow, and wrinkles press between his eyebrows as he studies me.

"Penny. She *didn't* like you." He takes a step back, and I grab on to his right wrist with my free hand. I'm sure it just cemented his opinion that I'm completely insane, but I don't let go. "I mean she *did* like you, but not like that. You're not her type." I laugh at that, a little too hysterically. "Zander from the coffee shop. Well, he's *Alexander*, really. Zander is AP, *he's* her type. Not you."

"Oooo-kay?" Asher says.

"It's not okay, it's great! Because it just so happens that you are *my* type." I step closer, still with a death grip on his wrist.

"Yeah?" he asks, his eyes finally relaxing and the corners of his mouth curling up into a smile.

"Yeah." I sigh. And wait. He gives a small nod that means a million things and nothing at all and tips his face down toward me. When his mouth reaches mine, I kiss him back and then laugh lightly. I can feel his smile against my lips. "Yeah," I whisper again.

I close my eyes and press my cheek against his soft T-shirt. I can see Penny there, in my mind where she's always been, where she'll always be. She smiles and nods then whispers, "See? It'll be okay," and I believe her. I don't know how, but I don't have to figure that out right now. I just know it will be.

I'll build a new okay.

acknowledgements

Thank you to the experts to made this professional: Editors Colleen McKie and Allister Thompson, cover artist Jillianne Hamilton and book designer Valerie Bellamy.

Thank you to the readers who made this worthwhile: if a story is never read, does it really exist at all?

Thank you to my family and friends who cheer me on.

Thank you to my Favourite Four and their Dad for everything else.

natalie corbett sampson

Natalie lives outside of Halifax, Nova Scotia in a home filled with kids and fur. She is a Speech Language Pathologist, a job that allows her to share her love of language and words every day. Natalie spends her evenings and weekends trying to squeeze time for creative work like writing and drawing between trips to the rink or basketball court with her husband and four children.

You can find Natalie online here:
email: **NCS@NatalieCorbettSampson.com**
web: **NatalieCorbettSampson.com**
Twitter: **@Nsampson17**
Facebook: **facebook.com/NatalieCorbettSampson**
GoodReads: **Goodreads.com** search Natalie Corbett Sampson

also by natalie corbett sampson

Game Plan (Fierce Ink Press, 2013)

"*Poignant, well-paced and compassionate,* Game Plan *is an achingly real look at how two families cope when life doesn't go as planned.*" — Tish Cohen, bestselling author of *The Truth About Delilah Blue* and *Inside Out Girl.*

Aptitude (Fierce Ink Books, 2015)

"*Akin to the haunting subtleties of Atwood's* The Handmaid's Tale *and Lowry's* The Giver, *Natalie Corbett Sampson delivers in Aptitude a richly-imagined dystopian world, which seems scarily all too plausible.*" — Jo Treggiari, author of *Ashes, Ashes*

It Should Have Been a #GoodDay (Clubhouse Press, 2016)

"*With an authentic tone grounded in gritty realism,* It Should Have Been a #GoodDay *shies away from morbid voyeurism and instead invites readers to consider the negative consequences of being labelled, and if any of us have the right to judge each other.*" — Bethany Myers, author of *Butterflies Don't Lie, Girl on the Run* and *ASP of Ascension.*

www.ingramcontent.com/pod-product-compliance
Lightning Source LLC
Chambersburg PA
CBHW020638250626
47154CB00008B/2729